A heated, skittery sw... sensual arousal spiraled through Sara as she recalled her first glimpse of him.

His shirtsleeves rolled up, his shirt open to reveal a strong neck and broad chest, his big, capable hands threaded dexterously between cotton strands and gears as he ministered to the machine. He'd looked...primitive, powerful—and perhaps dangerous.

Not at all like the highly educated, well-born, dedicated political gentlemen she'd previously found attractive.

Despite his gentlemanly demeanor, Mr. Fitzallen seemed the sort of man more likely to pummel his opponent into submission with his fists than persuade him with clever argument.

She should be equally wary of both.

She'd felt his gaze on her numerous times as he conducted their tour. A gaze that seemed to be admiring—and had set up that nervous flutter inside her. Perhaps it was the novelty that he'd seemed to find her attractive, as she found him, that had compelled her to linger behind and speak to him. She'd had the impression that he liked her—which was why she'd been so stung when he suddenly seemed to dismiss her.

Clearly, he had *not* liked her. Which was just as well.

Author Note

Little more than a hundred years ago, music could be heard only at a concert, literature found only in a library, and communication was in person or by letter. Now, with one small device, we can access vast treasures of music and books, and communicate with almost anyone.

A similar technological explosion began in the nineteenth century. Inspired by visions of a world in which machines made life easier for everyone, inventors were replacing laborious handwork with devices that could spin thread, weave cloth, and transport people and goods.

Hero Cameron Fitzallen is such an inventor. Born with neither wealth nor family, he has risen to become a factory owner through brilliance and perseverance.

After the marriage of her two friends ends her dream of living independently, heroine Sara Standish finds new purpose in helping host a Parliamentary committee inspecting factories. She's thrilled to be able to meet—and affect—the lives of the mill children she passionately champions.

Dynamic Cameron Fitzallen intrigues her. When chance offers an opportunity to further their acquaintance, both see no harm in it. But as they join forces to help factory children, their shared ideals and a strong attraction start each of them thinking the unthinkable—that in the bold new future Cam imagines, there might be a place for a Lady of Quality and a workhouse orphan to be together.

I hope you will enjoy their journey.

JULIA JUSTISS

The Enticing of
Miss Standish

HARLEQUIN®
HISTORICAL™

ISBN-13: 978-1-335-50565-1

The Enticing of Miss Standish

Copyright © 2020 by Janet Justiss

This edition published by arrangement with Harlequin Books S.A.

For questions and comments about the quality of this book, please contact us at CustomerService@Harlequin.com.

Harlequin Enterprises ULC
22 Adelaide St. West, 40th Floor
Toronto, Ontario M5H 4E3, Canada
www.Harlequin.com

Printed in U.S.A.

Julia Justiss wrote her first ideas for Nancy Drew stories in her third-grade notebook and has been writing ever since. After publishing poetry in college, she turned to novels. Her Regency historicals have won or placed in contests by the Romance Writers of America, *RT Book Reviews*, National Readers' Choice and Daphne du Maurier Award. She lives with her husband in Texas. For news and contests, visit juliajustiss.com.

To the Zombie Belles, who inspire,
encourage and keep me going.
Couldn't do it without you!

Chapter One

London—summer 1834

'Act as a *companion*?' Sara's aunt echoed, her horrified voice rising. 'Do you want to send me into a decline and be the death of your poor invalid mother? Why, society would think the Standish family had become indigent, like your poor friend Miss Overton!'

Sighing, Sara Standish gazed over at Lady Patterson, who occupied the other end of the sofa in the small back salon at Standish House where they were taking tea, Sara's mother, as usual, being laid down upon her couch.

Sara supposed it wasn't worth mentioning that her friend's sudden loss of fortune had turned out to be a blessing, since it had led her to find the man she would fall in love with and marry. 'Assisting a *marchioness* by accompanying her to meetings and society events would hardly suggest a sudden lack of funds.'

'Perhaps not,' Lady Patterson allowed. 'But you might as well put on a cap and announce yourself a spinster, beyond all hope of marriage!'

'Since I'm about to complete my fifth Season and have

reached the advanced age of three-and-twenty, I expect society already considers me one.'

'You needn't have been. If you'd made just a little more push to engage one of the gentlemen who have shown interest in you,' Lady Patterson argued. 'Mr Ersby or Mr Berwicke. Or that charming baronet's son, Mr Harlande.'

'Mr Ersby, who talks of nothing but hounds and hunters. Mr Berwicke, who merely wanted some gently born female who wouldn't baulk at residing year-round in the depths of Yorkshire and married Miss Woodward within a month after I politely refused him. And that charming baronet's son lives with his mother and intends on remaining with her, even if he weds.' Sweeping her hand down to indicate her plump, rounded figure, she said wryly, 'He probably thought I resembled his mama.'

'Not every man wants a tall, sylph-like beauty,' her aunt retorted. 'Some prefer a lady with a bit of flesh on her bones. True, you'd never be taken for an Incomparable, but your figure is elegant, your pale blonde hair is lovely and I've overheard several gentlemen describe your blues eyes as "very fine".'

'Be that as it may, *I* prefer a gentleman with a bit of sense in his head and a great deal of purpose in his heart!'

'Then why haven't you endeared yourself to one of those politicians you're always talking about? It's not as if you don't spend the vast majority of your time working with Lady Lyndlington's Ladies' Committee, writing letters in support of Parliamentary bills, or some such vulgar thing.'

A politician she could admire.

Sara pressed her lips together, trying to keep her countenance from betraying her as the unhappy memories escaped. After heady weeks of having consulted and encouraged her, handsome, dashing Member of Parliament Lucius Draycott asking her for a private interview. Her nervous jubilation, her certainty he meant to offer for her. The humiliation of discovering that all he wanted was her opinion on which of two well-dowered, crushingly conventional young ladies he should court.

She'd never shared that pain and didn't intend to divulge it now, since the resolution it produced—that she would never marry—would only prolong the argument with her aunt.

'No activity sponsored by a viscountess could be considered "vulgar",' Sara countered after a moment, keeping her tone light. 'I suppose you'd prefer me to devote myself solely to afternoon calls and shopping trips, and my evenings to soirées, routs and balls, meeting and talking with the same people about the same things I have for the last five years.'

'Of course I would. They are your peers, the elite of England, society's leaders.'

'Most of them *lead* rather pointless lives,' Sara retorted. 'I prefer to spend my time among the small segment of that elite who are working to change the nation and make life better for all England's inhabitants.'

'But to bury yourself away as a *companion*? After all the time and effort I've expended, trying to get you respectably s-settled!' Her aunt's voice breaking, she drew a handkerchief from her reticule and dabbed at her eyes.

'I know,' Sara said quietly, putting a placating hand on her aunt's arm. 'I'm grateful that you were willing to take over sponsoring me after Mama decided that going about in society was too…taxing for her delicate health. And I do appreciate all the opportunities you have tried to create for me—even if it appears as if I don't. I know you want the best for me. It's just—your view of what that is, and mine, are so very different.'

'You truly think you'd be happy living the rest of your days as a spinster, assisting some high-born lady to work on behalf of that orphan school and those legislative committees?' her aunt asked. 'Left behind, while your peers are raising their offspring, and left alone, with no child to comfort you, when your mother and I and the Marchioness pass? For I can't imagine you could abide living with your brother and that silly featherhead he married!'

Perhaps she was making progress, Sara thought. Her aunt's usual refrain was to recommend marriage—any marriage. Perhaps Lady Patterson was finally coming to see that wedding a typical society gentleman—a man with whom she had nothing in common—just wasn't right for Sara. Such a man would almost certainly disapprove of her opinions, try to limit or forbid her political activities and probably leave his modestly attractive, quiet wife to run his home while he took his pleasure with a prettier, more dashing woman.

As her father had.

Whereas, though a political gentleman might encourage her opinions and applaud her activities, when it came to *marriage*, he usually chose a conventional society maiden as his bride.

Which pretty much swept the field of matrimonial prospects.

Was it any wonder she now yearned only to live an independent life?

'I think I could be happy, yes. I have friends—and their children to coddle and love. I would be able to devote myself to working on causes that truly matter to me. I know I'm a sad disappointment to you, Aunt Patterson, but the usual rounds of entertainments and dinners and routs that delight most well-born ladies simply don't interest me at all.'

Her aunt sighed. 'So you've been telling me these last five years.'

'Perhaps, now, you're finally listening? Besides, both you and Mama had already agreed that at Season's end, you would allow—if not give your blessing to—my moving with Emma and Olivia to the house on Judd Street, where we would all pursue our political activities.'

'Except that Miss Henley and Miss Overton, quite sensibly, opted to marry instead,' her aunt pointed out, a triumphant gleam in her eye. 'Despite previously claiming, as you are now, that they preferred to remain unwed and devote themselves to good causes.'

'If I were to capture the affections of a gentleman whose mind, heart, and purpose captivated *me*, as Emma did with Lord Theo and Olivia with Colonel Glendenning, I wouldn't be opposed to marriage. But as you noted, I've encountered both society gentlemen and political gentlemen over the years, without any such miracle occurring.'

'But such a "miracle" will never happen unless you remain in society,' her aunt countered. 'Don't hide yourself away as a companion and resign yourself to spinsterhood!'

'Then perhaps we can make a bargain. If I agree to continue to forgo spinster's caps and continue to conduct myself like a marriageable maiden, will you allow me to assist the Marchioness? As you may remember, she still suffers from that fall she took riding two years ago and is often in pain. It's not as though I would be a *paid* companion—more a friend and assistant. To have someone to write out her correspondence for her, help her when she entertains and assist her to attend such meetings and social engagements as she wishes, would be a kind, Christian thing to do. For the present, when in London, I could still reside here with you and Mama. And assisting her would hardly mean hiding myself away! Despite her injuries, she moves in the first circles of society. Indeed, accompanying her might give me an even better chance of meeting that sterling young man who could tempt me into marriage.'

'Oh, very well,' her aunt said. 'I suppose you'd talk me around to it one way or another eventually anyway. Goodness, for all that you scarcely say a word in company, you can be persuasive when you want to be!'

'Then I may call on Lady Trent and let her know I can begin?'

'I never thought I'd see the day...my darling niece, a *companion*?'

'A kind, Christian assistant,' Sara substituted.

Lady Patterson shook her head, that gesture telling Sara the change in wording didn't make the proposition any more palatable to her. 'But...yes, you may call on her.'

'Thank you, best of aunts!' Delighted, Sara jumped up to give her Lady Patterson a vigorous hug.

'Goodness, now,' that lady grumbled, 'careful of my cap!'

'I'll go out at once,' Sara said, walking towards the door. 'Lady Trent has invited the members of the Parliamentary Committee who are to oversee the newly appointed Factory Inspectors to stay at Brayton Hullford, her country estate in Derbyshire. They will be touring the manufacturers in the region to check their compliance with last year's Factory Act. Lady Lyndlington and the other committee members were as concerned as I was about the Marchioness taxing her limited strength, trying to manage such a large house party on her own.'

'Why, you sly thing!' Lady Patterson said reproach-fully, shaking a finger at Sara. 'Securing my approval of your proposition *before* informing me that taking up the position will send you out of London before the Season ends!'

'The Season will be ending soon anyway. And you know you never stay in London after July. So I shall probably see you next in Kent.'

'Not until we're settled in Kent?' Lady Patterson wailed. Then, shaking her head again, she said, 'Oh, get on with you then, before I change my mind!'

Blowing her a kiss, Sara couldn't help grinning as she walked out. For the first time since her friends' unex-pected marriages had ended for good any hope of leav-ing her mother's house to live independently, she had the possibility of finding another way to take up the life the three of them had dreamed of since they'd met, bookish girls of serious natures, at Mrs Axminster's Academy for Young Ladies.

She would miss her friends, of course. And happy as she was for their happiness, going to assist Lady Trent wouldn't be like setting up a household with the two people dearest in the world to her.

With determination, she shook off the melancholy that always seized her when she thought of them, both now so far away, Emma with Lord Theo on their Grand Tour of Europe and Olivia back at her husband's estate in Somerset. Though she couldn't expect Lady Trent to be a replacement for her friends, she hoped the lady would turn out to be as congenial and interesting a companion over an extended period as she had been the short dura-tion of the Ladies' Committee meetings.

If they should prove to be incompatible—one couldn't blame a woman who suffered constant pain from being querulous, after all—after the trip to Derbyshire, Sara could gracefully bow out of any further commitment.

But in the meantime, there *was* Derbyshire. Her spirits rose again and excitement tingled her nerves, just thinking of it. Living independently at Judd Street would have allowed her to spend as much time as she liked on her Ladies' Committee work and assisting with Ellie Lattimer's school—but it would be political work at a distance. In Derbyshire, she and Lady Trent intended to accompany the committee members on their factory tours, giving her an unparalleled opportunity to see with her own eyes, rather than reading about it second-hand in a journal or Parliamentary report, the working conditions of the factory children whose plight so touched her heart and whose best interests she was determined to advance and protect.

As she mounted the stairs to her room to collect her pelisse, she had to chuckle. If Aunt Patterson had any idea that during the visit to Derbyshire, her darling niece would be visiting factories employing pauper children and indigent females, she would lock Sara in her bed-chamber.

Instead, she would shortly be on her way to inform Lady Trent she had her family's permission to assist her on the journey. She couldn't wait to begin.

But despite Aunt Patterson's fondest hopes, she sincerely doubted that among the members of the Parliamentary committee or the inspectors Parliament had appointed, she would discover any discerning gentleman interested in enticing *her* into wedlock.

In the afternoon two weeks later, Cameron Fitzallen stood by his desk in the manager's office of the Hughes Cotton Works near the village of Knively, trying not to grimace as the owner, Mr Hughes, informed him about the Parliamentary Committee that was to visit the mill later that afternoon.

'Shouldn't be anything to worry about, Cam my boy,' Mr Hughes said. 'We run a model mill and the working conditions here already surpass the standards established by the Factory Act.'

'Oh, I'm not worried about what they will find. But I can't help resenting the obligation to nursemaid yet another group of ignorant outsiders through the mill while they gather tales to amuse their London friends. A waste of my time! Only those who work in the business have the expertise to change things for the better.'

'Aye, I know you've little taste for visiting committees,' Hughes replied. 'But sometimes, a nudge from outsiders doesn't come amiss. In fact, I believe Mr Pennington, the committee member who represents Derby, wanted to bring the group to Hughes first for just that reason—so that they would see how a mill *should* be run, before they visit others that may need...improvements.'

'We're certainly proud of the establishment you've built,' Cameron replied, looking at his mentor with admiration and respect. 'Everyone from the over-lookers to the newest piecer will be happy to show off their work.'

'And I'll hear no more protest about having you do the tour, or the speech to them afterwards. Not for nothing did I insist you be trained up to talk like a London nob! They'll listen a deal more attentively to you than they would to me, with my thick north-country speech.'

'They ought to listen to you,' Cameron retorted. 'You've got as much expertise as I do. And a great deal more experience.'

'Well, as so often in life, it's the appearance that counts. Looking fine as five pence, and speaking as though you was one of them, always helps. Today, and when you'll be on the hunt for more investors for those expansion schemes of yours.'

Cameron smiled. 'I'll let you take care of investments. I'll concentrate on machinery. I might look and speak like a gentleman, but I wasn't born one.' The ugly memories of his time in London threatened and, with a dash of anger, he pushed them away. 'Not that I care one whit about their opinions, but those who were born gentlemen will never forget I wasn't.'

'Aye, 'tis the way of the world,' Hughes acknowledged. 'May we live to see the day when a man is recognised for his achievements, rather than his birth! True, I started the business and kept the capital flowing. But it's the improvements you've made to the machinery, your study of the work and techniques of others, that have kept Hughes Works so profitable.'

'Thank you, sir. I appreciate the vote of confidence.'

Mr Hughes chuckled. 'I should hope I have confidence in the man to whom I will be turning this operation over! The first of several mills you mean to direct, eh, my ambitious young lad? Aye, I expect you're itching to try out some of those novel new techniques you've been reading about! Well, keep the mill profitable is all I say. I'll handle any grumbling from the investors over your changes.'

'I intend to keep it profitable, sir.'

At that moment, a knock came at the door, followed by the entry of a child who worked in the card room. 'What is it, Jenny?' Cameron asked.

''Scuse me, Mr Hughes, but Lennox sent me up to fetch Mr Fitzallen. He's having some trouble with the oiling of one of the spinning mules.'

'With the committee due here any time, you'd better get the machinery working at once,' Mr Hughes said.

'On my way,' Cameron replied. 'Let's go, Jenny.'

As he followed the child out of the office, the noise of the machinery drowned out all other sound—and made him smile. Though the clatter had awed and intimidated him the first time he entered the mill as a nervous six-year-old, he'd loved the complex machinery at first sight and the thrill he felt every time he gazed upon it had never faded. The levers and pulleys, gears and wires, rollers, drums and bobbins fascinated him, their interplay an elegant language of motion and efficiency he'd been studying ever since.

He'd done pretty well for an orphan from the parish workhouse, he thought as he followed Jenny. Working his way up over twenty-five years from a scavenger cleaning lint and fly from the edges of the machines to overall manager, along the way looking for ways to improve both efficiency and safety. The small adjustments he'd made had first caught the eye of his supervisor, then of Mr Hughes himself. Recognising his potential, the owner had sent him away to school. And very soon now, he thought with a rising swell of excitement, Mr Hughes would turn over the factory to him, to improve and expand even more.

He mimed a goodbye to Jenny in the carding room and walked on to enter the larger space occupied by the mule spinners, the heat and humidity hitting him like a slap to the face. Lennox, one of the senior minders, must have been watching for him, for he waved Cameron over. Using hand gestures, he indicated the machine that was giving him difficulty. Though he'd shut it down, the problem had occurred on one of the least

accessible pulleys, a place difficult to reach even with
the machine not in motion.

Stripping down to his shirtsleeves in the heat, Cameron tossed his coat, vest and cravat to the minder. The
skinny workhouse orphan he'd once been had grown
into a tall, broad-shouldered, powerfully built man, so
he could no longer slither under the yard sheet to access
the part, as he had as a boy—nor could Lennox, which
Cameron figured was why the man had summoned him.
He'd have to reach through and around, a delicate process to avoid ruining the thread being made—or catching a hand in one of the shuttles.

But solving mechanical difficulties was the sort of
puzzle he loved—applying angle and torque and finesse
and an intimate knowledge of the machine and its workings to successfully make the repair. With a hand motion to Lennox to indicate he was studying the situation,
Cameron dropped to his knees and looked up at the recalcitrant part from below, then stood and peered down
at it from several different angles. Satisfied he'd worked
out the best way to proceed, he motioned to Lennox for
the oiler, got back down on his knees and set to work.

His concentration intensely focused on his task, it
wasn't until he'd finished and got back to his feet that
Cameron noticed Mr Hughes leading a group of strangers
into the room. The Parliamentary Committee, no doubt.

He'd just handed the oiler back to Lennox when
he realised that, among the seven or eight individuals
approaching him, two were female. He frowned at that
discovery, wondering why the committee had brought
ladies with them. One older woman in an elegant pelisse
and turban was leaning on the arm of a second female,
who seemed to be assisting her as she walked.

The second lady turned towards him and looked up.

A shock ran through Cameron as he realised this lady was not only much younger, but very attractive.

She looked like the pictures he'd seen of angels, he thought disjointedly. A twist of golden curls framed the soft, pale face under her bonnet, large, beautiful china-blue eyes looked at him enquiringly—and her deep blue pelisse accentuated curves much too voluptuous to belong to one of the heavenly host.

As his body had its inevitable reaction to that observation, the lady's eyes widened. Cameron suddenly realised he was standing there, gaping at her, coatless and cravat-less, his open-necked shirt revealing the top half of his bare chest. Which, to someone from the Polite World, was akin to being practically undressed.

His face heating, he grabbed his garments back from Lennox and hastily shrugged on vest and coat and wrapped the cravat around his throat. No time to tie it properly, but a quick knot would bring the edges of his shirt back together and render him decent.

What was a young, attractive, gently born lady doing at Hughes Works? Besides looking as out of place in this cotton mill as he would at a reception at St James's Palace.

Pasting a smile on his face, he tried to shake off the strong sensual reaction she'd elicited. As he walked over to meet the committee, he hoped by the time they finished the tour and returned to his office, where he would answer their questions, she would cease distracting him, else he might not be able to remember the speech he'd prepared.

After all, he had about as much business admiring the physical attributes of a Lady of Quality as he would those of a celestial being.

Chapter Two

After an exchange of hand signals that informed him the mill owner had not yet begun his visitors' tour, Cameron took over to guide the group through the various steps of the thread-making process, from the scutching, where the raw cotton was separated from its seeds and another debris, to the carding room where machines combed it into long strands, then back to the mule spinners where the rovings were further drawn, twisted into thread and spun on to the bobbins that would be installed in the weaving machines.

The power looms themselves being housed in another building, he then guided the group back to his office, where he expected Mr Hughes would await them.

The noise of the machinery making discussion during the tour impossible, while he waved a hand to indicate machines and mimed the processes being performed, he couldn't help having his attention continually stray back to the ladies. If the intent expressions with which they gazed around the factory were an accurate indication, it seemed they were quite interested in the mill. Why, other than simple curiosity, he couldn't imagine.

Mr Hughes met them at the office door. 'Gentlemen—

and ladies—please, come in. May I formally present to all of you my factory manager, Mr Cameron Fitzallen? Cam my lad, this is Lady Trent, who has been kind enough to house the committee at Brayton Hullford during their inspections of the factories in the area, and her companion, Miss Standish. And the committee itself: Sir Henry Wright, the chairman, Lord Cleve, Mr Pennington, the M.P. from Derby, and Mr Marsden.'

Cameron bowed, to which the visitors returned nods and curtsies.

'Won't you all have a seat?' Hughes continued, indicating the chairs he'd had brought into the room. 'Let's have some tea. You may serve now, Hannah.' Hughes motioned to a lady in a cap with a long white apron over her gown, who proceeded to bring a cup to each visitor.

After they had all had some refreshment, Mr Hughes said, 'So, what do you think of Hughes Cotton Works?'

'Quite impressive,' Lord Cleve said. 'Sir Henry, who as you know has seen a number of manufacturers, told us that Hughes Works was an innovator in its field, one of the first mills to integrate both the production of thread and the weaving of cloth. A very efficient process!'

'Our efficiency is increased by having a stable, well-trained work force,' Cameron said. 'We provide housing for many of them. Also schooling for all the children under the age of fourteen.'

Lord Cleve raised his eyebrows. 'Is schooling the children really necessary?'

The subtle sneer in the man's voice immediately fired Cameron's anger. Cleve must be another idle rich man's son who believed educating children of the 'lower orders' to be a waste of time and resources.

Children of the sort he had once been.

Before he could make a hot—and probably imprudent—reply, Lady Trent said, 'Surely, Lord Cleve, as a gentleman and a Christian, you want every Englishman—and woman—to be able to read the Bible for him or herself. For the father of a household to know his sums, so he may manage his wages to cover his living expenses, and to be able to write his name to contracts and documents.'

Lady Trent was a dowager marchioness, Cameron recalled—and thus outranked an earl's son with a courtesy title. Though he looked annoyed, Lord Cleve nodded. 'Of course, you are right, Lady Trent.'

'How many hours of schooling does your factory offer?'

Surprised to hear the question emanate from the lovely blonde lady he'd been trying so hard to ignore, Cameron allowed himself to look in her direction—and once again felt an almost tangible pull of attraction.

Fighting to resist it, he said, 'You have an interest in factory education, Miss Standish? I thought you ladies were just acting as hostesses to the committee.'

Sir Henry chuckled. 'Oh, they do—and have done—much more than that, Mr Fitzallen. Lady Trent and Miss Standish are members of a Ladies' Committee chaired by Lady Lyndlington, whose husband is one of the reform leaders in Parliament. They have done much good work, writing letters to lobby members to support legislation outlawing the slave trade, expanding the franchise and enacting protections for children working in factories.'

From the mists of childhood, hurtful memories resurfaced. A continuing succession of workhouse inspection committees, often headed by the first ladies of the parish, all raising hopes that were ultimately dashed.

Though Cameron tried to suppress them, the anger and resentment those memories stirred were hot enough that they should, he thought, snuff out his inappropriate attraction to Miss Standish. The one thing he still found almost impossible to tolerate were self-important gentry who amused themselves by dabbling in 'Good Causes'.

'Commendable,' he said drily, knowing he needed to dispense with the group before he lost his temper. 'Shall we finish off any questions? You have important work to do and must be anxious to move to your next destination.'

For the next several minutes, as the guests drank their tea, Cameron forced himself to answer the committee member's final questions about production, working hours, hiring practices and the efficiency of the new power looms over manual ones.

Their tea finished, Sir Henry expressed his thanks to Mr Hughes for accommodating their visit and the group stood. Thanking them in return for their attention, Hughes led them out of the room.

Miss Standish, however, lingered behind. 'You never answered my question, Mr Fitzallen.'

Because I didn't want to waste my time, indulging your idle curiosity about your Enthusiasm of the Moment.

Despite his irritation, though, he couldn't help noticing the subtle fragrance of violets that surrounded her, the gleam of her gold curls, the soft roundness of her cheeks. Or that kissable rosebud mouth and the ample curves evident despite the masking thickness of her pelisse.

The fact that, despite his disdain, he could not shake free of his attraction to her infuriated him. Irritation snapping his hold over his manners, he gave her a bow and pulled on his forelock, as exaggeratedly obsequious as a Russian serf kowtowing before the master. 'So sorry, miss. I meant no disrespect.'

To his surprise, she seemed to understand the gesture was contemptuous rather than conciliatory. Colour flooding her face, she dropped him a stiff curtsy and headed for the door—only to halt and look back at him from the threshold.

'Why do you mock me and avoid answering my questions? Because I'm only a woman and couldn't possibly understand the answers?'

'As to the depth of a woman's understanding, I offer no opinion. I just didn't think you'd need the information. After all, by next month, you and your committee will have moved on to your next little cause and forgotten all about the children at Hughes Works.'

'Oh, so I'm idle and inconstant? How dare you, sir! You know nothing about me!'

'That's true. I don't *know* you at all—my lady,' he shot back. And immediately regretted the remark, as its unintended sensual undertones registered in his brain, intensifying his body's regrettable response.

Her deepening blush said she'd understood the innuendo. But despite her discomfort, she stood her ground. 'I'm not a "my lady", I'm just a citizen deeply concerned about the education and welfare of children sent to work in the mills. A concern I have felt for several years and a cause I intend to pursue for many more!'

He had to admit, she argued a good case. But then, so had all the others.

'Perhaps your enthusiasm will last. If it does, perhaps then we can discuss the issue.'

'I assure you,' she replied, anger evident in her voice, 'my "enthusiasm" will last a good deal longer than your show of courtesy has. Good day, Mr Fitzallen.' Giving him a nod, with a quaint dignity that made him feel ashamed for provoking her, she walked from the office.

Hell and damnation! he thought, wiping a hand over his brow as the door closed behind her. It seemed his anger over the noble committees who visited the workhouse where he'd been incarcerated as a child, scattering vague promises that were never fulfilled, burned as hot as ever. Even so, he shouldn't have let it get the better of him.

She was right—he didn't know her or the sincerity of her interest in factory children. He'd been, at best, rude to one of his employer's visitors. And, at worst, unfair and flat-out wrong.

He probably owed Miss Standish an apology. Though exactly how he could explain his reaction without revealing his true opinions of her class and her activities, which would likely offend her further, he had no idea.

Fortunately, it was highly unlikely he'd ever have to give it a try. The factory committee was to make only this single visit to Hughes Cotton Works. He couldn't imagine any other place where Cameron Fitzallen, factory manager, and Miss Standish, companion of a dowager marchioness, would ever meet again.

Fury and chagrin making her cheeks hot, Sara hurried to catch up with the group. Beastly, arrogant, dismissive man! Belittling her concern because she was a woman? Or was there some other reason for his discourtesy?

Taking a deep, calming breath, she reminded herself that, by now, she should be used to the condescension with which so many men treated women who dared venture beyond the domestic realm, if that had in fact been the reason behind his response. Mr Fitzallen would be only the latest in a long line of gentlemen who apparently found her interest in parliamentary reform at best naive and uninformed, at worst unnatural and unwomanly.

Somehow, she'd assumed that, being a mill supervisor who must have risen to his current position of responsibility as a result of his own skill and hard work, he would have a higher opinion of a woman's intellect. That he might believe women were capable of playing a larger role in the world than the men of her class did. After all, a good number of his employees were female.

She knew Hughes Works was considered a model mill. Was Fitzallen impatient with her—and the committee—because they were outsiders taking him away from vital tasks? Or was he only anxious to rid himself of them before they could see or question his workers? Was he truly devoted to the well-being of the factory children who meant so much to her? Or only a manager who intended to profit from their labour?

He was certainly impatient with outsiders.

Having him ignore her question should have told her at once all she needed to know about his attitudes towards reformers—so why had she lingered to talk with him? Normally shy and not given to speaking out, she usually avoided confrontation. Had she truly thought he'd just been distracted into forgetting her query and wasn't going to deliver the officious set down she'd received?

Or had she persisted because she'd felt towards him a strong and most unexpected sense of… She didn't quite know how to describe it. Connection? Shared passion for reform? Attraction?

He conducted himself with the confidence of a man used to being in charge—and he was certainly attractive. With his tall, broad-shouldered physique, strong-boned, purposeful face with its dark, intelligent eyes, and luxuriant dark brown hair curling over his brow, he would draw the attention of any female who chanced to come near him.

Though he'd been attired and spoke like a gentleman, he clearly was not. No one born a gentleman would work with his hands in a factory.

Nor would a gentleman ever have doffed any of his garments when there were females present.

A heated, skittery swirl of what must be sensual arousal spiralled through her as she recalled her first glimpse of him. His shirtsleeves rolled up, his shirt open to reveal a strong neck and broad chest, his big, capable hands threaded dexterously between cotton strands and gears as he ministered to the machine. He'd looked... primitive, powerful—and perhaps dangerous.

Not at all the highly educated, well-born, dedicated political gentleman she'd previously found attractive. A man as at home giving a speech on the floor of Parliament as he was listening to the concerns of voters—or of factory workers. Courteous, accommodating.

Despite his gentlemanly demeanour, Mr Fitzallen seemed the sort of man more likely to pummel his opponent into submission with his fists than persuade him with clever argument.

She should be equally wary of both.

She'd felt his gaze on her numerous times as he conducted their tour—a gaze that seemed to be admiring—and had set up that nervous flutter inside her. Perhaps it was the novelty that he'd seemed to find her attractive, as she found him, that had compelled her to linger behind and speak to him. She'd had the impression that he liked her—which was why she'd been so stung when he suddenly seemed to dismiss her.

Clearly, he had *not* liked her. Which was just as well. When she imagined Aunt Patterson's reaction should Sara confess she'd lingered to speak to the manager of a cotton mill, she had to chuckle. Her aunt's scream before she swooned would be penetrating enough to be heard three streets away and there probably wouldn't be enough hartshorn in London to revive her.

Despite Fitzallen's obvious disdain for her, and that edge of dangerous attraction that should warn her off, Sara couldn't help being curious about the mill manager. He was such a vital, driven young man, obviously possessed of considerable expertise and just as obviously valued by his employer. Indeed, it suddenly struck her how unusual it was that Mr Fitzallen, rather than the mill's actual owner, had been the one to tour them through the factory and answer all the Parliamentary Committee's questions.

Where had Cameron Fitzallen come from and how had he risen to his present position? Was he a farmer's son lured from the fields by the promise of wages and advancement? Or had the man who, with an almost tender deftness, coaxed an enormous mule spinner back into running once been a boy fascinated by machinery? At some point, he had to have been schooled elsewhere, for he spoke without a trace of the strong northern accent Mr Hughes possessed.

She suspected if she were brave enough to press him on the matter of the children's welfare—if his opinion of her improved enough to permit that—his answers might be fascinating. He was far different, and far more interesting, than the boringly conventional society gentlemen with whom she normally associated. From whom he seemed as different as an India tiger was from a domestic house cat.

Her curiosity, and the pull of her surprising physical attraction to him, warred against her scepticism—and hard-earned caution.

What had come over her? she wondered wryly, shaking her head. Shy, soft-spoken Sara Standish had never been bold, or the least bit tempted to seek out a confrontation with unpredictable strangers.

Even should that odd inclination not prove to be fleeting, she wouldn't have much chance of pursuing it. As far as she knew, the committee intended to make only a single visit to each factory on their list. This one annoying, intriguing, unsettling glimpse of Cameron Fitzallen was all she was likely to have.

Dismissing an irrational pang of regret, Sara reached Lady Trent and, smiling, offered that lady her arm.

Chapter Three

In the evening a week later, Sara walked into the dining room at Brayton Hullford House, instructing the maid who followed her on where to set the several bowls of flowers she'd just finished arranging for the dinner being given tonight for the committee, some of the neighbouring gentry, and the owners of several of the factories the committee had recently inspected.

That task completed, she stood for a moment and looked the room over with satisfaction. Silver and crystal gleamed in the light of candelabras on the table, the sideboard stood ready to receive the dishes of the various courses she'd ordered and Thurston, the butler, was even now greeting the guests who'd begun to assemble in the drawing room.

Though the Marchioness was officially the hostess, Sara felt a sense of accomplishment in knowing it was really she who had planned the event and, after receiving Lady Trent's approval of her plans, she who had supervised their implementation. Placing the flowers was the last detail she had to complete before going upstairs to collect her hostess, who'd been resting in preparation for the evening.

Though she'd assisted her aunt at social functions Lady Patterson had hosted at Standish House, her role had always been minor, with her aunt firmly in charge. Sara found she relished having the authority to direct everything. Even greater than her satisfaction at how well the dinner had turned out was the knowledge that, by taking the burden of the organising of the event on her own shoulders, she was enabling a lady as intelligent, knowledgeable and gracious as the Marchioness to continue her involvement in political affairs. With the leg and back injuries that taxed her strength and the pain that often forced her to retreat to her couch, co-ordinating such an event on her own would have been difficult, if not impossible.

All of which reinforced Sara's conviction that coming to Derbyshire had been the right decision. When she thought of what she'd be doing instead, had she remained in London—dragged along to the last few balls of the Season, where the maidens who'd successfully found husbands would gloat over their conquests and the chaperons of those who had not—like Aunt Patterson—would huddle together in unhappy and increasingly desperate groups—she could only be even more glad she'd escaped.

If being able to run a household and earn the gratitude of a lady for whom she was fast developing a deep affection weren't delights enough, tonight, for the first time, she would not be just a minor guest at a political dinner—but the official co-hostess. Her lips curved into a smile at the very thought.

After only a week in Derbyshire, Sara was becoming convinced that being Lady Trent's assistant was the right path to an independent future. She couldn't wait to sit at table with the diverse assortment of lawmakers, captains of industry and local gentry, all of them exchanging views on the efficacy of the Factory Acts and predicting what additional changes might be necessary to make conditions for workers—and productivity for the factories—even better.

She let out a little sigh. Silly as it was, she had to acknowledge that a small cloud shadowed what otherwise promised to be a starry bright evening—knowing she wouldn't see, or be able to listen to the views of, Cameron Fitzallen. If, in fact, he could have been induced to express his views while dining with—how had he described them?—'a committee that by next month would have moved on to its next little cause'.

His thinly veiled disdain still rankled.

Despite that, the talk he'd given the committee when they had visited Hughes Cotton Works proved he had a deep knowledge of machines and how to utilise them to maximise production, while still looking for ways to protect his workers. She would have enjoyed hearing more of his observations.

Much as she prided herself on being calm and rational, some small, illogical feminine part of her burned to discover if she'd feel the same inexplicable draw to the man upon seeing him again that she'd felt at their first meeting.

Had Mr Fitzallen been remotely eligible, bitter experience would have warned her to avoid a man who attracted her that strongly. But with no possibility of a future between them, she could have allowed herself the indulgence.

Alas, illogical feminine curiosity would remain unquenched. Lady Trent's soirée was to include only factory *owners*. Even at that, Sara thought with a chuckle, some of the local gentry might be shocked that their aristocratic hostess would actually sit at table with members of the bourgeoisie, no matter how wealthy or influential they might be.

The chime of the mantel clock brought her out of her reverie. Time to collect her hostess and help her down to greet their guests.

A half-hour later, Sara stood in the salon beside the chair Thurston had brought for Lady Trent to sit in while she received their guests. Along with the members of the Parliamentary Committee, who were chatting in a group by the mantel, they had greeted the Squire, another local landowner, Sir Reginald, and his guest, a Mr Lawrence, as well as Messieurs Ward and Johnson, who owned factories the committee had recently toured. Just before dinner, Thurston announced the arrival of the last guest, Mr Hughes—adding after the mill owner's name, 'and Mr Cameron Fitzallen.'

As she swallowed a gasp of surprise, Sara's gaze shot to the threshold, quickly skimming over Mr Hughes, to whom she gave an absent nod, and fixing on Mr Fitzallen. She wasn't sure whether to be alarmed or intrigued as those insidious little eddies of nervousness and delight began swirling again in her belly.

How handsome and commanding he looked in evening dress! And somehow, in formal attire, with his neckcloth properly tied—no intriguing glimpse of bare chest tonight—he also looked more…civilised. Though the muting of that sense of danger that hung about him did nothing to diminish the pull he exerted.

Her appreciative gaze took in the strong chin, the prominent cheekbones and sharp nose, the dark brown hair curling over his forehead as his alert eyes scanned the group. Somewhat to her surprise, he seemed quite at ease. If he were nervous at the prospect of dining with aristocrats, Members of Parliament and some of the richest industrialists in Derbyshire, he hid it well.

Then he saw her. A hint of a smile, followed by a swift expression of chagrin, crossed his face before he nodded to her.

Warmth, along with an intensifying of those flutters in her belly, filled her as the two men approached, bowing to their hostess and thanking her for the pleasure of inviting them to dine, then turning to greet Sara.

Curtsying, she returned an embarrassingly garbled response.

Not until Thurston reappeared a moment later to announce dinner was served did Sara gather her wits together enough to wonder why Mr Fitzallen *was* here. His name had not been on the invitation list she'd sent for Lady Trent's approval.

As the highest-ranking gentleman, Lord Cleve came over to assist Lady Trent to her feet and lead her to the dining room, while Sir Henry offered his arm to Sara. As they exited the salon, Sara overheard Lord Cleve murmur to the Marchioness, 'I've heard you were broad-minded, but isn't this gesture a bit extreme, ma'am? Given our mission, inviting mill owners to eat at your table is understandable, but a mill *manager*?'

Though the Earl's son was voicing the same question she'd wondered about, he didn't have to pose it in such an arrogant, toplofty fashion, Sara thought with frown. She glanced quickly back at Mr Fitzallen who, as the lowest-ranking member of the group, walked last in the procession to the table.

If he'd heard Cleve's remark, he gave no indication.

'As for that, you shall have to see, Lord Cleve,' she heard Lady Trent's amused voice reply.

Since the dinner was intended to be a working meeting of those interested in discussing factory legislation, Sara and her hostess were the only two ladies present.

Wanting Sara to be recognised as co-hostess, Lady Trent had insisted they sit at opposite ends of the table, with the various gentlemen parcelled out between them. Another little thrill filled Sara as she took her place. How she looked forward to tonight's discussions!

Lord Cleve took pride of place beside the Marchioness, the other committee members following, while Sir Henry sat beside Sara, with Mr Hughes on her other side, Mr Fitzallen next to him, and the other mill owners in the middle. More conscious than she wanted to be of Cameron Fitzallen sitting only one chair away, Sara told herself sternly she would not glance at him except in the normal course of conversation. With determination, she turned to Sir Henry.

Before the first course was brought in, however, Lady Trent motioned for her guests' attention. 'Before we begin, I believe Mr Hughes has an announcement. Mr Hughes?'

Smiling broadly, the mill owner rose from his seat. 'If you would, gentlemen and ladies, I invite you to join with me in a toast. First, to our gracious hostesses, Lady Trent and Miss Standish. And then, to the new owner of Hughes Cotton Works, Mr Cameron Fitzallen, who as of today takes over both management and majority share ownership of the mill. To your health and good fortune, ladies, Mr Fitzallen.'

Surprised and pleased for the man, Sara's gaze flew to Fitzallen—who nodded, smiling faintly as he raised his glass to her.

Smiling back, she raised hers to him. 'Congratulations, Mr Fitzallen. Taking over ownership must be both an achievement and a challenge.'

'I'm sure it will be both, Miss Standish.'

'Well done, Mr Fitzallen. You've obviously made more from your patents than I imagined,' Mr Ward, another mill owner, said.

'You should know,' Mr Hughes said with laugh. 'You've paid enough for his designs!'

'You own patents that improve machinery, Mr Fitzallen?' Sir Henry asked. 'How commendable!'

'Much of the credit must go to Mr Hughes. He's encouraged and supported me from the first,' Fitzallen replied modestly.

'The only credit owed me is recognising mechanical genius when I see it,' Hughes replied. 'Fitzallen couldn't have been more than twelve when he came to me with a drawing showing how to modify rollers to keep the cotton from shredding. Aye, and then explained to the machinist how to go about making them! After he came up with two more improvements, I knew I needed to send him to school and get him trained up right.'

'Do you believe there is scope for more improvements?' Sara asked.

Raising his eyebrows, he looked at her. 'You have an interest in mechanical things, Miss Standish?'

'I have an interest in everything that affects the work children do in the mills.'

This time, rather than turn aside the question, as she half-expected, he nodded. 'There is always room for improvements. Mr Robert's new loom of 1830 replaced the traditional wooden frame with a much sturdier iron one and he's just patented a new carder—that's the part of the machine that combs the raw cotton into long strands that can be twisted into thread. It's backed in India rubber, rather than leather, which makes it much more flexible and better able to endure the heat and stress generated by the machine. But there's still much to be done to make operating all the machinery safer for the workers.'

'And you have ideas about that?' Sir Henry asked.

He nodded. 'I'm experimenting with some.'

Mr Ward laughed. 'You won't make money selling safety equipment to me! I'm only interested in what makes the machines more efficient.'

'Safer machines make the whole factory more productive. They reduce the time machinery has to be shut down for repairs and maintain a stable work force that suffers fewer injuries,' Mr Fitzallen replied.

Mr Hughes shook his head. 'He's got a headful of daft ideas! Like reducing working hours for the children even more than the Factory Act requires.'

'A Ten-Hour man, are you?' Sara asked.

'You *are* a close follower of the legislation affecting mill children,' Fitzallen replied, surprise and—she hoped—a touch of approval in his tone. 'Actually, I intend to reduce the children's hours to eight.'

'Eight!' Mr Johnson echoed. 'How can you expect to maintain the productivity of the mill by doing that?'

'Have you visited the mill at New Lanark?' Fitzallen asked. 'That property, gentlemen of the committee, ought to be the standard for all factories! Under Robert Owen's ownership, the mill established housing, communal dining facilities, co-operative stores, and schools for children from infancy on. Though most of the work force came originally from the slums of Edinburgh, there are very few incidents of drunkenness or vice. A rested, well-trained, well-fed work force is the most efficient and productive work force.'

'And so he intends to prove here,' Mr Hughes said. 'As I told him, he'll have free rein to try those ideas, with my blessing, as long as the mill remains as profitable.'

Totally engaged by the conversation, Sara only then noticed that the rest of the table had fallen silent, the diners turning to focus on the discussion at her end of the table.

'And you believe you can continue to make the mill profitable, even with reduced work hours for the children?' Lady Trent asked.

'I do, ma'am, while establishing the best education in Derbyshire for child mill workers.'

'An admirable goal,' the Marchioness said.

The arrival of the next course momentarily halted the conversation, which afterwards became more general. Sara noted that once the other diners moved on to other topics, Mr Fitzallen sat quietly listening, not commenting unless a direct question were put to him.

He seemed, she thought with admiration, remarkably comfortable in his own skin, neither needing to try to puff himself up by dominating the conversation, nor to be intimidated by the distinguished company.

Most of the discussion focused on how well the factories were meeting the requirements of last year's Factory Bill—and whether more legislation was needed. Some of the guests—mainly the mill owners—thought there were already enough rules in place, while Sir Henry and Mr Darlington, the member from Liverpool, argued that further action was needed, particularly more protection and shorter working hours for the child labourers.

In between inserting the occasional question or redirecting the conversation to draw in gentlemen who had not had much opportunity to talk, Sara listened, enthralled. How she loved this freewheeling exchange of ideas and opinions on matters of vital importance to the economy and the working people of the nation! When she compared the discussion around this table to what she would be listening to, were she in London—gossip about the latest *on dit*, newly affianced maidens discussing the style of gown to purchase for their trousseau, or matrons carrying on a lengthy debate on the merits of feathers or ribbons for trimming bonnets—she never wanted to leave Derbyshire.

After the last course was cleared, Lady Trent rose. 'We shall leave you to your brandy and cigars, gentlemen—but not for too long, please. We shall be awaiting the opportunity of rejoining this fascinating conversation over tea very shortly!'

The gentlemen didn't disappoint, coming in to join them just a half-hour later. As they poured for their guests, Lady Trent murmured, 'Are you enjoying yourself as much as you appear to be, my dear?'

'Oh, yes. Would that I might attend such a dinner every night! The only thing better would be to sit in Parliament itself, with the power to make the changes being discussed.'

Lady Trent chuckled. 'Some day, my dear, some day! But for now, being present while those who *can* make the changes talk them over is satisfaction enough. And I have you to thank for that. Had I been required to oversee all the preparations, by now I would have had to excuse myself and take to my bed. Let me express my appreciation again for your making this evening such a success. I hope we can repeat it often.'

'As often as you like!' Sara replied with a grin.

Breaking away from Sir Henry, who'd been engaging him in conversation, Lord Cleve turned back to the ladies. 'I'm to understand that you were responsible for arranging this dinner, Miss Standish? A superior job, as Lady Trent has just been telling you!'

'Miss Standish has an excellent command of running a household,' Lady Trent said.

'I had an experienced advisor to assist me,' Sara responded with a nod to their hostess.

'I'm sure she was. Still, any Member of Parliament would be fortunate to possess so skilled a political hostess.'

Somewhat flustered, Sara wasn't sure what to say. Was Lord Cleve merely being complimentary, or was he indicating an interest in her? She cast a glance at the Marchioness, whose lifted eyebrow told her that lady wasn't sure what to make of the remark either.

Electing for something light, she replied, 'A hostess is a fine thing, I suppose, but it was my understanding that most politicians preferred a wife with a large dowry to fund their careers.'

Lord Cleve laughed. 'A large dowry is never to be sneered at. But there are other valuable attributes for a political wife. Such as one who can make a success of a gathering, even one with such…inferior company.' Lifting an eyebrow, he nodded towards Cameron Fitzallen, who stood nearby in a group with Mr Hughes and the other factory owners.

Annoyed anew, Sara said, 'I thought all the guests were engaging and contributed much to the discussion. And some are such experts! Imagine, having present an industry representative who not only knows the business thoroughly, but is brilliant enough to have patented new equipment designs! If you'll excuse me, I must see if our guests need more refreshment.'

But as she turned to approach the industrialists, she saw that Mr Fitzallen had been watching their group. Chagrined that he had almost certainly overheard Cleve's disparaging remark, she was about to offer something placating when the expression on his face stilled her tongue.

With a smile that didn't reach the dead cold darkness of his eyes, Fitzallen said, 'You had something to say about me, Lord Cleve?'

Though his tone was polite, the intensity of that look and the commanding energy of his stance—like, Sara thought, a shiver running over her skin, a predator about to dispose of his prey—silenced them all. Eyes widening as his gaze met Fitzallen's unrelenting one, the Earl's son opened his mouth, then closed it.

A flush suffusing his face, he swallowed hard before stuttering, 'N-no, Mr Fitzallen. I have…nothing to say.'

'That's what I thought. You were about to offer us more tea, Miss Standish?' he asked, turning his attention to Sara.

'Y-yes,' she replied, stuttering a little herself after the impact of what she'd just witnessed. Had she ever seen someone quelled so completely by just a look?

While the other industrialists demurred, Mr Fitzallen followed her back to the tea table, from whose vicinity Lady Trent had borne Lord Cleve away to join several other members of the committee.

Perhaps she'd insulted Cleve by leaving his group so abruptly, Sara thought as she watched him led away. If so, Lady Trent would smooth things over. Cleve's hauteur regarding the industrialists annoyed her and his compliments made her uncomfortable.

Though if they were meant to indicate an interest in her, she ought to be gratified. Should Aunt Patterson be keeping a list of attractive matrimonial candidates, she'd be delighted to add Cleve's name. As a titled gentleman from a noble family who also was involved in the politics she loved, Sara should perhaps consider him, too.

After all, he knew all about her work with the Ladies' Committee and had just witnessed her active participation in the conversation at dinner. And he still seemed to look on her admiringly.

Although, as she knew only too well, admiration did not necessarily lead to matrimonial interest. Not that she would want it to in this case.

Something about the Earl's son made her uncomfortable, though not at all in the same way as the feral and compelling Mr Fitzallen. Though Lord Cleve was quite handsome, he didn't attract her in the least.

Unlike the man for whom she was currently pouring tea, of whose presence at her elbow she was acutely conscious.

Accepting the cup, he said, 'My compliments on a fine dinner. Lady Trent was telling me that you were responsible for planning and directing it.'

Though he was offering virtually the same praise as Lord Cleve, Sara liked it much better coming from Mr Fitzallen. There was no innuendo in his voice, no undertone that he was saying one thing but might mean more. No, this was just a simple compliment.

'I am so glad you were able to attend. I very much enjoyed listening to you talk about factory management. Once again, congratulations on your new position. It seems a…frightful responsibility.'

He nodded. 'It is. The other investors expect the mill to be run at a handsome profit. But I also owe my workers good wages and safe working conditions. I cannot consider myself successful unless I can achieve both. And might I ask a favour of you?'

A bit taken aback, she said, 'Of me? What can I do for you?' She felt herself blush as the most inappropriate things—like kisses—came to mind. Heavens, what *was* the hold this man seemed to exert over her senses—and her good sense?

'I was speaking with Lady Trent about the treatises that had been written about factory reform and she indicated she had copies in her library. I'm afraid she volunteered you to show me there, to see if I could find the one I was looking for. If you wouldn't mind too much?'

Had her interest in the young industrialist been obvious to her mentor? Sara wondered, feeling her blush deepen. If it had, Lady Trent must approve, or she wouldn't have provided Sara with an opportunity to speak alone with the man.

Despite her unease over how dangerously attractive she found him, it was an opportunity Sara couldn't help seizing.

After glancing over to her hostess, who gave an approving nod, Sara said, 'I am always happy to do what I can to spare Lady Trent. Walking tires her very quickly. If you would follow me, sir?'

Chapter Four

Brayton Hullford being a tidy manor house, rather than the enormous pile rivalling Blenheim in which the Marchioness's son and current title holder now lived, the walk from the salon to the library wasn't long enough to dissipate the nervousness that still sat in the pit of Sara's belly.

Firmly she told herself she was being ridiculous. True, the sheer dynamic energy of the man certainly drew her to him. But, unlike that day at the factory, Fitzallen cast no surreptitious glances her way at dinner that indicated *he* might have some personal interest in *her*.

He simply wished to find the political tracts. She would simply assist him to do so.

That conclusion did nothing to soothe her nerves.

After ushering the guest into the library, Sara walked around the room, lighting enough candelabra to make viewing the titles on the shelves easier, glad to focus on any small task that would lessen her fidgety agitation.

'I believe she keeps the political tracts in this corner,' Sara said, indicating the appropriate shelf.

Nodding, Mr Fitzallen came over to study the volumes. Sara lingered just close enough to render assistance, should he ask for it, but not so close that he might—embarrassing thought!—sense how strongly she was drawn to him.

The fact that they were alone in the library together might give Aunt Patterson palpitations, were she to know of it, but for Sara, who had long looked forward to escaping the ridiculous restrictions placed upon the behaviour of unmarried *ton* females, being able to escort him here with Lady Trent's tacit approval was refreshing. She wasn't ever going to marry and therefore felt no compunction about ignoring the rules that required an unmarried lady to have a suitable chaperon whenever she was accompanied by a gentleman.

As sensitive as she was to Fitzallen's proximity, however, she ought to step aside, or take a chair, but she found she couldn't make herself move further away. As he perused the shelves, she was able, without seeming rude, to frankly study him.

What a worthy object of study he was! She noted a few scars on those big, capable hands—injuries from tangling with machinery? There seemed to be some sort of barely leashed power about him, even as he stood completely still, as if at any moment he might leap into action, making him seem once again both primitive and powerful.

He was certainly handsome. She took full advantage of being able, unobserved, to admire the strong chin, nose and cheekbones, the lush curl of dark hair, the broad shoulders and the strength of that tall, solidly muscled body.

'Ah, here it is,' he said at last, jolting her from her reverie.

'What was it that you wished to find?' she asked. She ought to scold herself for having taken advantage of his absorption in the books to blatantly stare at him, but she couldn't muster enough conviction.

'Some tracts written by Robert Owen,' he replied, holding up several slim volumes. 'Since I'm about to utilise some of his systems at Hughes, I wanted to review his principles.'

'Mr Owen was the gentleman you mentioned at dinner, who ran the factories at New Lanark?'

'Yes. He married the previous owner's daughter, then later took over directing the mills himself. He wrote a report to Parliament about the conditions there in 1812, then *Essays on the Formation of Human Character* a year later. He believed the secret to creating citizens of character was for them to be brought up in the proper physical, moral and social conditions from their earliest years. He opened the first infants' school at New Lanark in 1817 and offered free education through adulthood to all his workers.'

'Something you would like to emulate at Hughes.'

'I would. It won't happen overnight, of course. I intend to gradually reduce the children's workday so they have the energy, as well as the time, to benefit from schooling. But now, I must confess that it wasn't only the chance to find Owen's treatises that prompted me to ask Lady Trent about her library.'

Puzzled, Sara angled her head at him. 'What else did you hope to achieve?'

He gave a rueful sigh. 'A chance to apologise to you. You were quite right when you took me to task the other day. I was rude, and condescending, and I had no idea of the depth of your commitment. Which, it appears from what Lady Trent was telling me at tea about the work of Lady Lyndlington's Ladies Committee and your involvement with a school for indigent girls in London, is deep indeed. I hope you will excuse my poor behaviour.'

Surprised and gratified, Sara nodded. 'I will forgive

it, if you will concede it's possible that reformers can both understand, and perhaps even help do something to advance, the causes in which they believe.'

'Perhaps,' he replied.

'Ah, so you still don't approve of Parliamentary Committees—you will just be more polite about your disapproval.'

He smiled, showing her those delightful dimples again. 'Perhaps you can convince me I am wrong.'

'Perhaps I can. I would like to talk more with you about the sort of school you now run at Hughes and what you want to do to improve it. So I may have an idea of what to look for at the other factories.'

'You might want to read Owen's pamphlets after I return them.'

I'd rather listen to you talk about them.

Squelching that reply before she could utter it, she made herself smile. 'Perhaps I shall.'

But as he gazed down at her, his own smile faded. A more intense look came over his face, and though he neither moved nor spoke, Sara felt a strong wave of tingling awareness wash over her. An intense awareness of him as a man. The certitude that he was aware of her as a woman, too.

Before she could react, he stepped away, breaking the contact. 'I should get you back to the party before the other guests notice your absence,' he said, looking not at her but down at the books he held. 'Wouldn't want to give Lord Cleve further scope to pontificate on the poor manners of "inferior" guests.'

Sara grimaced. 'Lord Cleve is a good deal too certain of his own superiority.'

Looking back at her, he said softly, 'I must thank you for your kind defence.'

Oh, dear. So he had heard her reply, too. 'I only spoke the truth.' She laughed. 'Though you had no need of my help! You put him in his place quite nicely.'

'You're not angling to become Lady Cleve?'

'The wife of that insufferable man? I should think not!' she retorted—before she realised she should have returned just a vague negative.

Mr Fitzallen laughed. 'I don't care in the slightest about Lord Cleve's good opinion—or lack thereof. Dealing with aristocrats like him is an unpleasant necessity of advancing my business, which I do when I must and avoid when I can. I'm glad, though, that you don't seek his approval. You seem too intelligent and independent to play the subservient role he probably envisions for a wife.'

'Being a mirror to reflect his splendour?' Sara tossed back—and then put a hand to her mouth. 'Oh, dear! That was most ungracious! Please forget I said that.'

His smile broadening, Mr Fitzallen gave her a little salute. 'Your secret is safe with me. Shall I blow out the candles for you?'

'Leave the ones on the mantel. Lady Trent may come here to read after the guests leave and she hates to walk into a dark room.'

After extinguishing the others, they paused while Sara blew out the last taper on the table beside the doorway. 'Some day,' Mr Fitzallen said, scanning the room, 'I shall have a library as fine as this.'

'It is excellent, isn't it?' Sara said. 'How I'd hoped to have one, too! Well, that won't happen now.'

'Why not?' he asked as they started back down the hallway.

'I had planned to set up a household with two dear friends from school, a place where we might live together, independent of our families and society, and pursue our political work. The most important thing we all wanted in a house was an excellent library. But, rather unexpectedly, both friends decided to marry. I haven't sufficient funds to live by myself, even if my family would permit it. So…no library of my own.'

She gave a rueful sigh. 'So you see, though in the world's eyes my situation is more fortunate than yours, you now have the advantage of me. With your intelligence, hard work and drive, you are carving out a successful place for yourself in the world. And some day, you'll build or buy that house with an excellent library. Something I, for all my advantages of birth, can never do.'

'Unless you marry a gentleman who possesses a fine one.'

'Then it will be *his* library, not mine. Not one I earn for myself.'

'The advantages of birth aren't to be sneered at. They make "carving out a place for yourself" a deal easier.'

'I'm sure they do. Still, were I a man, I would prefer your situation to Lord Cleve's. You have brilliance and vision—whereas he possesses only birth, the result of a random chance of fate that had nothing to do with his own efforts.'

'You think not? He probably considers it a great achievement to be born an earl's son.'

She laughed. 'You're right. He probably does.'

After hesitating a minute, he said, 'And if I were to tell you I was a foundling orphan who grew up in the parish workhouse, would that change your view of my… "situation"?'

She stopped short, staring at him. She'd supposed him the son of a farmer, or the offspring of a craftsman of some sort, a draper or milliner or draftsman. She'd never imagined he could have come so far after beginning as one of the lowest of the low, with literally nothing— neither home nor family.

'It does change my opinion, yes,' she said slowly.

Glancing at his suddenly taut body and grim face, Sara realised that Fitzallen was bracing himself. Waiting for her to move away, for her tone to cool as she made some non-committal remark before distancing herself from someone socially so far beneath her.

He'd been sent away to school, she remembered Mr Hughes saying. He must have suffered endless slights, overheard sly innuendo, perhaps even been dismissed outright because of his lack of birth. Yet, tonight, he'd been the most brilliant and compelling man in the room.

And, yes, the most attractive. An attraction that continued to entice her.

An enticement that ought to make her avoid him, despite the certainty that he would soon be out of her life.

A single dismissive remark now would accomplish that.

Still, his conversation at dinner and here in the library had convinced her he truly did want to help the mill children whose welfare she cared about so deeply. He'd taken steps to promote that welfare, steps that she wanted to know more about.

Making up her mind on the instant, she decided she would, for now, ignore the danger he posed to her peace of mind and give him an honest answer.

Pausing on the threshold, she said, 'I admire you all the more for beginning with nothing and having won your present position and the prospect of even more by your own efforts alone.'

She watched his expression go from guarded, to surprised, to…wondering. 'Thank you,' he said gruffly.

'Might I ask an impertinent question? About your name. "Cameron Fitzallen" suggests you are a Scot. But I don't hear any trace of Scotland in your speech.'

He shook his head. 'I was born in the north, but the name itself means nothing. It was the custom at the foundling home where I was left as a babe to name orphans after the institution's founders or supporters. Since the founder was Lord Cameron, and one of the chief benefactors Sir Ralph Fitzallen, I was dubbed Cameron Fitzallen.'

'Ah, I see. It…suits you, somehow.'

He chuckled. 'Those noble gentlemen would be distressed to hear that. Apparently the custom is being discouraged, as rascally orphaned "namesakes" have occasionally turned up on aristocratic doorsteps, claiming to be relations.'

'They need have no concern about that in your case! You will make your mark on the world with no help from the likes of them.'

Then, fearing her fervent avowal might have revealed her attraction to him all too clearly, she gave him a quick nod and headed down the hallway.

Oh, my, he certainly was fascinating, Sara thought as she walked. As she'd told Fitzallen, knowing how far he'd come only increased her admiration for him.

She found herself wondering how she might establish some sort of…friendship with him, despite their radically different experiences and places in society. But although he offered her the novelty of seeming to listen to her opinions, even conceding he might be persuaded by them, she needed to remember how risky it was to pursue friendship with a man who attracted her.

Heavens, no need to be so melodramatic, she admonished herself. It was unlikely they'd manage to become friends, much as his intelligence and his vision called to her.

Where, after all, would they ever meet again, unless Lady Trent repeated her dinner with local industrialists? The Marchioness might be forward-looking, but it was unlikely she would encourage a factory owner to pay her a social call.

Though if Sara were to visit Hughes's factory school, she might encounter him there...

As they entered the salon, Sara thanked heaven Lady Patterson was safely ensconced in Mayfair.

Still supremely conscious of his presence beside her, she walked over with him to Lady Trent, who was seated on a sofa by the fire, Sir Henry and Mr Pennington arranged beside her. 'Did you find what you required, Mr Fitzallen?' Lady Trent asked.

'I did, ma'am. I should like to borrow these volumes, if I may. And thank you for lending Miss Standish to assist me. What a magnificent library you have! Without her help, I might have needed hours to discover the volumes. Though I could never regret time spent in a library.'

Lady Trent nodded approvingly. 'Knowledge is the key to success—and power, as I imagine you know, Mr Fitzallen.'

'Also a path to pleasure, ma'am. I've never had as much time as I'd like for it, but when I can spare a moment, I thoroughly enjoy reading Burns, Shakespeare, Wordsworth and Keats.'

'Truly?' Sara exclaimed. 'I shouldn't have thought those works would appeal to a practical businessman and inventor. Mathematical tracts, perhaps.'

'Poetry, more than any other form of literature, reduces a topic to its purest form,' he replied, turning those compelling dark eyes on her. 'Just as a successful design strips away unnecessary detail and incorporates only the essentials.'

'So it does,' Sara allowed. 'I'd never considered the parallel.'

Somehow, the idea that this virile, intelligent, intensely driven man could also be moved by poetry made him even more appealing. A fact which, alas, was not at all helpful in trying to persuade herself it would be prudent to suppress the urge to see him again for more than a brief consultation about mill schools.

'You are a man of unexpected pursuits,' Lady Trent observed.

Fitzallen smiled wryly. 'One of which must be to arrive at the mill before daylight. So, reluctant as I am to take my leave, I fear I must. Thank you for a splendid dinner and a most interesting evening, Lady Trent, Miss Standish. Goodnight to you both.'

With that, catching the eye of Mr Hughes and giving him a nod, Fitzallen walked away.

She ought to be relieved he'd removed the compelling temptation he represented. Still, most of the energy, and a great deal of her enjoyment in the evening, walked out with him.

Chapter Five

The other guests took their leave shortly after Mr Fitzallen. After turning the rooms over to the housekeeper and her staff to clear, Sara lent Lady Trent her arm as they mounted the stairs.

'Stay a moment, won't you, my dear?' Lady Trent asked after Sara had assisted her into the sitting room adjoining her bedchamber.

'Of course, ma'am. What else can I help you with?'

Rather than return an immediate answer, Lady Trent took a seat in her favourite armchair by the fire. 'Ah, much better,' she said with a sigh as she settled back. 'I should be grateful to Mr Fitzallen for beginning the exodus of the guests. I'd about reached my limit for sitting on that sofa.'

'I'm so sorry!' Sara exclaimed, instantly solicitous. 'Can I bring you something? Perhaps some willow bark tea?'

'No, no. Just pour me a glass of that cordial, if you please.'

After taking a long sip of the herbal brew Sara brought her, Lady Trent looked back at her. 'So, what did you think of the enterprising Mr Fitzallen?'

Much as she trusted her mentor, a little voice warned Sara to be cautious in her reply. 'He's…most interesting. Obviously intelligent, talented, and driven to be successful. With such forward-thinking ideas!'

'Am I correct in observing that you found the gentleman himself as…attractive as his ideas?'

Sara smiled. 'If you're asking whether or not I thought him handsome and charming, I don't see how any lady could fail to do so.'

'Indeed! He's very handsome and his company manners were quite charming. I would just caution you to realise that they were…company manners. And warn you that, although he appeared quite gentlemanly, he is not a gentleman.'

Though Lady Trent was only telling her what she'd already told herself, Sara felt herself bristle—and was filled with a fierce desire to defend the man.

'I know he was not *born* a gentleman. But surely you will acknowledge that a man who has come so far by virtue of his own efforts and talent ought not to be disparaged because of his birth!'

'Oh, I'd no intention of doing that! I find him admirable, as well as attractive. If my years of observing people are of any worth, I think he will go far, perhaps expand his first mill into an empire of them. Even end up ennobled, as Sir Richard Arkwright did. What I meant is that, to come as far as he has from such low beginnings, he has had to be single-minded, perhaps even ruthless. The harsh environment in which he had to survive probably didn't allow for the development of the courtesy and consideration you are accustomed to receiving from society gentlemen. You do intend to visit the mill school, don't you?' At Sara's nod, she continued, 'If you are to encounter him again, you must keep that in mind.'

Sara nodded. 'I'm quite aware of how lowly his beginnings were. Indeed, he frankly confessed them to me. However, rather than being…ashamed of them, he seems instead rather contemptuous of a man like Lord Cleve, who has been handed every advantage without expending any effort of his own.'

Lady Trent said, 'I can understand why *he* might feel that way. The world, however, will take quite an opposite view of the two.'

'Sadly true. But though I know nothing about how he surmounted the challenges he faced growing up where he did, I do know we share *some* of the same values and goals,' Sara countered. 'A concern for child factory workers and a deep desire to have them afforded the education that will allow them to better their condition. A belief that the welfare of the workers is as important as the profitability of the enterprise. Indeed, Mr Fitzallen exhibits a compassion and concern for workers that our own class quite often lacks. Coming from where he has, surely even you admit such feelings are exemplary!'

'Exemplary, yes. And no doubt developed by observing—and experiencing—what he must have, to rise to where he is. But despite his views on equality, and all that he has achieved, you must be wary. Though you may choose to overlook them, the differences between you are quite real. I just ask that you remember that and not be carried away by a handsome face and a noble agenda.'

Since she could hardly dispute the truth of Lady Trent's observations, Sara took another tack. 'Is it not assuming a great deal to imagine Mr Fitzallen would have any interest in me? Such a handsome, dynamic young man probably has any number of feminine admirers eager to attract his notice.'

'Quite true. As you say, Mr Fitzallen is handsome and charming enough to arrest the attention of any lady he meets. He exerts…a powerful attraction. I'm just warning you not to let that attraction lead you into doing something you would later regret. I know you are hoping, under my more relaxed supervision, to dispense with some of the silly restrictions imposed upon an unmarried lady of Quality. It is rather ridiculous to suppose a gently bred girl must be accompanied everywhere, while females of other classes are able to move about freely. I believe that you are wise and intelligent enough not to need a chaperon trailing about after you, as I showed tonight in allowing you to assist Mr Fitzallen in the library. However…'

She paused, giving Sara a penetrating look. 'You must also know that if you dispense with a chaperon—or if you were known to associate with a man like Mr Fitzallen—you reduce your chances of attracting an eligible suitor of your own class, who has been brought up to expect that a well-bred unmarried female would adhere to those standards. I assume that doesn't concern you?'

Sara shook her head. 'Not at all. Had I wished to marry such a gentleman, I would have remained with my aunt in London.'

Though she nodded, Lady Trent gave a sigh. 'I've become very fond of you, my dear. Just be cautious. I'd not want to see you drawn into the spell of a compelling man who could break your heart, ruin your reputation, or, even worse, lure you into risking exile from your home, family and the world you've always known.'

Sara felt an inward chill, even considering such a dire outcome. She had some money of her own, enough to live on without becoming impoverished. But if her attraction to Fitzallen led her into doing something that society disapproved of so completely that she found herself cut off from everything and everyone…

Having Lady Trent summarise her vague misgivings in one stark, simple sentence was both shocking—and revealing. Sara knew herself well enough to realise that shy, quiet Sara Standish wasn't bold enough to take risks like that.

'I admit that I'm drawn to him,' she replied at length. 'But I'm also quite aware of the…gap between us. I hope to draw on his expertise about the best way to encourage education of factory children, should I encounter him when I visit the school at Hughes Cotton Works. But I shall be on my guard against anything more.'

'That's all I ask,' Lady Trent said, nodding. 'And I truly don't mean to disparage the young man—quite the opposite! I feel I'd have failed in my duty if I hadn't warned you, for if Mr Fitzallen could excite the interest and admiration of an old woman like me, he is dangerously compelling indeed! Now, I've kept you long enough. You must be longing for your bed, as I know I am. Ah, there's Jeffers now, to assist me.'

'Goodnight, ma'am. And thank you again for allowing me to be a part of such a splendid evening.'

'Thank you for doing all the work to make it splendid.'

Smiling at her hostess, Sara walked out.

But that smile faded as soon as she closed the sitting-room door. Attraction, desire and a strong urge to know Mr Fitzallen better and discover what had allowed him to make such a spectacular rise in station warred with her natural reticence—and the bitter memories of what had happened the last time she let herself be drawn to a man she admired, whom she thought admired her.

It was foolish for her to daydream about some sort of comradely, platonic friendship between them. She was too attracted to him—she felt a blush heat her face again to recall her instinctive desire for his kisses—to trust herself. She couldn't guarantee she could spend much time with him without being pulled further under the spell of the mysterious, mesmerising Cameron Fitzallen.

A man who'd given her no indication he wished for any sort of relationship with her.

A man with whom, in the eyes of the world, no relationship *was* possible.

Despite knowing that, she had to ignore an inner protest whispering it was a mistake not to pursue her acquaintance with a man to whom she'd been more strongly drawn than anyone she'd ever met.

But ignore it she would. She would carry out her original intention to pay visits to the factory schools. But she would not seek out Mr Fitzallen when she visited Hughes Works.

A vague sense of regret saddened her at the decision.

Suddenly weary, she reached her own chamber and rang for her maid. Lady Trent had paid her the compliment of thinking her wise and intelligent enough not to need a chaperon to protect her.

She only hoped she deserved such confidence.

Ten days later, Cameron Fitzallen paced briskly down the main street of the village of Knively, nodding to various acquaintances as he walked towards Mr Ardley's bookshop. After a more than usually intense two weeks of work, he felt he deserved a break—and a reward.

Though his transition from manager to owner-manager was going smoothly—he had already been supervising the day-to-day operation of the mill for some time before he became the owner—he'd remained each evening after finishing his usual work to make a full review of the mill's ledgers, going back the last ten years. Mr Hughes had shared details about the current profitability of the mill with him, but Cam wanted to study its history to determine how and when the operation had expanded, so he might better plan for the future.

After evenings of intensive effort, he felt he had mastered those details and reacquainted himself as well with all the particulars of how and where Hughes Cotton Works obtained the raw cotton and flax that the mill turned into thread and cloth. He'd also identified all the markets into which the finished goods were sold, making notes of several supply-line corrections that would make the manufacturing process more efficient, and jotting down ideas of where they might next expand the market for their finished goods.

This evening, rather than picking up a plate of victuals to carry back to the suite of rooms he'd rented after becoming Hughes's manager, he intended to remain at the Thistle and Bobbin for some convivial company while he enjoyed one of Mrs Lockwood's fine dinners. Then he'd retire to the wing chair before the fire in his sitting room to read the journals and the new book of poetry Mr Ardley had ordered for him, which he was about to collect at the bookshop.

The prospect of having books and poetry energised him—and brought back to the forefront of his thoughts his evening encounter with Miss Standish in the library at Brayton Hullford. A thrill of attraction, desire and an odd sort of warmth he couldn't put a name to rippled through him, speeding his heartbeat and curving his lips into a smile.

Though, to be honest, he had to admit that memories of that evening had teased at the edge of consciousness ever since he left Brayton Hullford. He'd kept them at bay through single-minded focus on work and by telling himself that, having given the lady the apology he owed her, he should now dismiss her from his mind.

He'd already spent as much time thinking about her as their circumstances warranted when, upon learning he was to be included in the dinner Lady Trent was giving for local mill owners and the Parliamentary Committee, he'd allowed himself several days of edgy anticipation, suspecting she would be present at that event.

The rush of delight that swept through him upon seeing her in the receiving line with Lady Trent—along with a deeper stir of sensual awareness—had both been stronger than they ought.

Though he immediately promised himself to be sensible and limit his personal interaction with her to delivering, if the opportunity presented itself, the apology he owed her for his churlish behaviour during the mill tour, he'd been surprised and charmed by her conversation at dinner. She truly did seem interested in the work that occupied his life and not just the welfare of the child workers. Eyes alight, an expression of avid interest on her face, she'd followed closely the discussion of innovations and improvements in factory machinery.

And he couldn't help but be both amused and touched when she'd taken umbrage on his behalf at the slighting remarks made by that supercilious, full-of-himself Earl's son, Lord Cleve.

Then, when he'd been granted that time alone in the library with her...

He recalled his heightened sensory awareness as he'd accompanied her down the hallway. The subtle scent of violets emanating from her hair and skin filled his head, the warmth of her body heated his own, while everything masculine in him appreciated the sweet womanly sway of her figure as she walked.

He'd had to work to appear calm and articulate and avoid stuttering, awkward as a green stripling stepping out with his first sweetheart. Which was rather an extraordinary reaction for a man of his experience.

Not that he was a ladies' man by any means. He was far too single-mindedly focused on work, his studies and his inventions to devote a great deal of time to dalliance. But he knew women found him attractive and he'd had his fair share of dalliances since his teens.

He'd never met a woman quite like Miss Standish, though. Perhaps because she was a lady. But then, he noted with a frown, though his acquaintance with upper-class females was admittedly slight, she didn't seem like any of other society females he'd encountered. They generally fell into one of two groups, either expressing tender sentiments over the plight of the lower classes without ever doing anything practical to alleviate it, or looking down upon them, with an elegant curl of the lip, as lesser beings whose contaminating company should be avoided.

Miss Standish had accepted his apology with more graciousness than he expected or deserved. Displaying not a hint of reproach for his rudeness, she seemed to have mastered or forgotten the anger and righteous indignation evident in her voice and manner when she'd swept out of his factory office that day.

Altogether, she'd been such a...surprise. Not just the soft, rounded, golden beauty that called to the physical in him, but her bright and gentle manner. Trying to resist his attraction to her, he'd forced himself to reveal just how lowly his origins were. Yet even then, she'd treated him with respect.

A reaction not at all like the one bitter experience had taught him to expect from persons of her class.

Small wonder the conundrum—and the wonder—that was Miss Sara Standish kept intruding upon his consciousness.

Thinking about her had been a harmless indulgence. At this point in his life, he had no intention of becoming involved with any woman—females tending to muddy a man's thoughts and deflect him from the single-minded focus essential to advancing in his profession.

Besides, he was unlikely to see her again. As time passed, the deep impression she'd made on him in their two encounters would fade.

A spring of anticipation in his step, Cam reached the bookstore and walked in, the bell affixed to the door tinkling as he entered. As he looked to the counter to call a greeting to Mr Ardley, he stopped short, the words dying on his lips.

Across the aisle by a bookcase, her head bent over a book she was examining, stood Miss Sara Standish.

Chapter Six

Cam felt again that mix of delight and desire he had experienced upon seeing her that night at Brayton Hullford—and quashed it with a frown. Airy daydreams were one thing, harmless if not too often indulged. Acting on the attraction that drew him to the lady would be the height of stupidity.

The entry bell didn't seem to have interrupted Miss Standish's concentration, for she didn't look up. Thanking heaven for that, he walked quietly to the counter, determined to pick up the order Mr Ardley was holding for him and depart before he attracted her notice.

'Ah, Mr Fitzallen, you are here for your books, I imagine,' the proprietor said in a hearty voice that carried through the small shop. Though he now stood with his back towards her, Cam swore he could *feel* her regard the moment Miss Standish raised her eyes from her book.

'Mr Fitzallen?' she murmured.

'That he is, ma'am,' Mr Ardley said. 'Knively's new mill owner is one of the bookstore's greatest supporters and not just because of his standing order for scientific journals and newsletters. He purchases a large number of the latest books as well.'

Telling himself it was a simple matter of courtesy—now that his presence had been noted, it would be rude to ignore the lady—Cam turned around and bowed. 'Good day, Miss Standish. If you are looking for a new novel to occupy you, I am sure Mr Ardley will be as helpful to you as he always is to me.'

He told himself not to notice how the gold of her hair lit up the shop like a ray of sunshine. Not to admire the smooth curve of her face, the faint blush of her cheek, the rosebud mouth that called to him, or the blue, blue eyes, cerulean as a cloudless summer sky. A hint of her violet scent drifted to him and he sucked in a breath as a tremor of response pulsed through him.

'Good day to you, too, Mr Fitzallen,' she said and hesitated.

For a fraught moment, Cam thought she intended merely to add a nod to that greeting and return to perusing her book, politely acknowledging him, but giving him no encouragement to continue the conversation.

Which, of course, was exactly what she *should* do.

For several moments, she stood silent, neither turning away nor saying anything else, her expressive face a picture of indecision.

He was torn between delight and irritation at himself for being delighted, when instead of looking back down at her book, she smiled. 'Mr Ardley has been most helpful. But I would value your expertise in this matter at well. If it wouldn't be imposing too much, might I trouble you to answer a few questions?'

His eyes never leaving hers, Cam found himself beside her without being conscious of crossing the room. 'No imposition at all. With what may I assist you?'

'Despite what you may think, I'm not seeking a novel to while away my idle hours,' she said, her tone a mix of amusement and gentle reproach. 'Over the last week, I've visited the factory schools at Wirksworth and Bakewell. Although there seems to be some attempt to instruct the children in their basic letters, they have almost no resources beyond chalk and a few slates. I've not yet visited your schoolroom at Hughes Works, but I had the impression that you also provided instruction books to help the children master their letters as well as story books with enticing tales to inspire them to learn to read for themselves.'

Telling himself to ignore her appeal and concentrate on answering the questions, Cam nodded. 'We give the children slates and chalk to practise on. But I agree that, after having worked a long day, there isn't much incentive for children to learn the alphabet and new words for their own sake. Rewarding their diligence with stories, rhymes and songs is much more likely to get results.'

'So I would think!' she said, her expressive eyes lighting. 'Which books do you use? Not the horridly improving "Little Henry and his Bearer", I'm sure!'

'Certainly not!' Cam replied, smiling back. 'If you'd like to discuss the selection of books further, may I invite you to a glass of cider at the Thistle and Bobbin? It would be more comfortable than standing here in the shop.'

The invitation slipped out before he could consider the implications. He realised at once that he shouldn't have issued it—spending *more* time in her company was hardly the best way to rid himself of his fascination with her.

Fortunately, she'd probably refuse his offer.

But to his guilty gratification, after a short hesitation, she nodded. 'Yes, that would be more pleasant. Thank you, Mr Ardley, for your assistance. Rest assured, after

I consult with Mr Fitzallen, I shall be back to place an order!'

'Happy to help you at any time, Miss Standish,' the proprietor said as he ushered them to the door.

'I've been trying to recall which books my governess used when I was learning my letters,' Miss Standish said as they walked towards the inn, Cam once again intensely aware of her beside him. 'I believe Mr Newbery's *Pretty Little Pocket-Book* was the first—it had rhymes to help one remember each alphabet letter. The ones I truly recall were more advanced—*Aesop's Fables*, for example. We had a copy published by Bewick, with his wonderful woodblock illustrations.'

'We've used the Newbery book at Hughes's school,' Cam said, trying to restrain his enthusiasm at being able to discuss his passion for educating mill children—and discuss it with *her*. 'Also Anna Barbauld's *Lessons for Children*, written in four volumes, each one increasing in difficulty as the children progress. Ah, here we are at the inn.'

Uncomfortably aware of the attention their entrance was sure to draw, Cam ushered her inside. Yet another reason why his impulsive invitation had been unwise—but too late to retract it now.

'Ah, Mr Fitzallen,' the innkeeper called, smiling as he looked up from polishing the wooden bar. 'Good day to you and to you, young miss.'

Trying to defuse as quickly as possible any speculation about his escorting this particular 'young miss', Cam said, 'Miss Standish, allow me to introduce Mr Lockwood, proprietor of the Thistle and Bobbin. Miss Standish is staying with Lady Trent at Brayton Hullford, assisting her in hosting the Parliamentary Committee that is inspecting the cotton mills hereabouts,' he explained as the innkeeper walked over. 'Miss Standish has a particular interest in improving the lot of the children at the factory schools.'

'Honoured to serve you, miss,' Lockwood said, giving her a bow.

'Could we have that table in the corner, by the window, where it is quieter? Miss Standish wishes to consult me about compiling a list of the books we've found most useful in the school at Hughes Works, so her committee might obtain them for the schools at other factories.'

'A right fine service you'd be doing those youngsters, miss,' Lockwood said. 'I'll have your cider poured in a trice. Mrs Lockwood has cooked up a fine roast today, Mr Fitzallen. Will you be stopping by to pick up a bowlful later?'

'I thought I might sample mine in the taproom instead, along with a mug of your finest homebrew,' Cam said.

The innkeeper's eyes lit. 'That'd be a rare pleasure, sir! Works through almost every evening, he does,' Lockwood said to Miss Standish. 'The missus is always saying how it's not good for the digestion, you eating alone over your books! She'll be right pleased to have you supping here tonight.'

'Tell her I shall be looking forward to it. Allow me, Miss Standish,' he said, pulling out a chair for her.

'Since I foolishly left Brayton Hullford without paper or pencil, I shall have to make a mental list of what you recommend,' Miss Standish said as she took a seat. 'So far we have Newberry's *Pretty Little Pocket Book* and Mrs Barbauld's *Lessons for Children*. Have you also used Charles and Mary Lamb's *Tales from Shakespeare*?'

'No, that's a bit too complex,' he began saying, then paused as the barmaid sauntered over with their mugs on a tray.

'Here you go,' she said, bending low as she set them on the table, the better to show off the breasts swelling above her low-cut blouse.

'Thank you, Ellie,' he said, keeping his gaze fixed on her face.

'Always happy to serve *you*, Mr Fitzallen,' she murmured, shooting him a look of invitation before moving off again.

Hoping her blatant display hadn't shocked—or disgusted—his companion, Cam flicked a glance at Miss Standish—and was relieved to find her smiling.

'A very...efficient young woman,' she said, humour quivering in her voice as her gaze following the girl's hip-swaying walk back to the bar.

'Very,' he murmured, resisting the urge to run a finger around his suddenly too-tight cravat.

'You were saying you found the Shakespeare tales a bit too complex for the children?' she continued, mercifully moving the conversational focus away from the seductive barmaid. 'Is there another book of stories you prefer?'

'The children are fond of Robert Dodsley's *Aesop's Fables*. The ones whose families originally worked on farms particularly enjoy having the animals speaking in their own voices.'

'How about *Tales of Mother Goose*?' she suggested. 'I remember loving the stories of Sleeping Beauty and Cinderella.' She laughed. 'What little girl wouldn't thrill to read about a kitchen maid from the cinders being rescued by a handsome prince?'

'I suppose. My tastes ran more towards *Ivanhoe* and *Swiss Family Robinson*.'

'There's a newer book of fables, German ones recently

translated into English. *Grimms' Fairy Tales*. My brother's children like them very much. Have you heard of it?'

'Yes. I preferred the intrigue of "Hansel and Gretel". Although I imagine you would like "Rapunzel", another tale of a maiden rescued, or "The Frog Prince".'

She chuckled. 'Now, that is a tale for an *older* maiden. I'm sure many of us wish a simple kiss could turn some frog of our acquaintance into a dashing prince! If your students prefer more exotic tales, perhaps we could have the teacher read to them from *One Thousand and One Arabian Nights*. I remember being enthralled when my governess—'

'Not that one,' he said flatly.

She broke off, looking surprised. 'You disapprove? Were the stories not…moral enough? I admit, the idea of a slave girl spinning tales to avoid being executed might not be thought precisely edifying.'

'It wasn't that.' He forced a smile, sorry that he'd overreacted. 'The book represents…an early and rather bitter disappointment.'

'The *book* was a disappointment? I can't imagine how—but excuse me, I didn't mean to pry. I'm sorry you didn't enjoy it.'

Her expression conveyed puzzlement, but also respect for his feelings and a warm sympathy. He found himself wanting to explain what had happened to create what must seem an inexplicable distaste for a book in one who otherwise had expressed nothing but praise for the written word.

That impulse to reveal the circumstances surprised him. He'd kept his emotions bottled up closely for a very long time, having had no one he trusted to confide in since he was a lad.

If she'd pestered him about it, he would have revealed

nothing and moved on. But in the face of her apparent concern, he found himself saying, 'It wasn't the story itself that disappointed me. In fact, *Tales of the Arabian Nights* was the first book I bought for myself, once I was earning more than I needed to pay for food and shelter.'

He halted, taking a deep breath, still not sure he wanted to go on. But she didn't prompt him, merely continued to look at him with that expression of compassionate interest.

She certainly appears to genuinely care about people, he thought.

The notion seemed to unknot his tongue. 'By the time I started working in the mill—I was six or seven—I already knew I loved books. There were no Factory Laws governing schooling then, although the children were supposed to be allowed to attend the village school several days a week. I don't know how it was at other mills, but our attendance at the local school was much more erratic. Even so, from the first day, I was fascinated by the books on the schoolmaster's desk. I was determined to learn to read them. To one day possess books of my own.'

Carried away by the tide of long-suppressed memories, he continued, 'About that time, a committee of local gentry visited the parish workhouse. One of them, a beautifully dressed lady, stopped to talk with me. She asked me what gift I'd like. When I told her I'd like a book, she described a book of fantastic stories and promised to bring me a copy for my very own.'

'One Thousand and One Nights,' Miss Standish said. He nodded.

'And she never brought it.'

'No.'

She shook her head. 'No wonder you are so wary

of committees full of well-wishers, who glibly shower promises one cannot trust to be fulfilled.'

He quirked a smile. 'It did make a rather strong impression. For weeks, months, I waited for her to bring my book. In the meantime, I sneaked out as often as I could to the schoolroom. I vowed I would master reading, so that when the book finally arrived, I would be able to devour every page. I suppose it was nearly a year before I finally accepted that neither she—nor the book—would ever appear.'

'And yet you didn't let that disappointment diminish your resolve to read, or your love of books. Or your desire to continue advancing.'

He nodded. 'It reinforced the lesson that I could rely only on myself to achieve, or acquire, what I wanted. A useful maxim to absorb at a young age for one situated as I was.'

'Situated where you couldn't count on anyone but yourself to help you achieve your aspirations. And so you did. Climbing up an admirable—if lonely—path.'

Cam shrugged. 'I don't know about "lonely". Having never had a family, I've never been anything but alone. But I have many friends, so you may wipe that pitying expression off your face. I have been quite content with my life.'

'With all your achievements, how could you not be? It's just… I can't imagine not having family, or my good friends, with whom to share my life.' Then she paused, grimacing. 'Although now that my two dearest friends have married, I suppose I'm going to have to learn to exist on my own.'

The sadness in her tone pricked at him. 'Just two shipwrecked souls, cast ashore on deserted islands, are we?'

he said in melodramatic tones, trying to coax her out of her melancholy.

'I suppose.' With a sigh, she drained the rest of the cider.

'Now, I should let you get back to your work—or remain for your fine dinner!' she said, her tone as she looked back up once again brisk and businesslike. 'I'll take my mental list back to Mr Ardley and order copies of the texts you recommend. Plus several copies of the *Grimms' Fairy Tales* and *Tales of Mother Goose* for the schoolmasters to read to the children. They will enjoy them so much!'

All traces of sadness gone, she was practically beaming now at the idea of the factory children being entertained by the tales she'd so enjoyed as a child. A little awed, Cam watched her face, once again both amused—and touched.

Was she truly the pure soul she appeared, guileless as the children about whom she expressed such concern?

Though her gentleness touched him, it also made him uneasy. He wasn't used to encountering kindness or softness. He'd fought and competed for everything he'd ever had, from his first job at the factory, to advancement up the ranks of responsibility, to attention and recognition from Mr Hughes.

That toughness had served him well, enabling him to rise to the position he occupied today. And had helped him survive the miserable half-year he'd spent at Cambridge, shunned by his aristocratic betters while he doggedly worked to marry the practical principles of mechanics acquired after a decade of tending and refining machinery to the theoretical principles of classical science.

He'd observed first-hand what happened to soft people, giving people, people with kind hearts. Only the strong and ruthless made it alive out of the parish work-house.

Miss Standish probably wouldn't have lasted a week.

Much as he didn't want to disillusion her, he felt compelled to add a note of caution. 'Did the schoolmasters at the mill schools request that you obtain books for them?'

'What schoolmaster would not want more books for his pupils?' she countered.

He levelled a frank look at her. 'One who has already determined the way he wants to teach. One who doesn't appreciate someone suggesting other ways to do it.'

'You think I will meet with resistance, if I attempt to bring in more books?'

'I think you should be prepared in case you do. So that you will not be…bitterly disappointed.'

She smiled at him, the grin a little impish. 'I don't intend to be. If necessary, I intend to be…very persuasive.'

With that, she rose from her chair and made him a curtsy. 'Thank you for your time, Mr Fitzallen, and for your recommendations.'

Cam stood as well. 'You are very welcome. Let me escort you back to the bookstore.'

'That's not at all necessary. It's but a few steps. Besides, I believe there is someone here, waiting to offer you…service.'

Startled, he whipped his gaze to her face, to discover her giving him a saucy half-smile. She was *teasing* him, the wretch! he thought incredulously.

She might be pure of soul, but she was obviously not an innocent.

Unfortunately, his body had its inevitable reaction to that thought. He gritted his teeth as his simmering sensual attraction fired back up.

Unsure what to reply—he certainly mustn't follow up his mistake of an invitation by actually *flirting* with her—he decided the wisest response was to ignore her remark. 'A gentleman never leaves a lady until she steps into her carriage or has her maid beside her to escort her home,' he countered, gesturing towards the door. 'My dinner can wait.'

'Very well, if you insist, I am being picked up from the bookshop. Mr Lockwood,' she called as they walked to the door, 'your cider is quite as delicious as Mr Fitzallen claimed. While our party remains at Brayton Hullford, I'm sure I shall take other opportunities to come sample it.'

'Any time at all, Miss Standish! Be pleased to serve you.'

They talked again of the books she would order as he walked her the short distance back to the bookshop. While he managed to carry on the conversation, he had to wonder if she was as conscious of the pull between them as he was.

Or was the sensual attraction that affected him so strongly on his side only?

All his experience with the female sex argued it was not.

He hadn't decided what he ought to do about that complication when her gesture towards the street distracted him. 'There, you see, the carriage to carry me safely back to Brayton Hullford,' she said, pointing out a landau whose horses a groom was walking up and down. 'You may safely relinquish your charge.'

She might be safe now…but he still felt uneasy about how she and her educational theories might be greeted at the other factories when she sailed in with her armloads of books.

Stopping by with the committee to observe was one thing. Trying to restructure the curriculum of a harried, and perhaps uninterested schoolmaster, whose employer was not enthused about having a school in the first place, might invite a good deal more opposition.

Even if this were true, it wasn't any of his business how other factories ran their schools. Nor was Miss Standish in any way *his* responsibility. If she tried to step in and was firmly rebuffed, that would be unfortunate. And yet...

'When do you intend to return to the other factories?' he asked abruptly.

'Not until after the new books arrive. Probably in a week or so. Do you...really feel I may not be successful if I attempt to deliver the books on my own?'

'I'm afraid there's a strong chance you will be refused entrance.'

'You truly think so?'

'I'm virtually certain of it.'

'In that case...' She gave a little huff of frustration. 'I know I shouldn't ask, but... I do so want to help the pupils...'

He knew exactly what she hadn't asked.

Just politely refuse, he told himself.

Heaven knew he had work enough at Hughes to keep him occupied. He didn't need to go jaunting about the countryside with a woman he found too appealing for his own good.

He opened his lips, fully intending to regretfully decline—but at look of hopeful entreaty on her face, the words died in his throat.

Knowing he'd be annoyed with himself later, he found himself saying, 'Let me know when you intend to go and I will accompany you to Wirksworth. The owner at

Bakewell resigned himself with good grace to the legislation requiring schooling for factory children, but Mr Crowden at Wirksworth was a vocal opponent. He's remained bitter that the Factory Act passed, considering it unwarranted interference in how he runs his business. I doubt he will be very receptive to outsiders, even those bearing gifts. There are always matters of business I can discuss with him. I would feel…better, being there when you take the books.'

'To further persuade him, should he or the schoolmaster resist my efforts? That would be a relief! It's very kind of you to be so concerned.'

'I do feel somewhat responsible. After all, it's the practices of my "model mill" school that have encouraged you to want the other mills to run their schools in a similar manner.'

'Are you sure? I know how busy you are and am loath to disrupt your work. Much as I would appreciate your escort, you must promise me you will not accompany me unless you truly can do business of your own at the same time.'

He *wasn't* sure and might well end up cursing himself for allowing her to distract him. But having offered his help, he wasn't going to back out now.

'You may count upon me to accompany you and count upon my conducting business as well.'

He heard the tinkle of the entry bell as Mr Ardley opened the shop door. As they both turned towards him, the proprietor said, 'I'm ready to take your order, Miss Standish. Don't want to let your horses stand too long in harness.'

'Very true, Mr Ardley.' Turning back to Cam, she said, 'All that remains is for me to thank you again. For your suggestions, your hospitality and your guarantee, when the time comes, to add your persuasion to mine with Mr Crowden and his schoolmaster.'

She made him a curtsy, to which he returned a bow, and glided up the stairs into the bookshop.

Shaking his head, Cam turned to walk back to the inn, his body still tingling, his long-deprived senses clamouring for satisfaction. With his single-minded focus on work, it had been a very long time since he'd indulged himself with a brief, passionate affair.

Except what he craved now wasn't a flagrantly eager barmaid or a willing widow, but the golden loveliness and subtle sensuality of Miss Standish.

With whom a casual intimate encounter would *never* be possible.

To begin with, one didn't dally with a woman like Miss Standish, one married her. And even if he amassed a fortune and built an empire of modern, model factories, in the eyes of her family he would never be considered eligible. He wouldn't be able to offer her the social standing that meant nothing to him, but would be all-important to them.

Although he wasn't so sure he ever would marry. After losing the one person who'd ever cared for him, his workhouse friend Molly, he'd grown up on his own, relying on nothing but his own wits, talent and determination. He'd never established another close relationship. He admired and liked Mr Hughes, had met a number of colleagues with whom he'd discussed scientific and mechanical inventions, and had several *chère-amies* in whose arms he'd rested sweetly after pleasuring them. But he'd never shared his innermost thoughts and dreams with any of them.

Yet this afternoon, he had told Miss Standish about the long-ago *Arabian Nights* incident.

Because she'd offered him a sympathy and kindness he'd not experienced for decades?

A sympathy and kindness he must not let distract him from the hard work necessary to succeed in a harsh, indifferent world.

Then, suddenly realising the direction of his musings, he had to laugh out loud. The only thing more ridiculous than considering the improbable prospect of marriage was letting himself be tantalised by Miss Standish. The lovely, unusual, desirable lady whom he must never forget occupied a world so different from his, she might as well exist on another planet.

Still, for a man who'd decided before that foray to the bookshop to think no more about Miss Sara Standish, he'd just pledged himself to a course of action that would involve him with her at least several more times.

He wasn't sure whether to listen to the happy singing of his heart—or the angry grumbling of self-preservation that argued a continued association with the delectable Miss Standish could only end badly.

Annoyed by those incompatible impulses, he told himself to concentrate instead on the real and tangible pleasure of anticipating a fine meal and an evening spent with his new books.

Chapter Seven

A few days later, Sara neared the village after walking from Brayton Hullford, bound for the apothecary shop to pick up more of the herbs Lady Trent used to prepare her cordial. She could have ordered the landau and been driven in, but, feeling restless and edgy, had preferred to make the journey on foot, explaining to her hostess that it was too fine a day to be cooped up in a carriage.

Though it was a fine day, she had not wanted to acknowledge—and hoped her hostess had not guessed—the true cause of her nervous energy. Which was her inconsistent and contradictory feelings about Mr Cameron Fitzallen.

After Lady Trent's warning had reinforced her own doubts the night of the dinner at Brayton Hullford, certain that he represented a greater enticement than shy Sara Standish could resist, she'd sadly concluded she must not see him again.

But when she'd unexpectedly met him at the bookshop, the heat of his smile had evaporated those doubts instantly. She'd not only spoken with him, she'd accompanied him to the inn, allowed him to treat her to a cider and more or less manoeuvred him into agreeing to escort her when she brought the new books to the Wirks-worth Mill Works.

She needed to make up her mind which alternative was wiser—to avoid him after they made the trip to Wirksworth, to which she'd already agreed, or continue to see him and work with him. Unlike every other important choice she'd ever had to make in her life, she couldn't seem to decide.

While she waited for Mr Ardley to obtain the books for the other mill schools, she had forbidden herself from making the visit she'd planned, before the book-shop meeting, to the school at Hughes Works. Were she to do so now, she knew she wouldn't be able to resist the temptation to let Mr Fitzallen know she was there.

Since he had pledged to accompany her when she went back to Wirksworth, she ought not do anything else that would take him from his duties, even though the desire to see him again smouldered within her like the banked embers of last night's fire.

Frankly, after he'd warned her that her reception at Wirksworth might not be as enthusiastic as she'd naively expected, she was grateful he'd offered to accompany her. Not that she intended to let some reactionary owner or recalcitrant schoolmaster stand in the way of deliver-ing books that were sure to delight the factory's pupils.

If she were prepared to be defeated by the opposition of men who didn't want to change their ways, or thought a woman shouldn't venture from hearth and home to in-terfere in matters they consider solely their own busi-ness, she could have remained in London.

Still, she would be foolish not to utilise every resource to forward her aims and Mr Fitzallen was a formidable one. He was well respected by those in the mill indus-try and his support of her visit would ensure its success.

Something, given the owner's hostility to outsiders, she could not guarantee to achieve on her own.

Not that she'd forgotten the warning Lady Trent had given her, nor mastered her own misgivings about the wisdom of furthering her acquaintance with the far-too-appealing Mr Fitzallen.

Those warnings and misgivings were easy enough to remember when she was alone, in the quiet of her room. But each time she encountered Cameron Fitzallen, some wordless force seemed to draw her to him, sweeping away every thought but the desire to be with him.

A force that went beyond mere physical desire, though that was strong enough. She blushed again, recalling how often she'd found herself daydreaming about what it might be like to kiss him. She was also drawn by something more, something deeper, a common bond, as if their very thoughts and aspirations ran in parallel.

When they were together, she had a hard time remembering he had grown up in a place and suffered privations she could not begin to imagine. Because each time they were together, he seemed to think and react...much the same way she did. From their passion for the education of mill children, to the marvels of advancing science, to the need for workers to be paid and treated well, their views on important matters were aligned. As they spoke together, it seemed to her that the goals and ideals they shared were far more significant than the status in life that separated them.

Then, after the euphoria and excitement of having seen and spoken with him, she would return to Brayton Hullford and the solitude of her room, or feel her hostess's concerned gaze upon her, and the doubts and misgivings would resurface.

She felt as if she were riding a seesaw of conflicting

impulses, sometimes on an excited high, certain that she ought to continue to meet him and work with him, with impunity, sometimes plunging to an agitated low filled with a wariness that warned her she must give up the connection while she was still heart-whole.

Having her emotions batted back and forth like a tennis ball between two energetic opponents was wearing down her patience and shredding her usual serenity.

Hence, her dispensing with the carriage today, so she might diffuse some of her agitation in exercise. At least, the beauty of a walk along the leafy lane through midsummer woods and fields should distract her.

Thus far, though, it had neither calmed nor distracted her.

Reaching the village, she halted at the crossroads near the Thistle and Bobbin. She was tempted to stop by the bookshop…but if her books had come in, Mr Ardley would certainly have sent a note to Brayton Hullford to inform her. Putting firmly out of mind the seductive memory of encountering Mr Fitzallen at the shop, talking with him, surrounded by the scent of leather-bound volumes overlaid with the subtle spice of his shaving lotion, she turned down the other lane leading to the apothecary shop.

The proprietor, Mr Greenford, greeted her politely and, upon learning she'd come to obtain for Lady Trent the ingredients for her usual cordial, quickly made up a packet of the necessary dried herbs. After apprising that gentleman of the Marchioness's current state of health and promising to pass along to her the apothecary's hopes that his herbal remedy would continue to be efficacious, Sara tucked the packet into her reticule and exited the shop.

Once again reaching the crossroads, she dawdled a

moment. She *could* visit the bookstore again on her own account—perhaps finding that new novel Mr Fitzallen had disparaged. Or stop by the inn for a glass of Mr Lockwood's excellent cider.

But what she needed was to stop dawdling and return to the manor to check with Cook about tonight's dinner. The Parliamentary Committee, continuing its work by consulting with some of the M.P.s in the northern part of the county, had spent the last several days at Mr Robertson's estate near Disley, but would return to Brayton Hullford tonight and Lady Trent wanted the meal to be a fine one.

No sense lingering in the village. Perhaps, she thought with a sigh, after the walk home she'd feel calmer and more settled, a result her meanderings thus far had failed to achieve.

Then, as she reversed course to turn in the direction of the manor, a familiar, tall, commanding figure strode out of the dry goods store across from the inn.

Sara stopped short, the shock of recognition sending her heartbeat racing as a thrill of anticipation zinged through her. Though she tried to tell herself she hadn't been drawn to walk into the village with the expectation of seeing Cameron Fitzallen, a guilty niggle of satisfaction proclaimed that, deep down, she'd *hoped* she might encounter him.

He looked up from the dossier of papers he was inspecting, spotted her and came striding towards her, smiling.

'Good afternoon, Miss Standish,' he said, bowing to her curtsy. 'What brings you into the village today?'

'A visit to the apothecary for Lady Trent,' she replied, trying to keep her voice calm despite the flutters in her stomach and the little skittery sensations that raced up and down her spine as he fixed his dark-eyed gaze on her.

'Not a notice from Mr Ardley telling you that your books had arrived?'

'Not yet. But why are you here? I should have thought, at this hour, you would be fully occupied at the mill.'

'I certainly could be. But although I have a supervisor who oversees the provisioning of the dining room the mill maintains for its workers, I like to occasionally check the supplies myself.'

'The mill provides a place for workers to eat?' she asked, surprised.

'Yes, we began that initiative when the mill residences were constructed five years ago. Recently, we opened the dining room up to all workers, whether they reside in mill housing or not. With the long hours required by the job, they have little time to fix nourishing meals for themselves.'

'That was one of the advances you mentioned at the dinner at Brayton Hullford, wasn't it? An initiative pioneered by Robert Owen at the New Lanark mills? I didn't realise you'd already incorporated it at Hughes Works. How very forward-thinking of you!'

'Don't nominate me for sainthood yet,' he said with a wry smile. 'True, establishing a place that provides meals on the premises is the right thing to do. But the move is not entirely altruistic. A hungry worker is a tired worker and a tired worker is inefficient and prone to accident. Which is not good for either the worker or the mill.'

'Just as an educated worker is a more informed and efficient worker?'

'Exactly. Are you awaiting your carriage? Would you like to have another cider at the Thistle and Bobbin until it arrives?'

Although she yearned to accept the invitation and steal a few more minutes with him, she knew she should return to Brayton Hullford. She had duties to attend—and couldn't trust herself not to linger far longer than she should, once in his fascinating company.

'That's kind of you, but I must regretfully decline. The Parliamentary Committee returns tonight and Lady Trent wishes me to welcome them with an exceptional dinner.'

For a brief moment, she imagined that his expression was as disappointed as she felt. But then his brow cleared and he nodded. 'Then your carriage had better hurry. Should we send one of the grooms from the livery to speed it up?'

'No, I didn't bring the carriage. It's a pleasant walk and, if I go about it briskly, I shall be back in good time.'

'If Lady Trent truly needs you, walking all the way back will never do. Can I drive you? My curricle is at the livery. I was going to drive back to the mill in any event. It won't take long to detour by Brayton Hullford.'

She paused, torn between the delight of the idea of spending another half-hour of his company and dismay at just how great that delight was.

The brevity of her stay in Derbyshire would prevent her from growing too attached to him, a little voice whispered. However, her attraction was strong enough that the prudent, sensible response would be to thank him politely for his offer and continue back on foot, alone.

But she couldn't quite seem to make herself utter the words.

While she dithered, he chuckled. 'I see you hesitate, but don't worry—I won't overturn you! Despite my origins, I'm an excellent driver. From childhood, horses have fascinated me as much as books. As soon as I could afford them, I obtained a curricle and pair. I've been riding, and handling a team, these last ten years.'

'I don't doubt your competence! I'm sure you wouldn't have offered to drive me were you not proficient.'

The warmth in his eyes suddenly faded. 'I see. Having me ride with you to the mills under the eyes of the grooms and coachman in Brayton Hullford's carriage is…acceptable. The mill manager escorting you to inspect mills. But you would prefer not to be driven in public, or arrive back at Brayton Hullford, in *my* curricle. A prudent precaution. I shall bid you good day—'

'No, that's not it at all!' she exclaimed, dismayed, only then realising how he'd interpreted her reticence. 'I am honoured to have your company, anywhere! It's… complicated.'

She felt the chill of his withdrawal like the shock of the first icy winds of winter. Distressed, she watched helplessly as his body stiffened and a shuttered look came over his face.

He must think that, despite her fine words, like the endless committees who'd continually disappointed him, although she *said* the right things, she didn't really believe them. That despite her avowals to the contrary, deep down, she considered him unworthy of her company.

Which was untrue and the furthest thing from what she wanted to convey.

'Please, would you walk to the edge of the village with me?' She didn't want to part on such a bitter note. Stronger than her sense of duty to Lady Trent or any concern about the embarrassment of confessing the real reason behind her reluctance was her need to restore harmony between them.

She only hoped she could somehow explain it well enough to mollify him.

His face still stony, he nodded. Once they'd transited the main street and progressed past the livery to where the fields began, he halted. Turning that intense gaze on her again, he said, 'Complicated, how?'

When she hesitated, still trying to marshal her thoughts, he shook his head and said curtly, 'I think it's best if I just leave you here, before curious eyes and wagging tongues see you with me. Good day, Miss—'

'Don't go yet!' she cried, putting a hand on his arm to stay him. 'You haven't given me a chance to explain and it's…difficult.'

He looked down pointedly at her hand on his arm. Despite the fact that the bare skin of her fingers was separated from the bare flesh of his arm by layers of glove leather, shirt linen and woollen jacket, she felt the contact as a jolt of energy passing through her, conveying in a flash the knotted strength of his muscles. His sheer masculine ferocity, rigidly controlled.

Did he, too, feel that *burn* of connection?

Belatedly realising she'd held on to his arm far longer than necessary, she made to move her hand away. He put his free hand over hers, retaining her hand against his arm as his eyes held hers.

That gaze scoured her face, igniting something wild and fierce within her. Some primitive force that urged her not to retreat from the danger of her attraction to him, but to embrace it. To pull down his head and boldly claim the kiss she'd dreamed about.

Inflamed by the idea, her face, her lips, tingled and burned.

'Explain, then,' he ordered and released her hand.

She couldn't help feeling bereft.

It took her an instant more to gather her wits before she could begin. 'It's not being seen with you that concerns me, I assure you,' she added ruefully, recalling that nearly uncontrollable desire to kiss him. 'The problem is, I am…very…attracted to you. Despite the fact that we come from vastly different backgrounds.'

'You've been warned against me,' he said flatly. 'Because I'm not a gentleman. Did they caution you that this rude workhouse orphan would have so little control, if he caught you alone without a chaperon, he wouldn't be able to keep himself from molesting you?'

That scenario was so absurd, Sara had to laugh. Startled, he stared at her, apparently not sure whether to be further aggrieved—or bemused.

'Good heavens, no, Mr Fitzallen,' she assured him. 'I sincerely doubt that a man as handsome and charming as you, who has so many feminine admirers, would be tempted past control by a lady of unremarkable looks who is teetering on the edge of spinsterhood.'

Looking mollified but wary, he tilted his head, inspecting her. 'Is that how you see yourself?'

She felt a blush reheat her face at being once again the object of his scrutiny—but at least, he no longer appeared quite so insulted. 'That is what the looking glass tells me. Along with a lack of beauty, I'm…not alluring, or talented, or skilled at the witty conversation so prized by society. I'm usually shy, with little to say for myself in company, and completely *ordinary*. Being around someone like you, who has achieved such incredible things, whose life has been shaped by experiences so different from mine, makes me…exhilarated and draws me strongly to you. Despite our differences, we have important goals and aspirations in common. You…seem to admire mine, as I certainly do yours.'

She sighed. 'I suppose it comes down to this. Prudence tells me I should resist spending time with you, lest I grow too…attached. My ability to continue pursuing my political work, to remain independent, is vitally important to me. I imagine you, too, would not welcome the idea of an…attachment. There, is that plain speaking enough?'

For a long moment, he stood silently, just looking at her. She swallowed hard, hoping that explanation was apology enough to heal the breach between them. The idea that he felt she'd insulted him and, in so doing, had forfeited his regard and the chance to see him again was unexpectedly painful.

Only because he'd not yet helped her achieve what she wanted for the children, she assured herself. Not because he'd already become too important to her.

Finally, he gave a curt nod. 'Apology accepted. I appreciate your plain speaking. And you are correct; I am no more eager than you to…form any attachments. My work is far too demanding. I also appreciate your trust—especially as I suspect it is given in the face of strong advice to the contrary. So, is your conclusion that you should avoid my company?'

'I don't wish to. Quite frankly, I suspect I will need your assistance to achieve everything I'd like to for the children at the Wirksworth Mills school. I think I can allow myself to continue our association, now that you are aware of my…problem. If you will assist me in maintaining a…proper distance.'

'Not encouraging you to throw yourself at my head?'

As her face flamed, he held up a hand. 'Now I owe you an apology. I shouldn't have teased you. And I must confess, I find you…intriguing as well. Shall we agree to mutually behave with circumspection? And ensure our association remains cordial but…restrained?'

She blew out a breath. 'That would be…very helpful.'

'Consider it done. I'm as anxious as you are to provide as much assistance to the mill children as your committee can muster.'

'So we can continue to work together to reach that goal.'

He nodded. 'We can continue to work together to reach that goal. Now, since you must return to Brayton Hullford before Lady Trent sends out a search party, I'll let you continue your walk...*unmolested*.'

He added the last with a smile that reassured her that she truly had been forgiven.

She released a breath she didn't realised she'd been holding. 'Thank *you*! I... I would be very sorry to lose your good opinion.'

'You have not. You will let me know when the books come in so we may arrange the visit to the Wirksworth mill?'

She nodded. 'I will.'

'I trust, with you planning it, the committee will return to a fine dinner.'

'I appreciate your confidence.'

Coming up with no further reason to linger, she made him a curtsy. 'Good day, Mr Fitzallen. I shall look forward to talking with you again soon.'

'Good day, Miss Standish,' he replied, giving her a bow.

Reluctantly, she turned to resume her walk to Brayton Hullford. But after a few moments, sensing him still watching her, she turned back.

'You're wrong, you know,' he said, a hint of a smile on his otherwise serious features. 'You are not at all ordinary.'

Chapter Eight

In the late afternoon a few days later, with the promised books from Mr Ardley's shop wrapped up in paper and tucked in a basket, ready to be delivered to the mills, an impatient and excited Sara paced the front drawing room at Brayton Hullford. As it turned out, the day most convenient for Mr Fitzallen to escort her to Wicksworth had coincided with a long-standing appointment Lady Trent had made to visit a friend several villages away. Rather than postpone their excursion until the Trent carriage was available, Sara sent Mr Fitzallen a note, asking if he might drive them to Wicksworth in his curricle. He had agreed and would soon arrive to collect her.

She'd not seen him again since their talk on the road back to Brayton Hullford. She hoped her invitation would underscore the truth of her avowal that she was unafraid to be seen in his company.

And demonstrate that she could control the attraction she felt whenever she was with him.

Although, thinking of how strongly he drew her, how powerful was the wave of attraction that washed over her whenever they were together, she wasn't sure she could honestly make that claim.

Still, she trusted *him* not to try to attach her any more than she already was. Knowing he would help her keep the necessary distance between them freed her to embrace the energising prospect of continuing to see him, consult him and work together with him for the welfare of the factory children about whom they were both deeply concerned.

That decision was enough for now. She deliberately turned away from thinking about the future, putting off any decision about what to do about their wary friendship once the committee finished their work and left Brayton Hullford. After the Parliamentarians departed and the manor had been tidied and put back in order, Sara knew Lady Trent intended to return to London.

Which meant Sara would have to return as well.

That likely signalled the end of her association with Cameron Fitzallen. She'd have no reason to linger in Knively—and no place to stay if she did. She wasn't even sure it would be prudent to write to him from London.

Despite knowing it would be better for her continued independence and serenity to break with him completely, the idea that their collaboration might end in the very near future sent a wave of protest through her.

Yet she couldn't envision what sort of relationship they might be able to maintain once she left Derbyshire.

Unable to resolve that dilemma, Sara had, most uncharacteristically, simply shoved the conundrum to the back of her mind. She would enjoy the time she had with him now and not worry over what might come next.

Now, she impatiently awaited his arrival, driven by the same edgy anticipation that had sent her to the village days earlier. Having made numerous circuits of the drawing room since seeing Lady Trent off to visit her friend, she halted once more by the window overlooking the drive. After gazing out towards the carriageway, on which no curricle had yet appeared, she decided to collect her bonnet and pelisse.

She'd pass the rest of the time before her escort arrived walking in the garden. The summer day was fair and the roses in the walled garden were just approaching full bloom, scenting the space with their wonderful odour of cloves and spice.

Perhaps she'd cut some to bring to the schoolroom at Wirksworth. At the very least, she could trade pacing mindless circles around the drawing room with some productive action.

A short time later, garbed in pelisse and bonnet and with her basket of books staged by the entryway, Sara carried scissors, a trug and damp paper in which to wrap the rose stems out to the brick-walled garden. As she walked through the gate, their soft floral scent wafted above the sharper, herbal smell of the clipped rosemary hedge that outlined the beds—and the acrid smell of a cigar.

Though she stopped short, before she could retreat Lord Cleve looked up and saw her. 'Good day, Miss Standish,' he called, smiling as he snuffed out the cheroot and walked towards her. 'Come to take a turn about the garden? And collect some roses, I see. Please, let me escort you.'

She suppressed a grimace of displeasure, but there wasn't a polite way to extricate herself from his company, at least not until she gathered the roses. As she waited for him to reach her, she thought how odd it was that she felt much more at ease talking with the workhouse orphan than she did with this young man from her own class and background.

She couldn't quite identify just what it was about Cleve, but the Earl's son made her uneasy.

She'd been thankful, for the most part, to have been spared his company the last few days. Since the committee's return from their consults in the north, the gentlemen had adjourned after dinner each night to continue their discussions until late in the evening over brandy and cigars in Brayton Hullford's library, while Sara retired with Lady Trent to take their tea in the salon. Conversation at dinner had been general and Lord Cleve, as one of the highest-ranking gentlemen present, had been seated near his hostess, sparing Sara the need to chat with him.

Though they hadn't spoken, she would occasionally glance over and find him gazing at her. Since she always looked quickly away, not wanting to meet his eyes, she hadn't been able to evaluate his expression. Still, the mere fact of his scrutiny disturbed her.

On the one hand, she couldn't believe that an earl's son could have any serious interest in her—a girl of only modest looks, birth and dowry. Surely his—or his family's—sights were set on securing him a bride far more moneyed, beautiful and brilliant than Sara Standish.

But neither could she believe his attention indicated some illicit interest. Even if his character were suspect—not that she had reason to believe it was—no gentleman would attempt to seduce a gently bred virgin currently under the protection of a marchioness who was also his hostess. Committing such a violation of honour would see the man, at the least, forced into marriage, if not also blackballed from his clubs, his reputation as tarnished as that of the girl he ruined.

So why did he stare at her? The last few nights at dinner, she'd deliberately kept her gaze from straying to his end of the table, hoping that eventually his attentions would cease.

Perhaps her distaste at being trapped in the garden with him could be put to good use—if she could figure out why he continued to watch her.

'I'll carry the trug for you,' he said, interrupting her thoughts.

Uncomfortably aware of his nearness, she reluctantly handed over the basket. Since conversation would be unavoidable, as they walked down the path towards the full, fragrant pink roses she intended to cut, she gamely began.

'Lady Trent believes the committee will soon finish up its work. Have your consultations been successful?'

'I believe the committee is finally about to conclude that we have seen all we need to see. And, I hope, is ready to report to Parliament that the Factory Act already passed is sufficient and no further legislation needs to be considered. The bill already in place impinges enough on the freedom the owners have to run their businesses as they see fit.'

'But the Factory Act mainly concerns the treatment of children. Surely the government should provide protections for them! They have no power at all, nor have they enough experience of life to know what is in their best interests.'

Lord Cleve shrugged. 'They have parents to watch out for them. Parents who sent them to the mills in the first place. Since they are not working in the fields or apprenticed to a trade, they'd likely be thieving, or running about causing mischief, if they were not in the factories. Schooling beyond a basic understanding of their letters and numbers is wasted on children of that sort. What would they do with more learning?' He gave a disdainful laugh. 'They are hardly likely to become men of letters or stand for Parliament.'

While she bit her tongue to forestall a sharp retort, he shook his head. 'I don't see that it was necessary for the government to mandate that they receive a certain number of hours of education. The local owners and schoolmasters know best what their children need.'

Sara resisted the urge to point out that one of those 'children of that sort' had become a well-educated, innovative inventor and factory owner. Avoiding the subject of Mr Fitzallen—were Lord Cleve to make another deprecating comment about that gentleman, she wasn't sure she could remain polite—she said instead, 'But one never knows how far a child can go, given the proper training and encouragement. Look at Sir Richard Arkwright, who went from barber's apprentice to inventor to industrialist, eventually earning a knighthood!'

He waved a hand dismissively. 'There are always a few exceptional individuals. But in the main, the mill children will end where they began, as common labourers. But then, with a female's typically soft heart, you continue to have a special interest in them, don't you?' He gave her an indulgent look, as if he thought her soft-*headed* as well as soft-*hearted*.

Trying to contain her growing anger, she turned away and decapitated the floral offerings on another bush. If Lord Cleve continued his belittling remarks about her, and causes important to her, the children at Wirksworth were going to have a bounty of roses to enjoy.

'I do have an interest in their welfare,' she replied, once she'd mastered her irritation enough to speak in a calm tone. Depositing another handful of roses into the trug he held, she moved away from him towards the next rosebush.

He followed, rather more closely than she liked. 'Lady Trent tells me you visited the factory at Bakewell, bringing more books for their schoolroom. And that you intend to deliver another set of books at Wirksworth…in company of Mr Fitzallen.'

'Yes. As he is acquainted with both the factory owner and the schoolteacher, he offered to assist me in seeing the books are properly placed.'

Lord Cleve frowned. 'If you think the project important enough, I would prefer to have you accompanied by one of the committee members.'

'As you know, the committee members are fully occupied with their own work. They are as anxious as you, I'm sure, to finish up and return to London.'

As anxious as I am for you to leave, she thought, snipping off several more blooms and moving away again.

'True, but if you can delay for a few days, I could probably arrange to escort you.'

She averted her face, fearing her expression would convey her distaste. She was looking forward eagerly to the adventure of visiting the Wirksworth schoolroom in company with Mr Fitzallen. Making that same journey with Lord Cleve, even if it accomplished the same goal of providing books for the children, wasn't at all an attractive prospect.

But she could hardly tell him that.

'I wouldn't want to inconvenience you or have you linger in Derbyshire any longer than necessary,' she said, trying to sidestep the invitation diplomatically. 'Besides, the children will benefit from having the books as soon as possible.'

Looking annoyed, Lord Cleve blew out a breath. 'Such a trip *would* be inconvenient. But much as I dislike speaking ill of anyone, especially a man as…energetic as Mr Fitzallen, I cannot be easy at the prospect of you travelling there under his escort. And so late in the afternoon! Granted, daylight lasts longer in summer, but if you intend going now, it may well be nearly dark before you return.'

'It's not possible to go earlier, if one wishes to speak with the schoolmaster. The lessons don't begin until after the end of the children's workday.'

'Be that as it may, I still cannot approve you having Fitzallen as your escort, even travelling, as I'm sure you mean to do, in an open carriage. Though he may put on airs and graces that suggest otherwise, he is…not a gentleman. Indeed—and I'm sorry to be the bearer of such shocking news—I regret to inform you that Mr Fitzallen's origins are very low indeed. An orphan, he was raised in a *parish workhouse,* offspring of unknown parents who undoubtedly came from the dregs of society.'

Did Cleve expect her to swoon at his dramatic announcement, like the heroine in one of those new penny dreadful novels? Once again, Sara clenched her jaw to avoid an irritated response.

Struggling to maintain her even tone, she said, 'You may be easy, then, for I am not shocked. I've known of Mr Fitzallen's true origins for some time. In fact, considering that he came from a background that offered him none of the advantages of birth, wealth, or connections, the fact that he rose to become a successful inventor and the owner of a business that employs so many people makes him even more admirable in my eyes. He also expresses the same concern I share for the children in his employ. I am honoured to work with him to promote their welfare.'

'Have you considered that you could better promote their welfare in London by remaining actively involved with your committee work? And perhaps, eventually, by serving as a Parliamentary hostess on a regular basis? You wouldn't wish to ruin your chances of achieving such a position by becoming...tainted by association with a man of lowly origins.'

Furious, Sara wished she could skewer him with a pointed and clever reply, like Emma would. But ingrained habits of politeness—and a decided lack of clever remarks—prevented her from venting her frustration in that manner.

Instead, she dumped the rest of the roses she'd just cut into the trug, yanked it out of his hand and made a quick curtsy. 'I fear I must depart imminently to deliver those books. Since my untimely arrival interrupted your walk, I will leave you to resume it and finish your cheroot.'

Turning on her heel, ignoring his exclamation of surprise, she paced out of the garden as quickly as her voluminous skirts would allow.

Was he hinting that he might want to make her *his* Parliamentary hostess?

Perhaps that was the value he saw in her—her zeal for government work and the delight, which must be obvious, she'd taken in the dinner with local owners and dignitaries she'd arranged. Traits that would make her a useful wife for a politician.

Being a Parliamentary hostess on a consistent, rather than occasional, basis *was* an attractive prospect. But if she had to listen to Lord Cleve's reactionary views—and share his bed—to achieve that goal, she'd rather abandon reform work altogether.

To her relief, as she stormed out of the garden, she saw the welcome sight of a curricle and pair approaching down the driveway, Mr Fitzallen at the reins. She didn't think Lord Cleve would follow her but, having had the foresight to stage the basket of books by the front entrance, she should be able to quickly make her escape.

Swiftly she wrapped the flowers in wetted paper to keep them from wilting, then turned to smile, her heart lightening and her spirits lifting as her escort brought the curricle expertly to a halt near the front entry.

'Good afternoon, Mr Fitzallen,' she called up to him.

'And to you, Miss Standish. I see you are ready to leave.'

'Yes, I didn't want to make you take any more time away from your work than necessary.'

He nodded. 'I appreciate that. Are the flowers for me, Mr Crowden, or the children?'

She gave him a reproving look. 'I thought the children would enjoy them in the schoolroom. The scent is wonderful.'

'I'm sure they will prefer the odour of roses to the stench of hot oil and iron machinery.'

After handing up the wrapped flowers and the basket of books, she let a footman, who'd appeared at the approach of the carriage, assist her into the curricle.

As Mr Fitzallen signalled the horses to start, she saw Lord Cleve emerge from the garden. The expression on his face turned as dark as the smoke curling from his cheroot after he spotted them together.

Apparently Mr Fitzallen caught a glimpse of Cleve as well, for he chuckled. 'The Earl's son does not approve of me driving you to Wirksworth, does he?'

'No. Fortunately, Lady Trent does not object and hers is the only permission I need.' She wouldn't mention the raised eyebrow and look of concern that had accompanied her hostess's nod of agreement, or the softly uttered, 'Are you sure you know what you are doing?'

She didn't, of course. She had drifted about as far off

the course steered by the normally shy, soft-spoken Miss Standish as it was possible to be.

But, after a covert look at her escort that sent the flurries of desire swirling through her again, she couldn't help but relish what she was doing. Nor was she prepared—yet—to abandon this potentially reckless path and return to the safe—and lonely—one.

'From the extra bloom in your cheeks, can I assume that Lord Cleve was imprudent enough to...advise you against this course of action?'

She blew out a breath. 'Insufferable man! Though to his credit, he does serve his country in Parliament, which requires more effort than most idle *ton* gentlemen display.'

Then she laughed, her ire dissipating as soon as they rounded the bend in the drive and the Earl's son was lost from sight. 'Not that I have much standing to criticise, I who have done little more than attend committee meetings and write a few letters. Until now. Which is why I've found it so exciting and fulfilling to actually visit the mills—and bring books to the schoolrooms. To finally be *doing* something!'

'That does make you an oddity among your class.'

Sara chuckled. 'I suppose I've always been an oddity, bored by a life centred around fashion and society events and the latest gossip. Uninterested in trying to lure some gentleman with whom I have almost nothing in common to offer for me. My one dream, to establish a household with like-minded friends who wanted to make life better for all in our nation, rather than simply idle away their time.'

'I imagine your family did not favour that plan.'

She sighed. 'Not one bit. I'm sure they were very relieved when both friends married. Not that I am anything but delighted about that outcome! Their husbands are men of purpose, Emma's Lord Theo a talented artist, Olivia's Colonel occupied in restoring his family estate, which was much neglected by his older brother. Moving on to assist Lady Trent has been very satisfying and she is the kindest and most undemanding of companions.'

Still, talking about her absent friends reminded her of how much she missed them—and the dream she'd been forced to abandon.

Shaking her head to stave off the melancholy recalling those losses always triggered, she continued briskly, 'So, what can you tell me about Mr Crowden and the schoolmaster at Wirksworth—Mr Henries, I believe? I must gather the most persuasive arguments to lure them into welcoming my books.'

Sparing her a glance from tending the horses, Mr Fitzallen raised an eyebrow. 'You are going to "lure" them?' Then his amused expression faded and his eyes took on that look of shiver-inducing intensity. 'Yes, I believe you could be…very alluring,' he murmured.

His gaze and the warm tenor of his voice triggered a wave of physical awareness that washed over her, clogging her throat, setting every nerve tingling.

'Sorry, I shouldn't have said that,' he muttered, turning his attention to the horses.

Despite his attempt to defuse the sensual tension between them, it took her several minutes to recover her composure. 'You mentioned that Mr Crowden had been an opponent of the Factory Acts?' she asked, once her pulse returned to normal.

'Yes. Like so many owners, he's a self-made man, son of a tailor who had a mechanical bent. He worked on spinning jennys and machine tools, banding together with several like-minded mechanics to experiment with and improve them. Once they had perfected the machinery, they gathered enough capital to assemble several power looms into a small manufactory. Crowden eventually earned enough to build a mill of his own. Having spent so many years of hard labour establishing his business, he does not appreciate an act of legislation or a government committee trying to tell him how to run it.'

'So he feels his rights as the owner have been infringed upon. That he knows better than a group of Parliamentarians in London how best to conduct the enterprise he built up from nothing.'

He nodded. 'That sums it up.'

'A view you share?' she guessed.

'Those most involved in an enterprise have the best perspective to find ways to improve it.'

So he did agree, she thought. 'What about the schoolmaster?'

'Mr Henries runs the school in the village. Rather than hire a teacher who serves only the mill, after the Factory Act mandated that his child employees must have schooling, Mr Crowden offered to pay the schoolmaster a bit extra to come to the mill after the children's workday concluded and conduct the required classes there.' He paused for a moment. 'I have the impression that Henries doesn't believe the mill children worthy of his time. Or perhaps he is just as tired as the children after having taught at his own school for the day. In any event, he makes the lessons as brief as possible. Which, I'm afraid, is more often than not perfectly fine with the students.'

'So he feels put upon, unappreciated, and wants to finish his job quickly, with as little effort as possible?'

'That was how it appeared to me when I observed him.'

Sara nodded, her mind busy assimilating all the information. 'So they will both need to be convinced that having additional books available, and giving the children greater encouragement to learn, is something *they* desire to happen.'

'And you intend to convince them of that?' He chuckled. 'This I have to see.'

'To manage it, I shall need to know more. So tell me everything you know about Mr Crowden—what jobs he personally performed before he was able to establish his own business, how long it took him to accomplish that, the principles upon which he now runs it. And for Mr Henries, I need to know which intellectual discipline most inspires him—mathematics, literature, philosophy?'

Mr Fitzallen raised his eyebrows, but made no further comment. 'Very well, ma'am. I shall tell you everything I know about them.'

Energised to be working with him as an ally in a common cause, Sara listened intently, determined to absorb every detail and figure out how to use them most effectively.

By the time Mr Fitzallen brought the vehicle to a halt before the Wirksworth Mill, Sara had planned out the general outlines of her approach. Eager to begin—to once again intervene directly with the children, rather than simply observe at a distance—she waited impatiently while he handed the reins to a mill employee and came over to help her down.

Her excitement must have been obvious, for his face lit in a smile. 'Forward into battle?'

'Forward,' she replied, as excited by the touch of his fingers on hers as she was by the thought of bringing the joy of her stories to the children.

As they walked in, it struck her what she would likely be doing right now in London. Accompanying Aunt Patterson to pick up some new gloves, or having a fitting of a new gown, or paying some boring afternoon call. At the contrast, she nearly laughed aloud with glee.

'How glad I am that I decided to accompany Lady Trent to Derbyshire!' she said and took the arm Mr Fitzallen offered.

Chapter Nine

Amused—and curious to see just what arguments the determined Miss Standish would summon to win over the reluctant owner and schoolmaster—Cam escorted her to the factory entrance, where another employee met them and led them through the din to the owner's office.

'Fitzallen,' Mr Crowden said with a nod, rising as the employee ushered them in. 'And—Miss Standish, isn't it?' Though the owner greeted them politely, his expression was guarded and his manner noticeably cool.

'That's right. It's a pleasure to return to Wirksworth Mill,' she said.

'A pleasure to see you again, Miss Standish. I understand the Parliamentary Committee has finished its appraisals?' At her nod, he added, 'Then there was no need to inconvenience yourself with another visit, though it is kind of you to stop by. Fitzallen, you had some business you wished to discuss?'

'Yes, but more of that later. My primary aim just now is to assist Miss Standish.'

After giving the owner a moment to recognise that his comment meant her endeavour had *his* support, Miss Standish said, 'I noticed during our previous visit that, although the schoolroom was well furnished with slates and chalk for students to practise their letters, it had few books for the children to read as they master them. My committee felt it would encourage them to learn faster if they knew a collection of amusing and entertaining stories were available to reward them, once they could read well enough. Mr Fitzallen was kind enough to accompany me to help deliver the additional books.'

Crowden gave her a tight-lipped smile. 'I'm sure I have already provided the schoolroom with everything Mr Henries requires.'

'As a gentleman known for running his business with meticulous attention to detail, I'm sure you have! However, wouldn't you agree that when a person is working to master a difficult task, knowing there will be a tangible reward for his efforts encourages him to persevere? I imagine seeing the superior performance of the machinery you redesigned and the increased efficiency that resulted when you integrated the machinery into one operation spurred you to continue working hard, in the belief that you would eventually be able to unite all those elements and create a successful mill. And what a magnificent result you have achieved! Wirksworth is truly impressive!'

'Thank you,' the industrialist said, thawing slightly. 'Yes, I suppose it is helpful to have a reward for one's efforts.'

Cam smothered a smile. So far, Miss Standish was handling Crowden like a skilled politician. But then, after spending a great deal of time on her political committee work, she'd probably learned a few politician's tricks.

Content to observe her, he remained silent as she continued, 'You know much better than I how many demands are placed on a business owner's time and resources. How difficult it must be to balance one need against another and how much expertise is required to decide which projects should take precedence, which can be cut back, in order to best advance the interests of the business as a whole. So that owners may devote their attention and resources to matters that directly promote the profitability of their enterprise, my committee likes to assist in areas that affect it less directly, like the provisioning of a schoolroom. Of course, you as owner, and your schoolmaster, have complete control over how and when the books are utilised. The committee would never presume to suggest how you should conduct *any* aspect of your business.'

Bravo, Miss Standish, Cam thought. *Disarm that objection before it can be raised.*

'If only all outsiders were as sensible,' Mr Crowden replied drily. 'Well, I suppose there's no harm in you leaving some books. There's room enough in the schoolroom for them, I expect.'

'Thank you, sir,' Miss Standish said with a smile. 'Very gracious of you and so I will report to the committee. Its chairlady, as you may know, is Lady Lyndlington, whose husband is one of the leaders in Parliament. I'm sure he, too, will be pleased when I tell him how accommodating you have been to the aims of his wife's committee.'

She paused, waiting until his widened eyes and sudden alertness of manner showed he'd absorbed the implications of *that* connection.

Once again, Cam had to suppress a smile. Rather than sailing in and demanding co-operation with aristocratic arrogance, or threatening to invoke the retribution of her elevated connections if he resisted, Miss Standish offered instead to reward Crowden by carrying back a flattering report of him to the powerful politicians he disliked—but could not afford to antagonise.

An excellent tactic...subtle, but masterful.

Eyeing her with grudging respect, Crowden said, 'A man does like to know that the wife is pleased.'

'It makes for a happier and more congenial home, does it not? Now, I don't mean to take up any more of your valuable time. If you could just have someone show us to the schoolroom?'

'I'll escort Miss Standish up and return later for a chat,' Cam said. 'I've been working on designing a safety bar to run along the side of the spinning mule. I'd be interested to hear your impression of it.'

Though Cam didn't think he would witness anything today more impressive than Miss Standish's diplomatic handling of Mr Crowden.

Mr Henries was setting out slates and chalk before the imminent arrival of his students when the employee ushered Cam and Miss Standish into the small room—a converted storeroom by the looks of it, Cam thought—that served as the Wirksworth school. As he looked up and saw them, the look of tired resignation on his face turned to annoyance.

Reading his expression, Cam suppressed another smile. He couldn't wait to see what approach Miss Standish would take with the visibly irritated schoolmaster. But first, to perform his role as escort.

'Good day, Mr Henries,' he said, once the employee left them and closed the schoolroom door, cutting off most of the factory noise.

The schoolmaster inclined his head. 'Good day, Mr Fitzallen. And...'

'Miss Standish, let me present to you Mr Henries,

schoolmaster in Wirksworth village, who also teaches the factory children here. Miss Standish, a member of the Ladies' Committee for Parliamentary Reform, has been assisting the Parliamentary Review Committee on their inspection tour of the manufactories in Derbyshire.'

Though the instructor schooled his face to politeness, the thinness of his smile and the brevity of his bow clearly indicated his opinion of outside reformers. Given his own experience, Cam had to sympathise.

But Henries had never met a reformer like Sara Standish.

'Good day, Mr Henries,' she said, returning a smile and a curtsy to his bow. 'I regret that I did not have the opportunity to meet you when the Parliamentary Committee visited Wirksworth, that visit occurring much earlier in the day than your school begins. Though I did have an opportunity to visit the schoolroom and note that you had very few books. Once I informed them, my committee was happy to rectify that situation.'

Without waiting for a response, she took the books from the basket and unwrapped them. 'As you can see, we've brought several copies of the *Pretty Little Pocket-Book*, which has simple rhymes the children can read as they learn their letters. Then a copy each of *The Tales of Mother Goose* and the new *Grimms' Fairy Tales*.'

The schoolteacher held up a hand. 'Kind of you, Miss Standish, but it's best if you just wrap them back up and take them with you. Most of the children have very little interest in lessons. I can barely get them to concentrate on learning basic letters and numbers. Neither I—nor they, should they ever prove capable—have time for reading.'

She nodded—but made no move to gather up the books. 'You face a difficult challenge, as I'm well aware. Attempting to instruct tired—and uninterested—pupils must be such a trial to a man of your intelligence! You are quite gifted in mathematics, I understand—winning the master's prize when you were a student?'

Shooting a puzzled glance at Cam, Henries nodded. 'I had that honour.'

'If the children had the Pretty-Pocket books to look at as they practised with their slates, you might be able to give more attention to the students with an aptitude for mathematics. Mr Fitzallen tells me Ed, or little Joey, both show promise.'

Frowning, Henries nodded. 'It's true. They both quickly master any work that deals with numbers.'

'Just imagine, being able to engage the others to work independently while you demonstrate to your two promising learners the beautiful language of algebra or reveal for them the elegant architecture of geometry! They might well be inspired to pursue their schooling further, perhaps even attend the Manchester Mechanics Academy. How could the heart of an instructor not thrill at the thought of having his hard work rewarded by seeing students go on to become successful. Perhaps even as successful as Mr Fitzallen!'

'Finding more time for mathematics,' Mr Henries repeated, a glow in his eyes. 'I've used the *Pretty Little Pocket-Book* in my own school and the students do like them. Perhaps using them here might work.'

'You could beguile the other students into wanting to work harder by reading some of the stories to them aloud, so they could become excited about the prospect of being able to read the stories by themselves.'

The budding light in Henries's eyes faded. 'That's all well and good, miss, but as I said, I haven't the time for more than the essentials. I doubt the children would pay much attention anyway. Let them sit still for longer than a minute without writing on those slates and they'd fall asleep.'

The door opened, cutting off conversation as the factory din once again intruded into the room. A gaggle of children with tired faces filed in and took their seats on the benches that lined one wall, the slates and chalk Henries had distributed set out on the long table in front of them.

Once the last child entered and closed the door, Miss Standish continued, 'They might well be too tired to care. You know the children best, of course. But would you permit me to give it a try?'

'Kind of you to offer, miss, but I must set them to work. So if you would just leave us to it—'

A steely-eyed look from Cam cut him off. After a long, silent moment, in which Cam held the man's gaze, his expression unrelenting, Cam said in pleasant tones, 'Why not give the lady a chance, Mr Henries? It won't take long.'

Ah, the power of connections! Cam thought wryly. An outsider Henries could brush off. But he didn't dare disregard the wishes of an owner well known throughout the mill district, a man who had the ear of his employer.

As Cam expected, after giving a huff of frustration, Henries capitulated. 'Very well, Miss Standish. Read if you must.'

'Thank you, Mr Henries. As Mr Fitzallen promised, I won't take long.'

Turning to the students, who were eying her curiously, Miss Standish said, 'I know you have all had a long day. Before Mr Henries begins your work, who would like to hear a story?'

For a moment, no one spoke. Then one of the older boys said, 'What kind of story?'

'A magical story. The story of Mother Holle. It's about a woman with two daughters, one lovely and one ugly.'

'The pretty one marries a king and the other one has to wait on her?' one girl offered shyly.

'Oh, no. It's much more exciting than that. Shall I read it?' She opened the book of *Grimms' Fairy Tales* and smoothed down the page.

And proceeded to read. Although at first the older boys pretended uninterest, by the time she reached the part where the pretty daughter, having pricked her finger and dropped her spindle in a well, jumped into the well to retrieve it and found herself transported instead to a magical meadow, even they had their attention firmly focused on her.

Who could help it? Cam thought, watching her. Her blue eyes glowed and her face transformed as she changed her voice to become the different characters: soft and sweet for the pretty daughter, bored and whiny for the lazy daughter, impatient and harried for the mother.

The children would certainly want more stories after hearing her read this one, Cam thought, though he doubted Mr Henries could entertain them as well.

When she reached the climax of the story, when the good daughter returns home rewarded by Mother Holle by being covered in gold, the lazy daughter covered in pitch, the girls clapped and the boys hooted with delight.

'That'll teach her to be mean to her sister,' one of them cried.

'Would you like to hear more stories like this?'

'Oh, yes, ma'am,' said the little girl who'd spoken first, a worshipful expression on the thin face she lifted towards Miss Standish.

'Then you must study very diligently with Mr Henries. As you learn, there will be tales you can read for yourselves in this book—' she held up one of the *Pretty-Pocket* books '—and Mr Henries will occasionally read you longer stories from the *Mother Goose* book, or this one. But once you can read well, you may read any of them all by yourselves—as many stories as you like.'

One of the boys looked to Mr Henries. 'Would you read for us, too, sir?'

After shooting a resigned grimace at Cam, Henries nodded. 'If you are diligent and finish your lessons quickly, I suppose occasionally I can read a story. But better that you study hard—and read those—' he gestured to the *Pretty-Pocket* books '—for yourselves.'

'Which of you are Ed and Joey?' Miss Standish asked.

Two of the boys exchanged alarmed glances. 'Are we in trouble, miss?' the larger boy asked.

'Not at all. Mr Henries told me that you are both skilled with numbers. If I can find a book that will help him explain more about mathematics to you, would you promise to study it well?'

The two looked at each other, wary but clearly interested. 'Yes, miss. I guess we would,' the first boy said.

'Very good! But you must pay close attention to Mr Henries. He is wise and very clever. He can teach you to be wise and clever, too.'

'Don't need to be wise and clever to work in a mill,' the biggest boy in the room said derisively.

As the room went deathly silent, Cam turned slowly towards the boy and fixed him with a hard stare. When the boy shrank back, Cam said, 'Remember my example, Peter. Be clever working in a mill and, one day, you might own one. As I do. Now, Miss Standish, we've disturbed Mr Henries's classroom long enough. He, and you children, have work to do.'

Turning to the schoolmaster, he said, 'Thank you for

letting us stop by your classroom and speak with your pupils.'

Henries's lips twitching at the irony—as if he'd had any choice in the matter—the schoolmaster nodded. 'It was an...illuminating visit. And, Miss Standish—could you really get me a copy of Parker's *Advanced Mathematics*?'

'I'm certain I could. I know you would put it to excellent use.'

A little of the sparkle returned to the schoolmaster's eyes. 'It would be...interesting to see just how far those two could go with it. Yes, I should appreciate having the book, if it will not be too much trouble for you to procure a copy.'

'It would be my pleasure. Let me echo Mr Fitzallen's thanks to you. And good day to you, children. You will all study hard, will you not?'

'Yes, miss,' they chorused.

'Excellent. Wonderful stories await you!'

With a nod to them and Mr Henries, she turned to Cam, who offered her his arm. Though she walked out of the room with a decorous tread, as soon as he closed the door behind them, she gave a little hop and turned towards him, her face alight and her expression so gleeful, he had to laugh.

Conversation being impossible over the din of the machinery, he led her back to the owner's office, where they both entered after a knock.

After greeting them, Mr Crowden asked, 'Was Mr Henries...agreeable, Miss Standish?'

'He was most co-operative. With such diligent and forward-looking men working for you at Wirksworth, no wonder the mill is so successful!'

'Glad to hear it. Fitzallen, you mentioned wanting

to discuss some design modifications for the spinning jennys?'

'I think we've taken enough of your time for today, Mr Crowden.' Pulling a sheaf of drawings from his inside coat pocket, Cam continued, 'With your permission, I will just leave these for you to study. You can let me know what you think of them.'

Looking relieved to learn they meant to depart, Crowden nodded. 'I'll review them and send you a note. Thank you for your visit and a good day to you both.'

After bows and curtsies were exchanged, Cam gave Miss Standish his arm and led her through the cacophony of the factory and back down to wait outside the entry, while a boy went running to collect their vehicle from the stables.

Still beaming, Miss Standish said nothing while they awaited the arrival of the curricle. But after Cam had hopped in, the employee had handed her up and he set the carriage in motion, she reached over to squeeze his arm.

'Oh, wasn't that marvellous?' she exclaimed.

Chapter Ten

Cam had to laugh, both at Miss Standish's exuberance and at the sheer pleasure of having witnessed her performance. Though he still wasn't completely sure whether the motivation for that display was the satisfaction of manoeuvring others into doing her bidding, or whether she truly was as devoted to the cause of education for the mill children as she'd claimed the other day.

The day she'd made the astounding announcement that she was reluctant to spend time in his company—because she found him too attractive.

He'd been flattered, incredulous…and moved. He couldn't imagine another woman making so personal an admission, or doing so with such raw, unflinching honesty.

Having always appreciated honesty, he'd then admitted his own attraction. Which was probably for the best, despite his initial dismay at speaking so frankly.

Both of them had missions they were determined to pursue. If they both remained on guard, they could avoid letting the strong bond that pulled them together derail either of them from those missions.

As impressive as her performance today had been, she deserved every encouragement to continue hers.

'What a shame ladies do not serve in Parliament! You are certainly a persuasive negotiator.'

'Oh, I don't know about that. It's my friend Emma who always comes up with the perfect, clever response. My equally quick-witted friend Olivia can talk around and around a point, battering you with argument until there is nothing for it but to agree with her. I have no talent for the sort of clever repartee so prized by society. If I *was* persuasive, it was only ardent desire speaking. You see, I love reading so much, I wanted more than anything to give the children the means to experience that joy. There's nothing like a *story* to transport one from one's dreary or difficult or dangerous everyday life into a place of enchantment!'

Cam couldn't argue with that. How many months had he waited and waited for the *Arabian Nights* to appear, yearning to escape from the grim realities of the workhouse? How many hours of satisfaction and pleasure had he found since obtaining that first prized book, caught up in the world of his favourite stories?

'Thank you, by the way, for being wise enough to expect I would need your help. Mr Crowden might have agreed to let me visit the schoolroom, but I don't think Mr Henries would have accepted the books had you not... encouraged him.'

She chuckled. 'My, what a look you gave him! I should have quaked in my boots! No wonder he didn't dare defy you. Nor did that recalcitrant student, Peter.'

'It's well to learn early on how to size up a man—and to let him size you up in return, so one knows when to advance and when to step back.'

She sobered. 'Yes, I expect that's a lesson you learned

early and well. I imagine knowing how to avoid a fight saved you a good many scraped knuckles and battered heads.'

He laughed ruefully. *If she only knew.* Trying to rise in the world while having nothing and no one to rely on but one's own wits and determination required the ability to evaluate one's foe—and swiftly decide whether to do battle, negotiate, or yield the field to fight another day. He had done all three in his time.

'Perhaps. But it was your reading that won over the children.'

She shook her head disparagingly. 'That was the easy part. *Everyone* loves a good story.'

'I expect the students would have appreciated any excuse to delay their lessons. But your dramatic reading *captivated* them. I imagine quite a few decided on the spot that making the effort to master reading would be worth it.'

'I certainly hope so!'

Shaking his head, he spared her a quick glance. 'It's as impossible an occupation for a lady as standing for Parliament, I know, but it's a shame you can't go on the stage. You'd make a wonderful player.'

She gave him a quick smile before he returned his attention to the horses. 'I was often alone as a child,' she explained. 'My brother was much older, my mother, an invalid from my earliest memory, had no time for me and I seldom saw my father. Fortunately, Finchton Green had a wonderful library. Practically from the moment I could figure out words, I started reading aloud, playing the roles of all the different characters for myself and my dolls.'

'You spent time on your own? Living in a household

as large as I imagine yours would have been, I wouldn't have thought it.'

'True, Finchton sheltered a fair number of souls. But servants do their work before the family is up. I saw my governess for my lessons, of course, but once they were over, she retired to her own room. And as I mentioned, I saw little of my family. At our country estate, in good weather, I would ride to a favourite spot overlooking the valley, bringing along the book I was currently reading. If it were cold or raining, I'd take the book to my room and read there. I didn't really have friends to talk with until I went away to school and met Emma and Olivia.'

The revelation brought him up short. He'd had few friends himself growing up—and none that had survived the workhouse. But picturing her living in the midst of a large household, yet still feeling herself as alone and friendless as he had been, saddened him.

Perhaps she truly did want to help the children. He knew it was his own experience as a friendless waif in the workhouse that compelled him to try to make the lives of other poor children, those most vulnerable members of society, easier than his had been.

Though he was gradually becoming convinced Miss Standish was exactly the sort of person she appeared to be, he didn't dare let himself admire her character *too* much. Despite their current camaraderie, the time they would have for working together was limited. Within a few weeks, or even days, she would leave Derbyshire and return to her proper place, in London.

But surely he could think of her as a…friend? An engaging, attractive, admirable—and *temporary* friend.

Somehow, that description didn't satisfy him. Disgruntled, he forced his thoughts back to the conversation.

'Emma and Olivia—those are the two friends you'd hoped to live with? Before they decided to marry?'

'Yes. They found their places—as I've found mine, helping the Marchioness.'

'You've set against marrying, then?' he asked in a teasing tone—and realised with surprise that he was truly curious about her answer.

She laughed. 'No, nothing like that.'

'Then why have you not married, as your friends did?'

'Really, Mr Fitzallen! One doesn't ask a lady such a question, any more than one would enquire about her age.'

'My deplorable background. I don't know that I should refrain from asking impertinent questions.'

'The fact that you describe them as "impertinent" tells me you know very well! But I don't mind answering. My family is respectable, but not important or brilliantly connected. I'm passably pretty, but no Beauty, with a modest dowry, but nothing large enough to attract a gentleman of high degree. Having found I have little taste for the banalities that comprise most society gatherings, since my first Season, I've tried as much as possible to avoid them and seldom have anything to add to the conversation when I do attend. Such behaviour has earned me the reputation of being a well-bred, prettybehaved, but rather dull and ordinary young lady. I'm considered suitable enough to be the wife of a man with no greater ambition than to live out his life as a country gentleman, but nothing more.' She sighed. 'I might have become such a wife.'

'But you never found a man who tempted you to take on that role.'

'None that tempted me enough to give up my independence. Marriage would mean putting my modest dowry under a husband's control and a respectable country gentleman of no particular ambition would almost certainly disapprove of my political work. He could make it difficult for me to continue it, unless I were prepared to defy him.'

Cam nodded. 'I suppose he might well demand that his wife confined herself to managing home and children.'

'Exactly. And if he married me only to gain himself a well-bred, comfortable wife, he might well ignore me. If I had Emma's ability to skewer a man's pretences in one pithy sentence, or browbeat him into doing my will, I might have chanced it. But…even if I could think of a stinging rejoinder, I don't know that I would be able to utter it. I'm not defiant and hate being surrounded by harsh words and turmoil. I would probably just…go along, no matter how unhappy or frustrated I became.'

'Having been too often surrounded by harsh words and turmoil growing up?' he guessed.

She shook her head a little, but didn't immediately answer.

Even more curious about what else she might reveal, he kept silent, hoping she would say more.

When she did begin again, her voice was so soft that he had to strain to hear her over the clomp of hoofbeats and the jangle of harness. 'I've always had a horror of becoming my mother. Like me, she's not alluring, or clever, or beautiful. After she provided my father with an heir, he started spending his time and taking his pleasure elsewhere.'

She looked away, her expression troubled. 'At first, there were…terrible arguments. After which, he spent even less time at home. Mama coped with his neglect by becoming an invalid, hoping, I suppose, that having an ill wife might make him more attentive. It did not, but she discovered that being always laid upon her couch, with a discreet ear for the latest gossip, made her the favourite confidante of her many friends. She idles away her days chatting about fashion, potions and the latest *on dits*. I want to remain independent, free of a man's ability to hurt or control me, so I can accomplish *more*. Use my intelligence and my desire to help others to do something more important.'

'Liking giving mill children the gift of education.'

'One is never alone if one can read. At least, once the children master that skill, they can have that escape— and with education, the chance to do more than work in the mill, if they choose to.'

He knew the truth of that. Reading could transport and education was the key to unlocking opportunity.

When she gazed up at him so earnestly, her voice vibrant with emotion, he had a difficult time holding on to any doubt about the nature of her intentions and the depth of her concern.

As he let himself gaze into her glorious blue eyes, he couldn't help but believe she truly was the gentle soul she appeared. That she really did care passionately about the welfare of the mill children.

But a female like that would be so rare, so unprecedented in his experience, he hardly dared believe she existed.

Reining in his roiling emotions, he returned to the one thing he did know for certain. 'Once again I must disagree on one point—you are not at all "ordinary". You look at people and see not just class and position, not what is "expected", but who they really are. Which is most unusual for one of your class. Let me amend that—it's exceptional for one of any class.'

'I hope I try to see people for who they are—as much

as I am able. I'm afraid we all tend to see what we *expect* to see and react to anything that differs from the expected with suspicion or disbelief. As if our tailor delivered to us a new coat of unusual design that didn't quite fit, we view it with puzzlement or indignation and quickly demand another one in our usual size and style.'

'That's quite an image,' he said drily. How many times had he been served up—to his classmates that term at Cambridge, to other factory workers as he battled his way upwards—as the coat of unusual design that didn't quite fit?

Just as in the society of her birth, she apparently often felt like the ill-designed garment, the one to be frowned over and rejected. Like him, an oddity who never quite blended into the milieu in which they were supposed to belong.

Maybe it wasn't so strange that, despite all the factors of class and birth separating them, he felt so curiously drawn to her.

Returning his gaze back to the road ahead, he spied down the hill and around the next bend the entry gates to Brayton Hullford. Realising their afternoon excursion was almost over, he felt a pang of protest.

When would they share another afternoon together?

The idea of her leaving Derbyshire without him being able to see her again seemed intolerable. Immediately, he cast about for a way to prevent that.

'You've not yet visited the schoolroom at Hughes Cotton Works, have you?'

'No, not yet.'

'Do you intend to inspect it—even though we have a model school, not much in need of improvement?'

She chuckled. 'I should like to see that model school so I know better what to try to establish elsewhere. If it wouldn't create too much of a disturbance, I should love to visit Hughes's school before my party leaves the county.'

'You expect to be leaving soon?'

She shook her head. 'The committee will surely depart shortly. I don't yet know Lady Trent's plans, but I doubt she will remain too long after they leave.'

'Then you must visit soon.'

She smiled at that. 'It seems I must.'

'Good. You'll let me know when you intend to come?'

'Of course. It's your mill. A visitor can't just wander around without your permission. You're acquainted with all the pupils, aren't you? I expect you must be, since you knew even those at Wirksworth.'

'I've tried to become acquainted with all the children in my own mill and I know some of those in the neighbouring ones. I am hoping to discover some youngsters of talent and ambition I can sponsor, as Mr Hughes did me.'

'And have you found any promising pupils?'

'The two boys at Wirksworth. There are several at Hughes who may aspire to more than remaining mill workers.'

'You must introduce them to me when I visit. That is, if you can spare yet more time away from your duties. I'm quite aware that I've already taken up a good deal too much of your time.'

'I enjoy visiting the schoolroom—how I wish there had been one at the mill when I was growing up! Would you read to Hughes's children, as you did for the Wirksworth students? We try to *encourage* them as much as we can, but your reading would *inspire* them. Well,' he added with a wry laugh as he called to mind the various class members, not all of whom were keen on schooling, 'you would surely inspire *some* of them.'

'That would be most gratifying.'

'I'll stand ready to welcome you to Hughes whenever it's convenient for you to visit. Our schoolroom doesn't yet have a copy of *Grimms' Fairy Tales*.'

'I will be certain to bring one.'

By now, the manor was close enough that he needed to slow the curricle towards a halt. A footman was already trotting down the entry stairs, carrying a lantern against the gathering gloom, ready to help Miss Standish alight.

There would be no need for him to tie off the reins and hop down to assist her himself.

No reason to linger, either. Day had almost given way to evening. Miss Standish would need to hurry inside and prepare for dinner.

A dinner to which she certainly could not invite him.

He gritted his teeth at the frustration that truth provoked. But he should view it as a prudent reminder. The intersection of his world and hers ended at Lady Trent's front door, beyond which Cameron Fitzallen could not pass, except on the most unusual occasions.

He'd never cared a bit about that exclusion...until now.

Just as well he returned to his own world before the chimera of their camaraderie became too beguiling. Before it turned into something he would have difficulty giving up.

So he pulled up the horses and held them steady, saying nothing as the footman handed her down. Merely nodding, his face averted, as she smiled and said, 'Thank you for escorting me to Wirksworth today. For giving me the opportunity to act upon what I believe and truly do something.'

'It was my privilege.'

Had he ever met another lady of *privilege* who would have done what she had today?

No, he had not.

She truly was extraordinary. Awe and respect and something oddly like tenderness curled small tendrils around his heart.

And then his will faltered, and he *had* to look at her.

As she stood immobile, gazing up at him, a faint smile on her face, he felt that compelling sense of connection wrap around them. Drawn from different worlds, yes, but yet somehow so alike. Two lonely souls bound together by a love of books, an appreciation for the power of education to enrich and advance the lives of the poorest, most defenceless members of society and a keen desire to offer it to them.

And underneath those shared convictions swirled a dark, sensual current of physical attraction, so sweet, so beguiling, he felt a nearly irresistible urge to lean down and taste the smiling lips she angled up towards him.

The footman cleared his throat loudly. Startled, Miss Standish looked away from Cam and stepped back, belatedly releasing her hold on the footman's arm.

'As soon as I consult Lady Trent and determine our schedule, I'll send you a note, indicating which days I would be free to visit the mill. Please let me know which of those dates would be most convenient.'

'I'll await your note, then.'

Still, she lingered, seeming as reluctant as he to put an end to their excursion. Not until the footman, who now held open the front door, his lantern angled to light her way up the stairs, once again cleared his throat did Cam make himself speak.

'You should go in before the night-time dampness falls.'

'Yes, I should. Well… Good evening, Mr Fitzallen, and thank you again.'

'Good evening, Miss Standish, and you are very welcome.'

He watched her walk gracefully up the stairs. Watched as the footman shut the door behind her.

Only then did he gather up the reins, the image of the door closing her off, shutting him out, sending an odd, hollow feeling spiralling through his gut.

Why should he feel...forlorn? He'd attained what he had on his own, without relying on the support of any friend or confident. He didn't need anyone in his life now—certainly not a fascinating woman who aroused curious longings in him, desires that went beyond the physical, stirring emotions he'd never before experienced.

Complicated, complicating emotions he didn't have time for. Cursing himself for a fool, he turned his attention to the road and set the horses in motion.

Chapter Eleven

Three days later, Sara sat impatiently at her dressing table as her maid braided her hair. Once the girl finished, she would go down to join Lady Trent for breakfast and later she would set off in the Trent carriage to stop by the bookstore in the village, have some cider at the inn—and mark time until late afternoon, when she would visit the Hughes Cotton Mill.

A glow of pleasure lit within her as she recalled how gratifying it had been to persuade the owner and schoolmaster at Wirksworth to accept the books she'd brought for the children. But satisfying as that was, actually meeting and talking with the children, being able to read to them and watch most of them respond with interest and delight, had been probably the most fulfilling experience of her life.

She couldn't wait to repeat the experience for the children at Hughes Mill.

Though the visit hadn't been all untrammelled delight. As the children first filed in, she'd had to struggle to mask her dismay at their frail and ragged condition. She'd seen poor children before, of course, selling their flowers in Covent Garden, or on street corners, the few times her carriage had strayed into less prosperous areas of London. But usually at a distance, from the window of her coach. To be surrounded by such waifs, most of them rail-thin and garbed in worn, frayed clothing obviously handed down from older siblings or parents, brought home to her as never before just how little the poorest of the poor possessed. Just how privileged a life she'd led.

Those of her class would say that everyone had been born to his proper place. But she couldn't see any reason why Lord Cleve possessed ease, wealth and power—why *she* had ease, wealth and a bit of power—while these children had almost nothing.

Surely Cameron Fitzallen's dramatic rise in the world demonstrated that birth was only the beginning point of a life. It did not necessarily define what that life could become.

And if a person could rise according to his abilities, should each one not be given a fair chance?

She'd already come round to that view after working with the homeless girls Ellie Lattimar found and educated at her school in London. Seeing the Wirksworth mill children—that little girl whose big eyes had begun to glow in her wan face as Sara read her story, the cautiously eager response of the two numerically talented boys at the prospect of learning more mathematics—reinforced a thousandfold her desire to do all she could to provide them that fair chance.

The visit also made her even more amazed that Cameron Fitzallen, who'd once been one of those ill-clad, ill-fed, overworked urchins, had possessed the energy and ambition not only to survive—accomplishment enough for a child from the workhouse—but to claw his way up to unqualified success.

How arrogant, indulged and unfeeling he must think

all those born into wealth and privilege—he, who had fought and struggled to gain all he had attained. Having been given so clear a view of where he'd come from, she now understood better why he'd initially been so hostile and unaccommodating.

Despite all that, she couldn't deny the strength of the bond she felt for this man who came from such a different background.

A bond that she *knew* was mutual. Despite his initial disdain for her work, he had been fair enough to recognise her genuine interest and use his influence to help her reach out to the mill schools. Although he had accomplished worlds more than she in his life, he had supported, rather than dismissed or disparaged, her own modest efforts.

Did that not reveal a character as sterling as his face was handsome?

Thanking the maid, who finally inserted the last pin into her blonde locks, she rose and headed for the stairs, her mind still full of memories of her visit to Wirksworth—and all she had shared with Mr Fitzallen on the journey home.

It must have been that sense of common experience— two friendless children alone in the world, though those worlds had been nothing alike—that led her to describe to him how the bleakness of her childhood had spurred her love of books. A bleakness her subsequent friendship with Emma and Olivia had relegated to the back of her memory, until the need to defend her passionate dedication to the cause of literacy recalled it. She'd wanted him to understand why she cared so deeply about bringing the gift of reading to all children—so everyone might have the means to escape their everyday existence, to dream of achieving more, as she had.

As he had.

She should be embarrassed, perhaps, to have then divulged to this relative stranger even more intimate details of her life. Confessing her compulsion to escape becoming a neglected wife like her mother, too ordinary and placid to bewitch a husband, trapped in a lonely cage of idle comfort.

But instead, she'd felt…safe. She knew *he* knew what it was to grow up determined to avoid a future of misery, wanting to become something other than what everyone believed one had been born to. He understood what it was to be alone, having no one who seemed to care about you.

They both now had found their purpose and she had her friends. From what she'd observed, though, it seemed Cameron Fitzallen, who knew everyone but lived a solitary life alone with his books, had never known anything but aloneness.

She mustn't long to give him what it seemed he lacked—an intimate friend who understood and cared about him.

Something that, having never had one, he might not even desire.

So once again, as she walked down the hallway to the breakfast room, she put out of mind all the implications of her conflicting emotions about him and all speculation about the future.

She would allow herself only to admit she was as eager to see Cameron Fitzallen again as she was to meet the children at his school.

Entering the breakfast room, she saw her hostess already there, sitting over toast and coffee. After smiling a greeting, Lady Trent said, 'That's a lovely carriage dress! You must be preparing to go out. Are you off to the village?'

'Yes—do you need anything? I plan to spend some time browsing through the bookstore and the shops. But my main mission will be to visit the Hughes Mill later this afternoon, so I may observe the factory school. You'll remember I told you after my trip to Wirksworth that I intended to inspect the local mill school as well. I received a note yesterday from Mr Fitzallen indicating that today would be convenient for me to visit and, as you'd previously said you wouldn't be needing me, I wrote to inform him that I would go over by carriage. If you *do* have something for me, of course, I can always—'

'No, no, you needn't alter your plans. I will be fully occupied consulting with the housekeeper and the estate steward.'

Sara thought she'd spoken in an even, matter-of-fact tone. However, she must not have masked her eagerness as well as she thought, for her hostess pinned a concerned, acutely penetrating look on her. 'I can see how enthusiastic you are about visiting the mill children. Are you equally enthused about seeing the mill owner?'

'I am looking forward to meeting Mr Fitzallen,' she acknowledged. Trying to deny it would be so obvious a falsehood, Lady Trent would certainly see through it and probably be even more concerned that she'd attempted to prevaricate. 'For the pleasure of his company, of course, for he is a very charming man, but even more for the help he has so generously given me in smoothing the way to bring books to the children.'

'I'm not surprised that he has been helpful. As we've already noted, he would have to have learned early the importance of education, otherwise he'd never have escaped the workhouse and become so successful. Just take care that you don't find him...*too* charming.'

'I'm quite aware of the need for us to remain in our... proper places.'

Lady Trent nodded. 'Just make sure you remember that...when you are in his "charming" company.'

Nodding agreement, Sara filled her plate and sat down with her coffee, trying to mask the churning uncertainty Lady Trent's pointed enquiries had reactivated.

Her impatience to see Cameron Fitzallen intensified the closer they came to end of the committee's stay in Derbyshire. If Lady Trent were spending the day consulting with the two chief members of her staff, did that mean their departure was imminent?

Might this afternoon's visit be the last she would have with Mr Fitzallen?

The thought chilled her.

Driven to discover how close to the end of their time they actually were, she said, trying to imbue her voice with a casual note, 'I understand from Lord Cleve that the Committee is about to conclude their discussions and return to London.'

'Yes, I expect any evening to have Sir Henry inform me that they are ready to depart. I imagine they shall be gone by the end of next week, if not sooner.'

'How long do you intend to remain at Brayton Hullford after their departure? Would you find a short stay here beneficial, so you might rest after the Parliamentary visit and rebuild your strength before you return to the busyness of London?'

That enquiry earned her another sharp look. 'Would you like to remain in the country after they depart?'

'I would like to stay long enough to visit all the mill schools again. To make sure the schoolmasters are satisfied with the books I've already delivered and find out if there are others they could use. I'd like to get to know the children a bit better, too, to discover if there are any more who might benefit from specialised instruction, like the two boys at Wirksworth I told you about. Or any girls for that matter who might be candidates for Ellie's school in London. It has been so…energising to feel, for the first time in my life, that I've actually *accomplished* something!' She shook her head with a rueful sigh. 'I have to admit, I'm not eager to return to London and go back to merely writing letters.'

'Our letter-writing campaign is hardly a negligible activity!' Lady Trent protested mildly. 'Any true improvement in the lives of mill children can only come about if those measures are supported by men of influence and power, who must be moved to pass the necessary legislation.'

'Oh, I don't mean to downplay the importance of the committee's work! Just that it's not as…inspiring as working directly with the children.'

'You work with children at Mrs Lattimar's school.'

'I do,' Sara acknowledged. 'But only after Ellie has already found the girls she places. Here, visiting the mill schools, I feel I would have a chance to discover for myself other children who are capable of benefiting from further education. To imagine that *I* might be the means of guiding them to a better life fills me with the same sense of excitement and satisfaction I imagine Ellie must feel when she takes a new girl into her care.'

'I can understand how fulfilling that might be,' Lady Trent said, looking thoughtful. 'I suppose we could linger at Brayton Hullford for another fortnight or so after the committee leaves. So I can, as you suggest, recruit my strength and you can pay several more visits to your mill schools. By that time, you should have discovered which students have potential, and decided what to do about it.'

Lady Trent smiled. 'You mustn't look so woebegone at the prospect of returning to London! You will still have the pleasure of working with Mrs Lattimar's students. And I must emphasise again how important our letter-writing campaigns have been in getting passed the very legislation that has brought into existence the mill schools you are visiting.'

'Yes, I know I can look forward to resuming both those activities. Now, were there any supplies you would like me to bring back from the village?'

Their conversation became more general, Lady Trent recalling several items, Sara taking note. Though no more mention was made of the schools, Sara was relieved to have been granted a short reprieve. She would have another two or three weeks to visit the students here, discover their needs…and consult with Mr Fitzallen.

Nearly three weeks was better than the handful of days she'd feared might be all she had left. But it wasn't enough. Everything within her protested the idea of leaving all she had come to care for in Derbyshire in less than a month.

After she finished her coffee and went up to her room to get her pelisse and bonnet, she knew with a sinking feeling that the joy she'd always felt in helping Ellie's students was not going to overcome the sense of loss that would overwhelm her when she left Brayton Hullford.

And gave up her association with Cameron Fitzallen.

Still, there was no way she could avoid leaving. She couldn't remain at Brayton Hullford on her own, nor was Lady Trent likely to agree to further delay their departure. Just the thought of returning to London set a pain burning in her chest.

So she wouldn't think about it.

She would simply enjoy visiting the schools, getting to better know the students and their needs…and spending time with Cameron Fitzallen. Savour every second of the unique, never-to-be-repeated experience of working with him as the clock ticked down to the moment when their time together would end.

At which time, in order to hold on to the independence she prized, she would have to leave behind for ever this dynamic man who stirred her emotions so deeply and filled her with admiration, respect…and desire.

Several hours later, the Trent carriage halted at the entrance of Hughes Cotton Works. Mr Fitzallen having assured her in his note that he would once again drive her back to Brayton Hullford at the conclusion of her visit, Sara alighted and dismissed the coachman. Excitement expanding her chest and the edgy attraction Mr Fitzallen always stirred in her swirling in her belly, Sara turned to greet the employee who was opening the door for her.

Once inside, the now-familiar clatter and bang of heavy machinery put an end to any further conversation. She followed the tall young man down a long hallway, up past the office where she had met Fitzallen and Mr Hughes the day the Committee inspected the mill and along another hallway, where he opened a door to a large, bright room with a wall of windows that overlooked the forest behind the factory.

How much more cheerful and pleasant it was than the windowless, storeroom-like other schoolrooms she'd seen!

Not only was the room filled with sunlight, it was… nearly silent inside. 'How quiet it is here!' she exclaimed to her guide.

'Ah, yes. Mr Fitzallen put in a second wall of boards, then had cloth and rags stuffed between them. Keeps the mill noise out, so the students can learn better,' her escort explained as he ushered her in.

Compared to the schoolrooms at the other mills, which, though certainly quieter than the work floors, still vibrated with the hum and the occasional louder bang from the nearby machinery, the schoolroom here was…peaceful. Almost a haven.

A world apart, where the children would no longer feel themselves in a mill, but in a special place. A place that, with enough stories, could become magical.

As magical as Mr Fitzallen felt in his private rooms, when his books transported him?

'Miss Standish,' her escort said, interrupting her thoughts, 'this is Mr Sellers, the schoolmaster.'

'Very pleased to meet you, miss,' the man said with a smile as he walked over to greet her. Tall, thin and bony, with spectacles perched on his prominent nose, he radiated a calm, quiet sense of contentment.

He wants to be here, teaching these children, Sara thought.

'I'll leave you now, miss. Mr Fitzallen said he would come by later.'

'Thank you, and please give Mr Fitzallen my thanks also for accommodating my visit,' Sara said, curtsying to her escort before turning back to the schoolmaster.

'My employer has told me much about the efforts of your committee to improve the mill schools and ensure that all of them are equipped with sufficient books and supplies,' Sellers said. 'How commendable of you and your committee, ma'am, to concern yourself with their welfare.'

'You must be equally concerned. Mr Fitzallen told

me that you volunteered to teach the students after your own workday concludes. That's a very generous gesture!'

Still smiling, he shook his head. 'Mr Fitzallen is too kind. True, I work as a bookkeeper for the mill, but he reduced my hours so that I would have time to prepare lessons—and he pays me extra for doing so. I'd had a bit of schoolmaster experience before—as the eldest child in a large family, I enjoyed teaching my younger siblings as they were growing up. But to assist my widowed mother, I needed to earn more money than the village school could pay me, so I left home to find work in the mills. That I happened to choose the town of Knively and a mill run by Mr Fitzallen was the luckiest move of my life! Mr Hughes was a kind employer, but not much concerned with schooling. Mr Fitzallen has a keen interest in helping all his employees, especially the children.'

Mill children like he used to be, Sara thought.

'Won't you show me your supplies? Though with Mr Fitzallen being a leader in setting up mill schools, I know everything will be first-rate. I'm already impressed with the facilities. Such a well-lit and *quiet* room!'

Mr Sellers chuckled. 'I had my doubts at first about the "quiet". The youngsters are pretty tired by the end of their workday and I feared they would soon fall asleep! Instead—as Mr Fitzallen argued—having this respite from the constant noise and motion of the factory seems to calm and *energise* them. They certainly seem better able to concentrate and even the ones who aren't much interested in learning like coming to this room. Now, this cabinet is where we store the books, chalk and slates.'

Inspecting it quickly, Sara nodded. 'Yes, Mr Fitzallen said you used the *Pretty Little Pocket-Books*. And I note the *Tales of Mother Goose*. I brought along another storybook, recently translated from the German. *Grimms' Fairy Tales*.'

'Ah, yes, Mr Fitzallen mentioned that you would bring us a copy. I'll be very interested to read it. The children do love stories.'

'You read aloud to them?'

Sellers nodded. 'Several times a week, if they finish their work early enough. Mr Fitzallen told me the children would have the pleasure of hearing you read to them today.'

'Yes, I shall be delighted to.'

'They will enjoy it—or at least, most of them will. We do sometimes have problems with Thomas, one of the older boys. Until Mr Fitzallen took over, he had never been to school and has no interest in reading or writing. He's a big, strong boy who aims to leave the factory and do "a man's job" at the forge in the village. The blacksmith has agreed to take him on soon, so Thomas thinks he hasn't any need for "book-learning".'

'I'll keep that in mind. Now, what of the others?'

By the time Sellers had given her a quick description of the other students, the children were beginning to file in. Sara took special note of the several that Sellers had indicated were most interested in learning—the small, slender Jenny, who worked in the cardroom, Alice, one of the lint-pickers, and Andrew, who had a quick mind and might, Mr Fitzallen had told Sellers, have the aptitude to become a machinist.

Once the students settled at their desks, Mr Sellers introduced her and announced that, before lessons began, they would have the privilege of listening to Sara read from a new book of stories.

As Sellers had cautioned, Thomas immediately stood

up. 'I don't need to listen! Them stories is jest for babies. If we ain't havin' lessons, can't I just leave?'

'No, Thomas, as you know very well, you must remain for the whole of the class period,' Sellers said. 'Sit down, please. You are being rude to Miss Standish. If you don't wish to listen, you may practise your letters.'

'If he changes his mind, he is welcome to listen later,' Sara said. 'It's always useful to work on one's letters.'

Sellers brought Thomas a slate and a chalk. With a shrug, the boy sat back at his desk, but did nothing, leaving the chalk and slate unused on the table before him.

Ignoring him, Sara took the chair Sellers placed for her in front of the students. 'I'm going to read to you today about Rapunzel, a beautiful maiden with glorious long, golden hair.'

'Pretty as yours, miss?' Jenny asked shyly.

'Much prettier. So pretty, it beguiles a prince! Shall I begin?'

'Oh, yes!' the students chimed.

Smiling, Sara opened the book. 'Once, there was a woman who desperately wanted a child...'

Chapter Twelve

Sara was about halfway through the story when the factory noise suddenly intruded, alerting her to a new arrival. Quickly closing the door behind him, Cameron Fitzallen smiled at her. 'Don't let me interrupt, Miss Standish. Please, continue reading.'

Able this time, since he wasn't driving or walking beside her, to observe the force of that smile full-on, for a moment, Sara simply stared at him. The wavy dark hair she'd love to brush back off his forehead, the dark eyes glowing with an energy and intelligence that seemed to speak to her…the firm, full lips she had too many times imagined pressed against her own. He radiated such a sense of command, an air that said this was a man who knew where he intended to go and would certainly get there.

'Oh, yes, miss, you must go on!' Alice said, jolting Sara from her rapt contemplation. 'What happens next? Does the sorceress find the Prince talking up to Rapunzel?'

'Yes, you must let us know,' Fitzallen said, giving her a little wink as he walked over to seat his tall, rangy form on the edge of the study table. Feeling her cheeks heat at having been caught staring at him, Sara looked back down at the book.

''Course she has to catch him,' Andrew said. 'If she didn't, there wouldn't be no story.'

'You are correct, Andrew,' Sara replied. 'A story isn't very interesting unless the characters have to struggle to win their happy ending. But before he is discovered, he convinces the maiden to let down her hair and let him climb up to the tower...'

Sara continued to read, stopping from time to time to ask the students to guess what might happen next and, towards the end, pausing to let them chant the refrain, 'Rapunzel, Rapunzel, let down your hair', which they did loudly and with gusto.

As she made her way through the story, changing her voice as she read in turn the part of the maiden, the Prince and the sorceress, she noticed that, though he didn't look at her directly, Thomas was tapping his finger on the desk, quite obviously listening.

Not even someone opposed to school can resist a story, she thought.

At last, after sighing when the maiden was cast out of the tower and the Prince was blinded, the children cheered and clapped when the two were reunited, the maiden's tears healing the Prince's damaged eyes.

'And, of course,' Sara concluded, 'they went off to his kingdom and lived together happily ever after.'

'That was wonderful!' Jenny said. 'Please, Mr Sellers, can she read another story?'

'I mustn't today—you have lessons to finish. But if Mr Sellers allows, I will come back and read another day.'

'Please, say she can come back,' Alice begged.

'What a skilled reader you are, Miss Standish,' Sellers said. 'I would be as delighted as my students to listen to you again, whenever and as often as you find it convenient.'

'I would enjoy that. But now, I should go and let you get to your work! Thank you, children, for letting me visit today, and thank you, Mr Sellers, for lending me your classroom.'

'It was definitely my pleasure,' the schoolmaster said as he walked to the door. 'I know they all loved it— even if some might not admit it,' he added, with a nod towards Thomas.

'If he wants to have his own smithy some day, he'll have to learn how to read and cipher,' Sara said. 'He'll need to keep a ledger with the names of his customers, account for how much they have paid him and what expenses he incurs, so he can run his business profitably.'

Catching Thomas looking at her, she smiled at the boy before he quickly looked away. 'He may come around,' she murmured to the teacher.

'I'll see Miss Standish out,' Mr Fitzallen said. 'Continue the fine work you are doing here, Mr Sellers. I expect to have Jenny leave the carding room and join you in the bookkeeping shop by the time she finishes here and maybe Alice, too.'

'Until later, then.'

Nodding to the group, Fitzallen opened the door and guided Sara out.

Though she placed her fingers with the lightest touch on the arm he offered as he guided her across the factory floor and down the stairs to the entry, Sara was acutely conscious of his heat and sinewy strength...as if she could almost feel the pulse beating fiercely beneath the layers of shirt and coat. Once again, she felt the sheer power of his masculine presence beside her, a strength and energy that might intimidate—as it had

Wirksworth's schoolmaster and disobedient student—but, directed protectively towards her, was reassuring and comforting.

Walking beside Cameron Fitzallen, she felt...*safe*. This was a man who had overcome incredible adversity to battle his way to the status and prosperity he now possessed. She had absolute confidence that he could protect those he cared about from whatever buffets of misfortune life might throw their way.

Would he protect her?

Before she could wonder from whence that outrageous thought came, they reached the entry door and stepped out of the factory noise into the pleasant calm of the fading afternoon.

He turned to face her, smiling. All other thoughts fading in its glow, she revelled in the glorious wonder of that smile.

'Once again, you were masterful. Like Sellers and his pupils, I could listen to you read all day.'

'Thank you. Reading to real children is a great deal more enjoyable than reading to my dolls when I was a child! Who, though I am sure they appreciated the story, were always rather reticent about voicing their opinions.'

He chuckled. 'The pupils certainly appreciated you. Even Thomas, though he'd probably rather have his fingernails pulled out than admit it.'

'Well, as I said before, everyone loves a good story.'

'Indeed they do, when it is told as well as yours. But now I should drive you back to Brayton Hullford, as promised. Both the students and I want you to visit the mill and read for them again, so we mustn't annoy Lady Trent by making you late for dinner. That is, if you would truly like to read again and weren't just offering out of kindness.'

He wanted her to come back.

Suddenly, Sara realised she'd just been handed the answer to how she could both continue the work she so enjoyed *and* see more of Cameron Fitzallen.

'No, I would truly like to return. I do so enjoy reading to the children! The other factory schools are too far away for me to return there frequently—and I'm not sure Mr Crowden would appreciate seeing me again in any event! But Mr Sellers did not seem to find my visit an imposition. And if the master of the factory agrees...'

'The master of the factory agrees wholeheartedly.'

Almost giddy with delight at the marvellous prospect of being able to return to Hughes Mill as often as Lady Trent could spare her over the few weeks she had left in Derbyshire, it was all Sara could do to refrain from clapping her hands. Instead, she made herself stand decorously by the entry door as an employee brought up Mr Fitzallen's curricle. After he sprang up into the carriage and took her the reins, the man helped her up and they were off.

'You will have sufficient time after your return to prepare for dinner, I hope,' Fitzallen said as he expertly turned the corner and guided the horses on to the drive leading from the factory back to the country lane that ran to Brayton Hullford.

'Yes,' Sara replied. 'How I love these long summer days! The sun hasn't even set yet. Which is fortunate. Since I, too, am looking forward to reading to the students again, I certainly would *not* want to annoy Lady Trent by being late for dinner.'

He smiled slightly. 'You...almost seem to glow when you are reading. As if some vital force takes over and inhabits your body.'

'Doesn't a great story take over and inhabit your mind?'

'It does,' he admitted. 'So completely, you no longer notice anything else around you.'

'Exactly! Much as I enjoy reading stories, it's even more exciting to think that I might play a part in encouraging Jenny, or Alice, or Andrew, to learn faster and achieve more.'

'You will be an encouragement to those who *want* to learn. I... I only hope you don't become disappointed.'

'Disappointed? Why?'

'As fulfilling as it is to work with a Jenny or an Alice, the sad fact is that most of our students are more like Thomas. Not quite as resistant, perhaps, but certainly not eager.'

She gave a little wave of her hand. 'Perhaps Thomas can be brought round, if one figures out the correct approach. Something that makes learning to read worthwhile to *him*. And even if I can't reach him, even if I only reach one or two, isn't that still worth making every effort?'

He spared her a glance, his expression wondering. 'You really do care passionately about helping these children.'

'Another relic from the past, I suppose.'

He tilted his head at her. 'A "relic"? How so?'

'Do you truly want to know, or are you just being polite?'

'I never pose a question unless I want to know the answer.'

She sighed. Having already divulged so much, she might as well tell him this story, too. 'Very well. The spring I turned twelve years old, we were in London for the Season. One of the chimneys in the back drawing room had been smoking, so a chimney sweep was summoned. I was sitting in there alone, reading, when this little boy…fell out on to the hearth. With his clothes and skin covered in soot, I remember seeing only big, frightened eyes staring back at me. He begged me not to tell the sweep he'd fallen, else his master would beat him, and tried to scramble back up the chimney.'

She shook her head, tears threatening as she recalled the shock and distress she'd felt. 'He was so thin and there were sores on his hands and his bare feet. I was… appalled. I ran out to find the housekeeper and pleaded with her to do something to help him. She…she told me not to take on, that the boy was simply doing his job and wouldn't appreciate our bringing him to the attention of his master. So I went to find the butler, but he just repeated what the housekeeper said and told me to take my book into the front room, where no one would disturb me.'

She took a deep breath. 'I was twelve years old. I couldn't help that poor child myself and I couldn't persuade anyone else to help him. I cried about him every night for a week. And I vowed that when I grew up, I would do something about poor children like him. Even if I ever helped just one. Just one soul saved is worth the trying, don't you think?'

'It's worth it to that soul you save,' he said quietly. 'But now you choose to help mill children instead of climbing boys.'

She smiled. 'Fortunately, Parliament has taken over to help the sweeps. There was a bill read this year that should pass very soon—they're calling it the "Chimney Sweeps Act"—that will outlaw apprenticing children under ten years of age and forbid any child under fourteen from going up into chimneys. So I can in good conscience turn my attention to mill children.'

'I suppose government can actually make itself useful when it champions the protection of children.' Fitzallen laughed. 'Perhaps Parliamentary Committees have their uses after all.'

'And committee reformers who snoop about in factories, sticking their outsider noses into places they don't belong?'

He turned from his horses to spare her another glance. 'Sometimes it seems they *do* belong—when their hearts are pure and their intentions noble.'

Did he see *her* as 'pure and noble'? Though gratified, she had to protest. 'I only try to do what I see as right, as we all do.'

Fitzallen gave a humourless laugh. 'I only wish everyone did, Miss Standish! I'm afraid I encounter far more people who try to do what will advance their own interests, with little concern for what is "right".'

'Which is why people who act for the right have to try harder.'

To her disappointment, by now the curricle had climbed to the bluff on which stood the entry gates to Brayton Hullford. As he slowed the carriage to pass through the gateway, Sara caught a glimpse of the manor house, set up on a small hill beyond the drive that wound down from the bluff and back up again. The last, slanting rays of the afternoon sun cast a golden glow on the stone façade and lit up the windows with dazzling reflections.

'Could you stop the carriage for a moment? You must admire this view.'

Obligingly, Fitzallen pulled up the team and looked in the direction she pointed. 'See how the windows reflect the setting sun—and how sunlight gilds the whole building? Isn't it lovely?'

Nodding, he turned towards her as if to speak, then inhaled sharply. His body seeming to tense, he murmured, 'The late sun gilds your hair, too. Which is just as lovely as Rapunzel's.'

He looked down at her with that intense, dark-eyed gaze, immobilising her. As she sat, scarcely breathing, her eyes locked on his, he raised a hand to touch the sunwarmed curl at her ear.

'Were you to let down that golden braid, I would be tempted to climb up to your window.'

'Were you the one climbing, I would be tempted to open it,' she whispered back.

Then, as she had dreamed of and wished for so often, he leaned over and brushed his lips against hers. Gentle, tender, enticing.

Almost before she realised she'd been kissed, he pulled away. Before she could protest and beg him to continue, he snapped the reins and set the carriage back in motion.

She put a finger to her lips, which tingled in the aftershock of his touch. Her thoughts froze, refusing to consider anything beyond the wonder of it.

After a few moments, his gaze fixed on his horses, he said, 'Well, Miss Standish, you would be well within your rights to—'

'Don't you dare apologise!' she found herself exclaiming. 'Or I *will* have to slap you.'

He chuckled at that. 'I'll say nothing more, then.'

'That would be best.'

And so, for the remainder of the drive, they continued in silence, she marvelling over the wonder of her first kiss.

It had been rash, impulsive, thrilling—and she must never allow him to repeat it. The wave of need that arose in the wake of his touch would be so overwhelming, she might strip his hands off the reins and throw herself into his arms, begging him to kiss her again.

A prospect that thrilled her.

A prospect that should appal her.

Even if it weren't too dangerous to take the first step down a path she couldn't follow to its end…even if she didn't have her position to consider, or find the possibility of distressing and disappointing Lady Trent intolerable, she, Sara Standish, was not put together to be able to handle a clandestine affair of secret trysts.

With her stay in Derbyshire about to end, that was the only sort of relationship possible between them.

There couldn't be another kiss.

Sensible, responsible Sara Standish ought to berate herself for allowing—most certainly craving—a kiss whose consequences could threaten her hard-won independence. Instead, the giddy, irresponsible Sara she'd become pushed away every negative and alarming thought and simply relived the kiss again and again as she revelled in the solid, tantalising strength of the man beside her, silently guiding his curricle back to Brayton Hullford.

Far too soon, Mr Fitzallen drew up the carriage before the front entry.

As before, a footman immediately trotted down the steps to help her alight, while a groom stepped forward to steady the horses. Loath to climb down and end the interlude, knowing she must, Sara turned to gaze up at him—and saw the same longing and desire she felt reflected in his eyes.

For a moment, they simply gazed at each other, both

held immobile by the pull of need and a sense almost of... kinship. As if they belonged together and it was wrong for them to part.

Then Fitzallen put a hand on her shoulder and gently turned her towards the footman. 'Your attendant awaits.'

Resisting the urge to raise her hand and press his more firmly against her shoulder, she turned instead to take the hand the footman offered. 'Thank you for escorting me home, Mr Fitzallen,' she said as she alighted. 'I shall try to visit the school several more times before my party leaves Derbyshire.'

'You are quite welcome, Miss Standish. The children will be delighted to welcome you whenever you have time to visit them. Good day to you.'

Had there not been a footman and groom to hear him, would he have added that he, too, would be delighted to welcome her?

'Good day to you, Mr Fitzallen.' Marvelling at the strength of her resistance to the necessity of bidding him goodbye, Sara made herself walk up the stairs and through the door. Without looking back.

Chapter Thirteen

As he had the last time he drove her home, Cam found he couldn't make himself set the carriage in motion until he'd seen Miss Standish disappear inside the manor house.

What a marvel she was, he thought as he watched her walk away. Having listened to her describe the childhood events that prompted her to love reading and earnestly desire to help unfortunate children, having watched her delight as she entertained the mill students, Cam could no longer doubt either her sincerity—or the reality of the bright, shining spirit that glowed within her as brilliantly as the late afternoon sunlight that had lit up her golden hair.

In his wondering mind and uncertain heart, he felt a…stirring of something he hadn't experienced in a very long time. The sense of being mentally, as well as physically, close to someone.

And then in a flash, it came to him—why he'd had this odd, niggling sense of her being somehow familiar. She reminded him of Molly, the older girl who'd become surrogate mother and protector of the small boy who'd been thrust from the foundling home into the grim, un-caring space of the workhouse.

Not that they were alike in any physical sense. Molly had been thin, rather than alluringly rounded, her eyes and her lank hair dark, rather than blue and golden. But she'd had the same purity of heart, her smile project-ing the same gentleness and sense of caring as Sara Standish's.

Molly had looked after him, protecting him from the older boys who would have stolen his food, showing him the spots furthest from the cold draughts that swept through the sleeping room, offering him the only warmth and kindness he remembered from that bleak period.

Then she'd died, leaving him all alone. A flicker of anguish stirred inside as he recalled the devastation he'd felt.

No wonder he'd buried the memories of her kindness so deep. He never wanted to experience so searing a loss again. Besides, he'd done well enough relying only on himself ever since, hadn't he?

Time for him to return to the mill, in any event.

'You may give them their heads,' he said to the groom. 'Good day to you.'

'And to you, Mr Fitzallen,' the groom said, letting go of the leader's halter.

A cacophony of disparate thoughts tumbled about in his head as Cam drove the curricle down the carriage-way and back towards the factory.

Wise as they'd been in pledging to keep their asso-ciation decorous and proper, he hadn't been able to re-sist kissing her.

And after that impossible kiss, he could no longer tell himself that he felt only the natural attraction of a healthy male for an appealing female. He knew what lust was, that sharp desire that could be aroused and satisfied by a pleasant interlude with a willing lass.

He'd lusted for Sara, yes, but even more, he'd felt... tenderness and a deep desire to give her joy. He'd known she wanted him, been delighted that she wanted him, but felt compelled to treat her passion with the gentleness her innocence deserved.

Even more dangerous was the allure of her pure, bright spirit, unique among all the people he'd ever met. Her modesty, her compassion, her thoughtful, perceptive interest in those around her—especially those less advantaged than she—and her compulsion to do more in the world, all drew him to her, arousing an admiration and respect as great as his physical attraction.

Nor had he ever met another individual whose goals were as similar to his. One whom romantics might describe as a 'kindred spirit'.

But any relationship between them warmer than a distant, respectful friendship would risk her reputation, perhaps threaten her continuing the work for Lady Trent that afforded her the independence she so prized. Any relationship between them beyond a distant friendship would threaten the self-sufficiency he'd painfully built after losing the only confidant of his life.

Both risks were far too great for him to continue blindly down a path that, unless he caught himself now, would end with more kisses—and disaster for them both.

Ignoring the pain that stabbed in his chest at the conclusion, Cam resolved that when Miss Standish returned to read to the factory children, he would make sure he was too busy to see her.

Ten days later, Cam looked up at a rap at his door, mentally preparing his excuses if it were an emissary from the schoolroom requesting his presence. Sara Standish had returned to the mill and read to the children four times since he'd watched her disappear behind the front door at Brayton Hullford.

He knew precisely when she'd arrived on each occasion, exactly how many minutes she'd spent with the students and had listened to glowing reports from both Sellers and the children when he visited the schoolroom after she'd departed.

On the first two occasions Sellers had sent a child up to announce she was there and would be pleased if he were able to come to the schoolroom. He'd sent back a polite refusal, telling the child to inform her that, regretfully, he was too busy to stop by.

On her last two visits, he'd received no such invitation. She'd understood the unspoken message he'd been sending and respected it.

He couldn't help wishing she had not. If she'd continued to extend him invitations, he wouldn't have been able to continue refusing them without giving offence, which would be unthinkable after all she was doing for the children.

He would have been obliged to go to the schoolroom—and bask in her presence.

Though she'd stopped sending for him, knowing she was there, he still had to struggle to resist going to the schoolroom of his own volition. His excuse—that he was too busy—had become truly laughable, since struggling to resist doing what he badly wanted to do made him so agitated and distracted, he accomplished nothing useful during the time she spent at Hughes Mill.

That distraction and agitation would pass, he promised himself. In another day or week, she would leave Derbyshire for good. He would never see her again.

He would forget her...as she would him, the moment her carriage arrived back in London, if not sooner.

Probably far sooner. After he'd kissed and then avoided her, she might well have felt rebuffed, if not insulted. She had probably already written him out of her life—if she had, in fact, ever included him in the first place.

Which would be the best outcome. The last thing he wanted was to cause her anxiety or distress, or to place in danger the life she'd chosen. Indeed, she called up in him a deep desire to shelter and protect from the insults and injuries of a callous world a gentle soul who wanted to believe that others worked only for good.

But that wasn't a role he could ever play. The best way to protect her was to do what he was doing right now: keep himself, and the temptation they posed for each other, far away from her.

The bleakness he'd felt ever since deciding on that course of action stirred in his gut again.

A tug at his sleeve brought him out of his dismal reflections. 'Mr Fitzallen!' a small voice piped. 'Mr Fitzallen, excuse me, but you must listen.'

Pulling himself together, he looked down at the child standing beside his desk—who had evidently been trying for some minutes to catch his attention.

'Yes, Alice, what is it?'

'Jenny didn't come to work today. Miss Standish asked about her when she read to us and one of the other girls told her Jenny was sick. Miss Standish was worried about her and said she wanted to go check on her. I tried to wave at him not to, but that lackwit Andrew told her where Jenny lives. You know her da drinks and he's been kicking up at the pub lately—'

Shock, followed by panic, zinged through Cam. Before Alice could finish her sentence, he was out of his chair and pacing towards the door. 'When did she leave, Alice?' he asked over his shoulder.

'Just a bit ago. She said her carriage was waiting, so it won't take her long to reach the village.'

'Thank you for warning me. I'll go after her at once.'

Relief flooded the girl's anxious face as she followed him out. 'Thank you, Mr Fitzallen. I'm so worried—'

The rest of the girl's sentence was lost in the din of factory noise, but Cam didn't need to hear it to understand her concern. A concern he shared.

Perhaps there was a drawback to being a pure and gentle soul, he thought grimly as he jogged down the stairs, out the front entry and set off at a run to the stables. Being an optimist who looked for the good, rather than the evil, in her fellow man. Being a gently born lady who'd been sheltered and protected all her life, who had probably never ventured outside her own back garden without some attendant in train.

Who had undoubtedly never in her life been confronted by an angry, drunken man.

Sober, Frank Harrison was a good enough sort. But a man with his wits dimmed by gin would likely not see Miss Standish's status or her desire to help, only that an outsider was invading his home, interfering between him and his child.

Would that be enough to incite his brawling tendencies?

Please, God, he prayed, his mouth sent in a grim line as he rushed into the stables and ordered a groom to saddle his horse, *let her be prudent enough to take a footman with her when she enters the house.*

Far too many minutes later, on the lane just outside the village of Knively, Cam pulled up his galloping horse in front of the dilapidated, thatched-roof cottage occupied by the Harrison family. To his relief, the Trent carriage stood nearby. But to his outrage, both coachman and footman were dawdling beside it.

'Did you allow Miss Standish to enter that house alone?' he demanded as he tossed his reins to the coachman.

'Yes, sir,' the footman answered. 'She instructed us to wait here, said that she'd call if she needed us. She said there weren't but a sick child inside—'

'Idiot!' Cam cut off the footman in disgust. 'You come from the village, you know it's likely Frank Harrison is within as well. You should have escorted her inside, regardless of her instructions.'

The rest of the footman's disjointed excuses were lost as Cam jogged to the door and, after a perfunctory knock, burst in.

As his eyes adjusted to the dimness, he saw Miss Standish by the hearth, adding a few sticks of fuel to the meagre fire—and Frank Harrison, advancing unsteadily towards her.

A red haze of fury filled Cam's head. But before, fists clenched, he could launch himself to intercept the man, Miss Standish looked over and saw him. Shaking her head, she held up her palm, motioning him to remain where he was.

'I know you are concerned about your daughter, Mr Harrison,' she said in a soothing voice. 'I'm going to fetch a doctor, but you must not feed her any more of that gin.'

'Keeps her from coughing, it does,' Harrison said.

'This warmed water will help more.'

Cam might respect Miss Standish's desire that he not throttle Harrison, but he couldn't allow the unpredictable man to come closer to her. 'You!' he barked at Harrison. 'Get back to your chair.'

At his imperative tone, Harrison turned towards him, almost oversetting his precarious balance. 'M-Mr Fitzallen?' he stuttered. 'What be ye doing here?'

'Assisting Miss Standish, who was worried about your daughter. We will handle this now. Sit!'

Looking befuddled, the man shook his head, then shuffled back to three-legged chair by the fire. 'Jest tryin' to help the lady,' he muttered, reaching behind him for the jug of spirits.

A paroxysm of coughing came from what looked like a pile of rags in the corner. Miss Standish side-stepped around Harrison and went to kneel beside it.

Cam followed, realising as he reached the spot that the shape was the child Jenny, lying on a rough pallet.

'Rest easy, now, my brave girl,' Miss Standish said softly. 'I'm going to bring back a doctor, then visit the apothecary to get enough herbs to make a tea for that cough. We'll have you feeling better in a trice.'

'I'm sorry you're ill, Jenny,' Cam said, alarmed as he observed the girl's wan face and listless manner. 'We'll bring you help.'

The girl shook her head weakly. 'No…doctor. Mama said…can't pay him.'

'Don't worry about that,' Miss Standish said. 'Mr Fitzallen takes care of his employees—don't you?'

Her tone was as much challenge as affirmation. 'Of course I do,' he assured the child. 'Especially when I have someone to kindly remind me of my duty,' he added in an acerbic undertone, for Miss Standish's benefit.

After raising an eyebrow to acknowledge that jibe, she looked over to the father. 'Has Jenny had anything to eat or drink today, Mr Harrison?'

'Her ma give her a bit o' bread, afore she left for the factory. Didn't have nothing else,' he added defensively.

Cam gritted his teeth to avoid pointing out that Harrison had found coin enough for a jug of spirits. But rebuking the man would only embarrass Jenny.

'I'm sure you did all you could,' Miss Standish said soothingly, leading Cam to once again bite his tongue to forestall a derisive comment.

After patting the child's hand, she rose to her feet and once again addressed Harrison. 'Make sure Jenny stays covered and quiet. We will be back soon with the physician.'

At that, she nodded to the father and walked briskly to the door, Cam following closely behind her.

'Do you want to accompany me to find the doctor?' she asked, turning back to him after they'd exited the house. 'If so, we can take my carriage.'

'Yes. Thompkins, tether my horse behind the carriage,' he instructed the coachman. 'We'll drive to Dr Winthrop's house on Winding Lane. Martin,' he called to the footman—also sending him a scathing look that told the man Cam hadn't forgiven his negligence in not better protecting his mistress. 'You'll run in when we arrive and see if the doctor is home. If not, find out from his wife where he's gone.'

'Yes, sir,' the footman said, looking chastened.

While the coachman did his bidding, Cam walked Miss Standish to the vehicle and handed her up. As he hopped in after her, relief that she was unharmed turned to angry exasperation.

Waiting only until the carriage was underway, he burst out, 'What on earth were you thinking? Or did you think at all? How could you be so imprudent as to go running off alone to check on a sick child in a ramshackle dwelling with her drunken bruiser of a father inside?'

'I might have sent for you first, but you have been too *busy* of late to bother with me,' she snapped back. 'And I didn't know until after I went in that her "drunken bruiser of a father" was at home.'

'I would have accompanied you, had I known you meant to call on a sick child!' he retorted, uncomfortably aware that she had good reason to doubt his willingness to assist her. 'Especially if I'd known it was Jenny. Frank Harrison has a good heart. He's a former soldier. But there weren't any jobs to be had in the county of his birth after he returned from India, so he brought his family to look for work in the factory. Unfortunately, the unskilled labour in the mills requires small bodies, small hands and the dexterity to get under and around looms, work more suited to women and children than full-grown men. It is hard on the men, not being able to support their families as they once did. When he's under the influence of strong drink, Harrison's anger leads him to violence. He's been taken up several times by the constable for attacking other men at the pub. I shuddered to think how he might react to a stranger "invading" his home.'

'How difficult for him,' she murmured. 'I don't think I was ever in any actual danger. Besides, my coachman and groom were just outside. I could have called for assistance, had I needed any.'

'Unless he grabbed you from behind and covered your mouth, preventing you from crying out,' Cam countered. 'He could have thrown you to the floor or against the wall! Once you discovered the man was at home—and smelled the odour of spirits—you should have gone back out immediately.'

'I suppose having him catch me unawares was a possibility,' she acknowledged. 'Despite what you seem to think, I'm not completely naive. True, I probably could not fend off a strong man in full charge of his faculties. But Mr Harrison was...impaired by drink and I'm very handy with a fireplace poker.'

His alarm and tension beginning to dissipate, Cam had to laugh. 'You're as innocent as a child, if you think that would have helped you against a male set on harming you.'

'Ah, but you haven't seen my dexterity with a poker,' she countered with a smile. 'I've come to know Jenny rather well over the last few weeks. That cough of hers has grown steadily worse. When I asked her about it the last time I read at the school, she said she couldn't afford to stay home, that the family needed her wages too badly. So when she did miss work, I knew it must be something serious. Surely you understand that I *had* to come.'

'You should still have let me know at once.'

She gave him a wry smile. 'You're probably correct. I will do so next time.'

'Heaven forbid there is a next time! You mustn't go haring off, trying to help people in areas and places with which you are unfamiliar, with only an idiot footman to protect you! It's far too dangerous.'

'Perhaps so. But neither can I stand by and do nothing when a child's welfare, perhaps her very life, are at stake.'

The echo of another rattling cough filled his head. Might Molly have been saved, had there been someone like Sara Standish concerned about her? A swell of suppressed grief mingled with his ragged emotions of anxiety, relief, rage—and awe.

He looked at her, shaking his head. 'Much as I admire your dedication, you must temper bravery with more caution.'

'I suppose I am more dedicated than cautious,' she agreed cheerfully. 'I've accompanied my friend, Mrs Lattimar, who runs a school for indigent girls in London, on several of her forays to collect children in some of the less…salubrious areas of the city.'

'I don't even want to think about that,' he said with a shudder. 'Nor can I imagine how you convinced your family to permit it.'

She chuckled. 'Simple. I never asked their permission.'

Looking at her again, he shook his head wonderingly. 'I begin to believe you are even braver than you are dedicated.'

Colouring a little, she looked away. 'I'm nothing special, really. Anyone with a concerned heart would have done the same.'

'That statement just proves you're an innocent!' he retorted, making her laugh.

At her chuckle, the last of his tension eased, leaving him enclosed within a bubble of relief—and joy. He would have denied himself the pleasure of her company, but now that circumstance had intervened to require it, he would enjoy this stolen interval to the fullest.

By then, the carriage had pulled up in front of the doctor's house. The footman finding him at home, he soon joined them in the carriage, ending any further private conversation between them.

As they drove back to the Harrison house, Miss Standish described Jenny's symptoms to the doctor. 'I'll have to examine her to be sure,' he responded, looking grave, 'but it sounds like an inflammation of the lungs. Where does the child work?'

'The carding room,' Cam responded.

Doctor Winthrop nodded. 'I suspected as much. It's

the dust created when the fibres are pulled. Gets into the lungs.'

Cam felt the comment like a blow—knowing that as factory owner now, he was responsible for the working conditions at the mill, and therefore for not better controlling the floating fibres that might have caused Jenny's illness.

'Dust is a problem everywhere in the mill,' he acknowledged. 'I'm working on some ideas to try to combat it, but they are not perfected yet.'

'I'm sure you will keep working on them until they are,' Miss Standish said.

She did understand how committed he was committed to the welfare of his workers, Cam thought, gratified—and a little alarmed at realising how much her good opinion meant to him.

He forced that troubling thought away as the carriage pulled up in front of the Harrison cottage and the threesome quickly made their way back inside.

'Let's take a look at you, young lady,' Dr Winthrop said as he knelt beside the child.

'My chest…hurts so,' she said as Miss Standish helped her sit up.

The doctor murmured comfortingly as he looked her over, then stood. 'It's the lungs, for certain. She must rest and eat as much nourishing broth as she'll take.'

'Is there nothing else to be done?' Cam asked.

'I thought a syrup to soothe the cough might help,' Miss Standish said. 'I can get a quantity of dried herbs from the apothecary and boil them into tea, have the cook prepare a syrup and bring it all back tomorrow.'

'What sort of tea and syrup did you have in mind?' Dr Winthrop asked.

'Thyme tea to combat inflammation and syrup of

strained onion essence mixed with honey to soothe the throat.'

'Well, it can't hurt,' the doctor said as he stood and moved towards the door.

'Tell me what time you expect to return with it, Miss Standish, and I'll meet you here,' Cam said. 'Promise me that you'll not go back in until I arrive.' He might not be able to protect her everywhere, but he'd make sure she was adequately escorted as long as she remained in Knively.

'I'll send you a note—and I promise. Now, Jenny,' she said, turning back to the child, 'after I visit the apothecary, I must return to Brayton Hullford. I'll have Cook make up some broth for you, but Lady Trent needs me in the evenings, so I'll have to send Martin back with it. You must drink as much as you can tonight.'

'Thank you, miss,' Jenny whispered. 'I'll…try hard… to get better.'

'You just rest and I'll see you tomorrow.'

Cam gave her a hand up, relishing that small touch, the only intimacy possible with the child, her father and the doctor hovering around them. But her squeeze of his fingers before she released his hand and her quick smile showed him she enjoyed the contact as much as he did.

A fervent desire for a great deal more contact surged within him.

Forcing it back, he looked over at the child's father, still sitting in his chair by the hearth. 'Mr Harrison, you will be more presentable when we return tomorrow, won't you?' Cam gave the man his most intimidating look.

Harrison had the grace to look abashed. 'Aye, sir, I will. It's been right hard, seeing the child so sick and me not able to do aught for her.'

'We all hope to see her better soon,' Miss Standish said. 'Until tomorrow, then.'

Nodding a goodbye to Harrison, Cam walked her to the carriage and gave her a hand up, his fingers tingling again at her touch.

'Will she recover?' Miss Standish asked the doctor after the carriage set off.

Doctor Winthrop sighed. 'I'm afraid that depends more on the strength of her constitution than any remedies we can offer. Lung ailments are…difficult.'

'Then we must see that she gets all the broth, syrup and care she needs.'

How she intended to manage that, Cam couldn't imagine. He doubted Lady Trent would agree to delay her departure long enough for a child with a lung ailment to recover—if she did, in fact, recover.

A vision of Molly's thin face recurred, sending a chill through him.

But Jenny was younger, and stronger, and he would personally make sure she was well tended. Something he doubted Miss Standish would have time to do, despite her best intentions.

After they dropped off the doctor, Miss Standish directed Thompkins to drive back to the apothecary's shop in the village.

'Do you really mean to make up the medicine yourself?' Cam asked. In his limited experience, ladies in households as opulent as the Marchioness's at Brayton Hullford didn't personally attend to routine household tasks.

'Of course. I never offer to do something I have no intention of doing.'

'I would have thought you rather young to be an expert on syrups and potions.'

She smiled. 'You may remember that my mother is a great invalid. I took up physic at a young age, watching Cook and Mama's maid as they prepared her tonics, reading all the herbals I could find in the library, hoping to find something that would restore her to health.' She smiled ruefully. 'I must have been in my teens when I finally realised that she wouldn't be cured, that having chosen to play the invalid role, she didn't *want* to be. But by then, I'd learned a great deal and had become rather the household's expert in concocting remedies.' She chuckled. 'Along with becoming very familiar with all the local herbs and plants and all the ingredients stocked by the apothecary.'

'A good knowledge of physic is a useful skill.'

'Yes, especially for a lady who meant to set up a modest independent establishment in which she would tend to most household tasks herself. You will…return to the mill when we stop at the apothecary's?'

'I'm afraid so.'

'I thought you must. You've been absent for some time and mills don't run themselves.'

'They can, but badly.'

She drew in a breath as if to speak, then hesitated. Blowing it out in a huff, she said, 'I should probably remain silent, but before we part, I really must know. You've been deliberately avoiding me, haven't you?'

Before he could frame an answer, she continued quickly, her face flushing, 'I know I shouldn't have asked and please don't think I mean to take you to task for it! I expect that my…brazen behaviour that day you drove me back from Hughes Mill must have given you a disgust of me—'

'No, no!' he cried, putting up a hand to silence her. 'You must never think that! I found your behaviour that day…delightful. So much so that I wanted nothing more than to…repeat the incident, as soon and as often as possible.'

She gave a little smile. 'You did?'

'Yes. But I realised almost immediately how dangerous that would be. I would never want to…to take advantage of you, or have you suffer harm because of your association with me. The thought that my escorting you might put your reputation at risk, perhaps cause Lady Trent to end your association, exiling you from the political sphere that you love… Well, the idea was intolerable. Since I'd just demonstrated that I couldn't rely on myself to control my behaviour around you, the only alternative that would keep you safe would be to…not see you at all.'

'Because people might talk, you mean. About us being together, as…friends.'

'Yes.'

'You are not telling me this just to turn me away politely, are you? You truly do enjoy my company and would continue to see me, if you were not concerned about…unhappy consequences?'

'Absolutely.'

She gave him a smile so brilliant, it was all he could do not to haul her into his arms and kiss her on the spot.

'Then let people talk. I have only a week or so left in Derbyshire. Once I'm gone, people will find other things to gossip about. But until I leave, I'd like to enjoy your company as often as possible. If you will permit it?'

Not until she asked that did he let himself acknowledge how much he'd missed seeing her, talking with her, sharing his plans and aspirations. But excited as he was about continuing to see her, he knew he must establish some boundaries lest, in his weakness, he ended up compromising her—and threatening her future.

'I should like that. But to be prudent, I must not drive you, just the two of us. Or be alone with you, anywhere.'

She made a little moue of displeasure. 'No drives together?'

'No drives,' he confirmed quickly, before her disappointment could weaken his resolve. 'But I will meet you in the schoolroom.'

'And we may share a cider at the inn of an afternoon, with the innkeeper and the villagers all around?'

Though heretofore, he'd seldom left the factory during working hours, no force under heaven could stop him from adding another locale where he might safely meet her. He nodded. 'Yes, the inn would be acceptable, too.'

Reaching over, she seized his hand and squeezed it. 'Thank you,' she whispered.

He linked his fingers with hers and stared down at their joined hands, not daring to look into her eyes. For if the ardent desire he felt were mirrored there, he feared conscience would lose the battle with need and he'd end up kissing her again.

Which must not happen, no matter how desperately he wished for it.

'No, my intrepid Miss Standish, thank *you*,' he replied at last.

Belatedly, he realised the carriage had halted and managed to pull his hand away from hers just before Martin swung open the carriage door. A glow of happiness expanding inside him, he handed her down.

She had thought she might need to apologise to *him*? He shook his head at the wonder of it. Another woman would likely have felt scorned and angry at being kissed and then avoided. His previous *chère-amies*, during the short course of their associations, had been ready to blister his ears if they thought him not attentive enough. Yet Miss Standish had forgiven him his rebuff with that sweet modesty he found so compelling.

His spirits soared even higher as he contemplated the prospect of seeing her, not just tomorrow when she visited Jenny again, but every day Lady Trent could spare her, until the Marchioness bore her back to London for good.

Praise Heaven, there would be more stolen interludes. He intended to savour every moment of every one.

Chapter Fourteen

After Mr Fitzallen escorted her into the apothecary's shop, Sara lingered by the door to watch him ride away. Her cheeks heated again when she recalled how forward she'd been, demanding to know if he'd been avoiding her. Aunt Patterson would have fainted upon the spot to hear her ask a gentleman such an improper question.

Of course, Aunt Patterson would faint upon the spot if she knew how much time her darling niece was spending in the company of so unsuitable a gentleman.

A rash course of action she had no intention of abandoning during the short time she had left in Derbyshire, now that she knew he truly desired her company.

Did he also *desire* her…as much as she desired him?

She closed her eyes, allowing herself to recall once again the wonder of his kiss.

Much as she regretted the precautions he'd insisted upon, he was doubtless wise to insist they see each other only when in company, which would preclude a repetition of such dangerous behaviour.

Ah, but how she craved from him another kiss—one long, deep, passionate kiss—before she had to leave him!

One couldn't always get everything one craved. At

least now she had the satisfaction of knowing Mr Fitzallen was eager to see her as often as possible before she left Derbyshire, a boon she wouldn't have dreamed possible just a few hours ago.

She would see him again *tomorrow*. Excitement and anticipation buoying her spirits, she was too thrilled at the prospect to heed the alarm simmering beneath her delight—a warning that being with him had come to mean so much to her.

Surely she was too wise now to repeat her mistake— becoming attached to a man who merely wanted her as a compatriot for his political career. Much as Fitzallen appeared to relish her company, she knew his mind and heart were fully devoted to his work, as they must be, for him to attain the success he desired and deserved.

But in the short time left to them before the Trent party returned to London, she intended to relish every minute spent in his company.

'Can I help you, Miss Standish?' the apothecary's voice recalled her. 'You need additional herbs for Lady Trent's tisane, I expect?'

Abandoning her happy daydream of walking side by side—if not hand in hand—with Cameron Fitzallen, Sara turned towards the shopkeeper and recited a list of the ingredients she required.

The next day, her tea and syrup prepared, Sara wrote a quick note to Mr Fitzallen, informing him she meant to set out for the Harrison house just after noon. Only a few more hours and she would see him again, she thought, heady anticipation making her feel like skipping down the stairs to the breakfast parlour.

She found Lady Trent already within, a plate of toast before her as she sipped her coffee.

'Good morning, my lady,' Sara said, smiling at the Marchioness as she made her a curtsy. 'Are you still certain you will not require my assistance this afternoon?'

'No, I shall be resting, as I usually do in the afternoon. Did you finish brewing your remedies?'

'I did. I plan to deliver them and check on Jenny this afternoon.' Sara sighed, concern for the child submerging, for the moment, her soaring delight at the knowledge she would soon be meeting Cameron Fitzallen again. 'I hope she's been able to get down some broth. She seemed so very weak, but having the syrup to ease her cough will help and the tea should combat the inflammation in her lungs.'

'Good nourishment is certainly important to her recovery. You have a fondness for the child, I believe.'

'Yes, she is one of the brightest and most enthusiastic of the pupils at the mill school. I'm thinking she might be a good prospect to have more formal schooling and Mr Fitzallen agrees. I'm going to see if he would sponsor her education, as Mr Hughes sponsored his.'

'Will he be there when you return to see the child?'

Was her excitement that obvious? Sometimes Lady Trent could be too perceptive—but once again, Sara felt that trying to sidestep the question would draw more attention—and incite more alarm—than giving a frank answer. 'Yes, he's to accompany me. Jenny's father is unemployed and…sometimes the worse for drink. Mr Fitzallen is keen to check on the child, but he's also adamant about seeing that I am protected—even though I don't think her father would do me any harm.'

Lady Trent nodded. 'That speaks well of him. As does his commendable concern for his employees. I expect his own experience as a mill worker has led him to be more enlightened than most in that regard.'

'Yes. As you discovered when the Parliamentary Committee visited, Hughes Mill has several forward-looking programmes to benefit their employees, the school being just one. In Jenny's case, he informed the doctor yesterday that the mill will pay the doctor's fees for as many visits as are required and told the apothecary that he would cover the cost of any medicine made up for her.'

'All in all, a commendable young man and one who seems as keen to help mill children as you are.' Lady Trent gave her a penetrating look. 'It's a great pity he is so…ineligible. Were you of equal status it's a relationship I would encourage you to continue.'

Sara felt her throat constrict. Though a part of her wanted to argue that, if anything, Cameron Fitzallen's intelligence and ability placed him far *above* her, no one in society would see him—or her—that way.

Before she could think of something to reply, Lady Trent sighed. 'As long as you remain aware of that unhappy fact that he is *not* eligible, I suppose there is no harm in him accompanying you, or in you visiting the Hughes Works school. Though, had I any solid ground to do so, I would like to forbid both. I… I fear you are becoming too attached to Mr Fitzallen. I don't mean to be unkind, but surely you recognise there can be no… long-term association between you.'

Sara had to curb her tongue to avoid a sharp reply. Mastering herself, she said in as even a tone as she could manage, 'I'm well aware of that. But as we share the same concerns for Jenny and educating the mill students, it seems…silly to *avoid* him, simply because Lady Patterson would never consider him as a suitable…associate. And as you know, I have no intentions of…allying myself with anyone.'

'Just be sure you remember that,' Lady Trent said

drily. 'And if you wish to avoid sending your aunt into strong hysterics when we return to London, I'd not mention how often you've spent time with that young man.'

'I wouldn't wish to alarm my aunt—or you, ma'am. You have both been far too kind to me.'

Lady Trent reached over to pat Sara's hand. 'The shoe is very much on the other foot, my dear. You have not only made my life so much easier, your company has enriched it! But I cannot help telling you I will be considerably relieved when we safely are back in the city— away from the influence of the much-too-charming Mr Fitzallen.'

Though Sara knew she would do better to believe that as well, she couldn't make herself murmur an agreement. Settling for a vague smile, she poured her coffee, filled her plate and returned to the table to listen as Lady Trent detailed the various tasks that must be completed to close up the house after the committee's imminent departure.

A departure she viewed with dread, since their own would have to follow close on upon it. For she was becoming ever more convinced that when they set off for London, she would be leaving behind the mission, the children—and the man—who had already claimed a large piece of her heart.

A few hours later, submerging all her fears and worries, Sara felt a smile curve her lips as she watched Mr Fitzallen drive his curricle down the lane to the Harrison cottage. As she'd promised, anxious as she was to check on Jenny and give her the first dose of cough syrup, she'd waited in her carriage for his arrival.

Fortunately for her state of anxiety and anticipation, she'd not had to wait long.

By the time he'd pulled up his team, she'd already descended from the carriage and reclaimed her basket containing the straw-cushioned bottles of medicine. 'Good afternoon, Mr Fitzallen,' she called. 'Shall we go check on Jenny?'

'At once,' he replied, handing the reins of the team to her coachman before extracting a basket of his own from the vehicle. 'Walk them for a bit, will you, Thompkins? I'm afraid they are overheated. A last-minute problem delayed my departure from the mill and I had to spring them to arrive on time.'

Turning back to Sara, he offered his arm. 'Shall we?'

She knew her smile was too wide and welcoming, her enthusiasm for his company too apparent. But she didn't seem able to school herself to maintain a properly restrained decorum.

Devil take decorum! She'd concern herself with properly restrained behaviour after she returned to London.

'You brought provisions, too?'

'Yes. Broth is all well and good, but she'll need something more nourishing. I had the mill kitchen make up a stew of chicken and potatoes. Enough for her and the rest of the family.'

'That was kind of you!' she replied, surprised at his thoroughness.

'A lady once said I took good care of my employees. I wanted to demonstrate that she was correct.'

To Sara's surprise, after their quick knock, Mr Harrison himself answered the door—looking worlds better than he had the previous afternoon. His clothing worn, but clean, his face and hands washed, his clear eyes—and the absence of the odour of spirits in the room—testified to his sobriety.

'How is Jenny today?' Fitzallen asked quietly.

'At little better, I think,' he replied in a hushed voice.

'She had some of that broth last night, miss, and her ma got more of it down her this morning afore she left for the factory. She's been resting since.'

Sara nodded. 'We won't disturb her for long, just time enough to give her some medicine. Rest is the greatest healer.'

The two men followed as she walked over to kneel by the child's pallet. To Sara's critical eye, the child did seem improved. A trace of normal colour brightened her formerly waxy cheeks and her breathing seemed easier and more even.

'Afternoon, sleepyhead,' she said, gently shaking the child's shoulder. 'I've brought you some cough medicine. I added extra honey, just for you, so it shouldn't be too difficult to swallow.'

After struggling to open her eyes, Jenny looked up. 'Miss... Standish!' Her effort to speak prompted a fit of coughing, after which she continued, 'You...came back.'

'Of course I did—and made up the tea and cough syrup for you, just as I promised. No, don't try to talk any more! I'll help you sit up and give you a good spoonful, then you must sleep again. Mr Fitzallen brought you some stew, too, for when you are feeling stronger.'

Jenny peered past Sara to see the factory owner, who was standing behind her. 'You, too, sir?'

'Yes, Jenny. Everyone in the carding room misses you and Alice said to be sure to tell you to get well quickly so you may continue your lessons together.'

Turning towards her father, Fitzallen handed him the basket. 'There's enough stew in there to last the family a while. Hang the pot by the fire, so it stays warm, and add more water as it simmers down.'

'We be very grateful, sir—to you both,' Harrison said.

While Sara helped Jenny to sit up and spooned in

some medicine, then laid her down again, Harrison took Fitzallen's basket to the fire, carefully pulled out the stew pot and hung it on the rod on the hearth's edge.

When he returned, Sara handed him the jar of cough syrup. 'Give her a spoon of this each time she wakes. Try to get her to drink some tea and broth, too. If she's strong enough, tomorrow you can offer her some stew—but only a bit at a time.'

'Much obliged to you, miss.'

Turning back to the child, she said, 'You rest, now. I'll be back tomorrow to check on you. If you are feeling well enough, I'll read you a story, too.'

Smiling up at her, Jenny touched her hand. 'I love… your stories.'

'Then you shall definitely have one. Now, though, you must sleep. Rest well!' Affection for the brave little mite warming her heart, she smoothed the child's hair from her face and patted her cheek, then accepted a hand from Mr Fitzallen to help her rise.

'I shall check on you, too, Jenny,' Fitzallen promised. 'Everyone at Hughes Mill is anxious for you to get well and come back to us.'

'I'll…try, sir.' Then, as if holding open her eyes was too great an effort, her lids closed and she drifted immediately back to sleep.

Harrison walked with them as they exited the cottage. Paused outside the door, he said, 'Thank you both again for all you be doing for the family. And, miss,' he added, his face reddening, 'I'm right sorry about my… condition yesterday. Wasn't meself, but I've come to now and I mean to stay that way.'

'Think no more about it, Mr Harrison. We all make mistakes.'

Tears gathered at the corners of the man's eyes. 'That's

right Christian of you, miss. You can't imagine what it does to a man, not being able to provide for his family. Watching his wife and little dab of a girl go off to work to earn the coins that buy his bread and a bit of the ruin that helps him forget.'

'Mr Fitzallen told me you were in the army and, when you returned, there was no longer a job for you at home. What did you do in the country, before you went off as a soldier?'

'As a lad, I worked for the gamekeeper on Lord Howich's estate up near Nottingham. But when I got back, the gamekeeper had retired, another man taking his place, and him telling me he didn't need no assistant. So I come here. But there weren't work here neither.'

'Would you like to do such a job again?'

The man's bloodshot eyes lit. 'Back in the country, tromping the woods and fields, watching out for the deer and coverts? Didn't know how good I had it, foolish boy wanting to run off to see the world. Found I'd left the best part right back here.'

'I shall write to my brother, Lord Wendover. Finchton Green, our family's estate in Kent, has a large home woods and we may be able to use another experienced hand. It's likely a small cottage comes with the position and the village has a school Jenny might attend. Even become a teacher herself, which she told me she'd like to be. If this were possible, would you be interested?'

Harrison swallowed hard. 'It'd be like a prayer answered, miss.'

Sara nodded, sure she could convince her brother to take on one more employee. 'I will write to him at once. I should have his reply within a week.'

Harrison nodded. 'Bless you, miss. You, too, Mr Fitzallen, for all you've done for the family.'

'Just take good care of Jenny,' Fitzallen said. 'Good day to you.'

'And to you,' Harrison said before going back into the cottage.

'Can you walk with me for a moment?' Fitzallen asked. 'I don't need to return to the factory just yet.'

A little glow of warmth lit within her. 'I should enjoy a short stroll.' Calling to the coachman, she said, 'I'll be just another minute, Thompkins.'

Careful to remain in full view of the carriage and its waiting attendants, they turned to walk down the lane.

'Do you think your brother will be able to find Harrison a job?'

'I'm reasonably certain he will. There's always work to be done on an estate. The depressed prices for crops after the wars ended—and the prospect of a more exciting life in the city—has lured many away from the land, so I know there are cottages now vacant. Besides, he'd better find something. Harrison fought for England! It's not right that he be brought so low.'

Chuckling, Fitzallen shook his head. 'My firebrand Miss Standish, always championing the right.' Sobering, he added, 'Which means you will always have a cause. There will always be things "not right" for those without money or power.'

'Well, if one allowed that depressing thought to overtake one's thinking, nothing would ever get done!' Sara retorted. 'If *you* had thought that way, you would still be working in the factory, rather than owning it.'

He smiled wryly. 'True. We must keep on forging on.' Angling his head at her with curiosity, he said, 'Jenny told you she wanted to be a teacher?'

'Yes, the last time I saw her at the school. She's a fast learner, interested in every subject, and often helps tutor the children who don't understand the lesson, Mr Sellers told me.'

'I had thought to have her join Sellers in the book-keeper room—but if she longs to teach, I wouldn't want to stand in her way.'

'I was rather hoping you would sponsor her education. But if the Harrisons move to Kent, that won't be necessary, as my brother pays for the estate school—and being in the fresh air will certainly help her lungs heal!'

'It would probably be the best for all of them, if it can be worked out. A man needs to feel as though he's providing for his family and I'd like to get Jenny out of the carding room for a good long while. I imagine Mrs Harrison, like so many of the women we employ, would be relieved to have more time to tend her home and family.'

'Jenny will be able to continue her studies, too. The village school at Sallshurst is quite good. Before I moved to London for my come-out, I used to visit often, lending books from our library and providing supplies.'

He raised an eyebrow. 'So this bent to provisioning schools began a long time ago.'

'After that searing experience in London when I was twelve, I tried to find ways to help children whenever I could.'

'Did you make calls on the sick as well? Your handling of Jenny seemed very experienced.'

She nodded. 'By the time I was in my teens, Mama had long been an invalid, so I took over the mistress's role consulting with the vicar's wife about the sick and indigent in the parish.' She chuckled. 'Since I'd gone to such pains to acquire a knowledge of physic, it seemed a shame not to put it to use. I suppose it helped me feel more...useful, after I'd failed to be of any use to my mother,' she concluded, that ancient pain still throbbing a bit when memory poked it.

'You are a woman of many talents.'

'Nothing out of the ordinary!' she protested. 'Or at least, it didn't used to be out of the ordinary. Once, it was expected that the mistress of a comfortable manor would help provide for the poor and the sick in her parish. After my father died, I continued to pay the visits, since my brother's wife, the new Lady Wendover, had spent much of her youth in London and hadn't been raised in the custom. To be fair, her time is consumed by her growing family, which increases nearly every year.'

'So a lady of mercy, too.'

She looked at him sharply. 'It's not kind of you to mock.'

'I wasn't mocking! I'm entirely serious! I believe you are a paragon.'

'That's even worse than mocking,' she snapped back, flushing. 'I am certainly no paragon! I have as many faults as anyone else.'

'Name one.'

Looking at his expression, his eyes dancing, his intense gaze focused on her, she wasn't sure whether he was serious, or still teasing. Not sure how to respond, with an exasperated sigh she said, 'I have no allure and nothing to say for myself when out in society.'

'Are you truly concerned about what society thinks?'

'With my lack of interest in fashion, entertainment and eligible London gentlemen, I'm a constant disappointment to my aunt, who has expended so much time and effort trying to get me respectably settled.'

'Perhaps she is pushing in a direction in which you are not meant to go.'

Swallowing hard, she added, 'I have never been able to help heal the griefs of those closest to me.'

'Perhaps they didn't want to be healed.'

'I'm too frequently impatient and annoyed with those who wish only to idle away their days.'

'Well, naturally. They need to do something of value with their lives.'

'I find all I want to do is spend time with a man whose company Lady Trent and everyone else warns me I should avoid,' she found herself blurting.

The teasing look on his face fading, he halted. 'That is a grave fault indeed.'

She stared up at him, painfully aware that the ever-strengthening passion she felt for him must be clearly mirrored in her eyes. 'Alas, I fear there is no cure for it.'

For a timeless interval, he stared back at her, yearning on his face, his lips parting as if to speak.

Then the light in his eyes died. Looking away, he said shortly, 'Doubtless, distance will do the trick. We should get back. Your carriage awaits.'

Though he expressed only what she—and Lady Trent—had been telling her, she felt his answer as a blow.

Yes, he was willing to see her while she remained in Derbyshire. But he had no thought of continuing the relationship after she left.

Well, what had she expected? Why tease and torment herself, yearning for a long-term friendship that was never going to happen? As for imagining something *more*… Between modestly competent Miss Standish and the dynamic, exceptional Mr Fitzallen? The very idea was absurd!

Hadn't her humiliation with rising Parliamentarian Mr Draycott taught her anything? A man of purpose, one she could admire, might value her company, her intelligence, her dedication to others...but he didn't want *her*.

Angrier with herself for her idiocy than with him for his bluntness, she followed him back to the carriage.

Silently, he handed her up. Then, just before Martin shut the carriage door behind her, Fitzallen said, 'Will you be visiting the schoolroom again soon?'

The expression of conflicted pain and longing on his face eased her bruised heart. So he knew what they must do...but was finding it as hard to accept as she was.

Well, probably not as hard. She would soon leave this place, where she'd felt more fulfilled and energised than at any other time or place in her life. He would remain, building his enterprise, refining his inventions, going from one achievement to the next.

Firmly suppressing a wave of bleakness, she told herself not to let that desolate vision of the future overshadow the pleasure of the time she had left.

'Tomorrow. After I visit Jenny, I'll come tomorrow.'

'I'll let Mr Sellers know to expect you. Thank you again for your care of Jenny. Good day, Miss Standish.'

'Good day to you, Mr Fitzallen.'

Seated in the carriage, she watched him walk over and take the reins of his curricle from Thompkins, then swing up into the vehicle. She lost sight of him after the coachman climbed on to the box and her own carriage started off in the opposite direction.

Soon that opposite direction would carry her all the way to London.

A painful squeeze of her heart warned her again not to succumb to the danger Lady Trent feared and that she recognised, even as she struggled against it.

She mustn't lose her heart completely to a man she could never have—one who didn't really want her.

Chapter Fifteen

In the late afternoon the next day, Cam looked up at a knock on his office door to find Andrew on the threshold, gesturing upwards. Nodding to let the boy know he'd understood the message, Cam finished up the last of the papers on his desk, trying to quell the mix of anticipation, excitement and yearning that roiled in his gut at knowing he was about to see Miss Standish again.

For his own peace of mind, he needed to resist the ever-strengthening urge to find some way to keep her in his life and instead work on rebuilding the serene self-sufficiency that had sustained him since childhood. He ought to know by now that he could only rely on himself.

He made a wry grimace. For as long as he could remember, he'd been a problem-solver, figuring out what was wrong, contemplating possible solutions and setting out with single-minded intensity to implement the best option. For the first time in his life, a compulsion to solve a problem—their incompatible worlds—collided with a tangled web of emotions that swung from impatience to find a way to certainty that it would be madness for him to pursue such an outcome.

Irritated at being unable to resolve that battle, Cam

told himself to put the arguments aside for now and focus only on the pleasure of assisting her with the children.

Still, he couldn't forestall the leap in his heart and the heightened sense of well-being that buoyed his spirits as he exited the factory din into the quiet of the schoolroom. He spied her at once, her golden head bent over her book as she read to the students.

Absorbed in her story, her voice alternating in tone and timbre as she read the parts of the different animals—a Mother Goose tale today, apparently—she didn't look up at his arrival. It gave him the rare opportunity to study her, soaking in the loveliness of her voice and the animation of her figure as she brought the story alive for the pupils—who, enthralled, hadn't noticed him either, not even the education-resistant Thomas.

Fondly, his eyes traced from her profile—the fine nose and soft lips—down to the outline of her body—the soft curves of her bosom and hips, the legs disappearing in a froth of skirts. Though that scrutiny produced its inevitable result, as desire rose, thickening his throat and tightening his body.

Lusting after the princess in the tower again, he thought, quelling his desire by sheer will. This princess wouldn't—mustn't—let down her hair.

Then she did look up, her eyes widening as she recognised him. 'Mr Fitzallen! Excuse my rudeness!' she said, rising to give him a curtsy. 'I didn't notice you come in.'

'No need for apology,' he said, returning her a quick bow. 'It would be wrong to interrupt your story—as I'm sure the children would agree.'

Chuckling at the chorus of assent that met that remark, he said, 'Please continue.' Taking a seat beside the schoolmaster, he settled in to enjoy her dramatic performance.

And if, in a weak moment, he had a flash of wondering what it might be like to have her in his home, reading to their children, he quickly suppressed it.

After Mr Sellers agreed to the clamouring children's request that Miss Standish read 'just one more story', the students settled back at their desks to begin the day's lessons.

'I sent that letter to my brother this morning,' Miss Standish told him as she joined him at the side of the schoolroom. 'I hope that the Harrison family will be able to make their way to Kent, as soon as Jenny is well enough to travel. That is, if Mrs Harrison agrees. Do you think she will be willing to leave her factory job and return to the country?'

'It may be hard for her to step away from the independence of earning wages. But despite my efforts to make conditions in the mill as good as they can be, there is no denying that the hours are long and the work is hard. I think she will agree to leave, especially as she knows having a happily employed husband again will be best for her and her daughter.'

'You don't resent my intervening between you and your employees?'

'Of course not! You are concerned only with their well-being. As, I would hope you believe, am I.'

At that moment, Mr Sellers walked over. 'Excuse me for interrupting, Mr Fitzallen, but I wanted to show you Andrew's slate. He has done so well with algebra that I've begun to work with him on geometry, too. Will you look at this proof? He figured almost all of it out on his own! I think he has a real talent for numbers and for envisioning how objects work in space.'

After studying the slate for a few moments, Cam nodded. 'That is impressive. I believe he may have a real aptitude for mechanics. Shall we see if he has any interest?'

After Mr Sellers waved his hand towards the boy, Fitzallen walked over to him, carrying the slate. 'Your geometric proof is insightful, Andrew. Geometric principles are the underpinning of how all machines operate. Would you like to go from theory to practice and have a look at the machine I'm experimenting with?'

'Go to your workroom, you mean?' the boy asked, his eyes widening.

When Cam nodded, he burst out, 'Would I ever! I'll go any time you say, sir!'

'Very good. I'll take you tomorrow afternoon, after your shift ends.'

'Yes, sir! I'll be ready! Thank you ever so much!'

There was an outcry of surprise and delight among the pupils, who stopped their work to offer congratulations to Andrew, the closest ones slapping him on the back.

'Enough, children,' Cam said, smiling at them. 'You must get back to your lessons and accomplish what Mr Sellers has set out for you today. I'll bear Miss Standish away before we distract you any further. Good day to you all.'

'And to you and Miss Standish, sir,' Sellers said. 'I know you will be leaving Derbyshire soon, miss, but please do come read as often as you can. You can see how much the students love listening.'

'Indeed I will, Mr Sellers. Thank you all for being so welcoming.'

Cam escorted Miss Standish out, wishing he had an excuse to make her linger, knowing he did not. So he slowed his normally brisk pace, taking as long as possible to escort her to the front door.

'Thank you again, Miss Standish,' he said as they

stepped out into the relative quiet of the mill yard. 'You must know you've made yourself a great favourite with the students.'

'Working with them has become my favourite activity,' she said.

'When…do you think you might return?' he asked, not able to make himself let her go without knowing when he would see her again.

'I had intended to read to the children again tomorrow but…would you allow me to accompany you to your workshop instead, when you take Andrew? Though I don't expect I will understand your machines as well as he will, I would love to see what you are working on and have you explain how it will function.'

Did she really have an interest in the mechanical tinkering that was his chief delight? He was about to ask her if she truly wanted to go, then remembered her remarking, as he had once to her under similar circumstances, that she didn't ask about anything she didn't wish to know.

He would love to show her the workshop where ideas and theories turned into practical, working equipment. And share with her his vision for a future that skilfully designed machinery would make better for everyone.

'Of course you may accompany us. I suppose Andrew would be chaperon enough,' he said, considering the options. 'Or do you think it better to bring your maid?'

'Heavens, no!' she said, wrinkling her nose. 'I wouldn't want to drag along the poor girl, who has neither knowledge of nor interest in mechanics! She'd be bored to flinders. I am sure she treasures the time I am away, so she may do her mending in peace and have a good gossip with her friends.'

Nodding, Cam said, 'I could have my assistant accompany us. He's the chief minder in the spinning-mule room, but they could spare him for a short time.'

'I'm sure the presence of a small boy and a hale fellow inventor will be enough to forestall my nefarious designs on you,' she said with some asperity.

He laughed, then added in a more serious tone, 'And mine, on you.'

As Sara looked at him, her exasperated expression softened and her lips quirked in a wry smile. 'This really is impossible, isn't it?'

'It's the only possibility we have,' he replied. 'We must make the best of it.'

'So we must,' she said briskly, the melancholy he thought he'd glimpsed vanishing. 'Now, I must let you get back to your office, lest that mill of yours begins running badly again. Is your workshop nearby? Would Thompkins know where to find it, or should I meet you here?'

'Meet us here. After I'd showed him my first few designs, Mr Hughes let me convert a small storage building behind the mill into a workshop.' He chuckled. 'At first, I think he wanted to keep an eye on me, to make sure I was truly working rather than lazing about. Later, he wanted me nearby so he could easily walk over from his office to check on the progress of my designs.'

She gave him that brilliant smile that made him want to kiss her. 'I'm sure he was as eager to look over your work as I am! I can't wait to see more of your world. Until tomorrow, then, Mr Fitzallen,' she said, making him a curtsy.

'Until tomorrow, Miss Standish.'

He watched her walk to her waiting carriage and turn to give him a little wave before Martin handed her in, then watched as the carriage drove her away.

He couldn't wait to show her his designs either.

It struck him then that he'd never discussed his inventions with anyone but the assistant who helped him turn design into reality, and Mr Hughes. Even with them, he'd discussed mechanical details, but never his love for the work or his view of the future.

And when he imagined taking any of the handful of *chère-amies* he'd had over the years to his workshop, he had to laugh. To a woman, they would have been as bored and uncomprehending as Miss Standish's maid.

Whereas, somehow, he just *knew* Sara Standish would understand and appreciate his vision. Excited for what the morrow would bring, he went back into the factory and headed up to his office.

Chapter Sixteen

The next afternoon, Andrew and Lennox trailing behind him, Cam hurried from the factory floor down to the mill entrance, where Miss Standish awaited him in her carriage. Though Lennox looked only mildly interested in the proceedings, Andrew skipped behind him, almost as excited to tour the workroom as Cam was to show it off to the visitor.

He was also relieved that she'd finally arrived. He'd been pacing his office for the last hour, too distracted to keep his mind on the orders he was supposed to be reviewing. Once he'd given her the tour and she departed, he might finally focus on his work and accomplish something.

Though at the same time, he wanted to take as much time as her degree of interest demanded, so he might explain to her all the details about the improvements he was working on. Fortunately for the mill's need to get some useful work out of him today, his willingness to while away the whole afternoon was countered by the fact that Lennox mustn't be away for long from the mule-spinner room while the machinery was running.

Still, he would have her company for an hour.

Also important, he'd have the opportunity to judge if Andrew had the mechanical aptitude to match his interest.

She must have spied them approaching, for Martin was already handing her down from the carriage when the threesome halted beside it.

'Thompkins, why don't you and Martin drive into the village and have a glass of ale at the Thistle and Bobbin?' Miss Standish said after greetings had been exchanged and introductions made. 'I expect this visit will only last an hour or so—Mr Fitzallen and these gentlemen will need to get back to work. Tell Mr Lockwood to put those glasses on my account.'

Martin grinned, and Thompkins gave her a nod. 'That we will, miss. And right kind of you to offer.'

'You may as well enjoy yourselves as much as I intend to.'

'Looking over a bunch of parts and gears?' Thompkins said, shaking his head. 'Odd way for a lady to amuse herself, if you don't mind my saying so, miss.'

'Ah, but I'm interested in many things that are "odd for a lady", aren't I? Mill schools, books, inventions.'

'Excuse me—weren't my place to say anything, miss,' Thompkins said. 'We'll be off, and thank you again for the ale, miss.'

As the coachman and footman climbed back up to the box, Miss Standish turned to Cam with a sigh. 'Poor Thompkins, trying to make sense of the Quality. But if my aunt, after all her exhaustive efforts, hasn't been able to divert my interest towards more "ladylike" things, I doubt there is any hope for me now.'

'Society's loss is the mill children's gain,' he said, offering her his arm, the sizzle of her touch a guilty pleasure as they set off.

The mill children's gain...and mine.

A few minutes later he escorted her into the work-room, the wall of windows on the south side lighting the space to a pleasing brightness. Rows of workbenches beneath the windows displayed pieces of equipment in various states, some completely disassembled, the gears and cogs laid out neatly, some partially put together.

Cam felt his chest expand with pride as Miss Standish inhaled sharply and Andrew exclaimed, 'What a wonderful place!'

'It is indeed,' she echoed. 'Shall we start at one end and proceed all the way down? Tell me about everything!'

And so he walked her down the line of work benches, explaining how he was studying the disassembled machines to try to determine if there was a way to improve the gearing ratios to make them more efficient, how the partially assembled ones worked well enough, but had some flaw in their function that made him think there could be a better way to design it. Finally, on one of the last tables was placed a long, large machine next to a drafting table with a drawing pinned down, a stack of rolled drawings stored in shelves along the wall beside it.

'This is what I'm currently focusing on,' he told her, gesturing towards the large machine. 'It's the side section of a spinning mule. The levers must operate freely, but I'm trying to determine how a safety bar could be installed on the outside edge that would still allow the levers unimpeded motion, but protect workers from inadvertently getting a hand too close and catching it in the moving parts.'

'This bar?' she asked, pointing to a long piece of iron. She waved her fingers towards it, the bar catching them before her hand could get close to the levers. 'It seems to be quite effective.'

He grimaced. 'It's effective at protecting your hand, and it does allow the machinery to operate freely. Unfortunately, though, it's too heavy and, when the machine is running at full speed, unbalances it enough to cause an unacceptable level of vibration. I'm still working out how I might make it thinner and lighter, without having it become so small that it is no longer an effective barrier. If the iron is pulled into too thin a strand, it becomes brittle and the movement of the machinery causes enough strain to crack it. I shall have to keep thinking. The answer might be a better alloy of iron, but I'm going to experiment more with the design first.'

'And this?' She pointed to a long pole with a flanged end that resembled a rake. 'What is this intended to do?'

'I'm trying to construct something that could be inserted under the machinery to draw out the small bits of cotton fibre that come off during the spinning process—"flies", we call them. Right now, it's the job of the smallest employees to crawl under the machines and remove it. Which, as you can imagine, can be dangerous. Although the spinning mule is supposed to be shut down while the flies are removed, with the noise level in the shop, sometimes a child will begin, believing the minder has seen him signal that he's about to start, when due to some distraction or other, the man has not.'

Miss Standish shuddered. 'Does such a misunderstanding always result in injury to the child?'

'Not always. But often enough that it would be much better for the mill, and the children, if the fly could be removed with a device like this.'

'So what else needs to be done to perfect it? Since I

assume, if you were satisfied with it, you would already be employing it on the mill floor.'

'Exactly. The fly rake is reasonably effective, but right now it is still not as efficient as a child's skilled fingers. I'm experimenting with adding a covering of material over the iron, to which the fly might be attracted.'

'Like wool? Our housemaids prefer dusters made of wool to ones made of feathers. They say it attracts and hold the dust better.'

Cam nodded. 'Silk would be even better, but the cost would be prohibitive. Best of all would be some sort of fan that could blow the loose flies off the threads into a receptacle. But no one has yet devised a fan small enough—or efficient enough—to work.'

Looking down at Andrew, who had followed along raptly as they progressed through the room, Cam had to smile. In the boy's shining eyes and fascinated expression, Cam saw himself as a lad, when he'd first discovered the magic of machinery.

'So, Andrew, would you like to take apart one of those flywheels and figure out how it works?'

'Oh, yes, sir!' the boy exclaimed. 'Would you let me?'

Cam nodded to his assistant. 'Lennox, take the lad down to the second table and let him finish disassembling the flywheel there. Keep a watch on him, though, so he doesn't lose any parts! And answer his questions, too, if you can. Andrew, we can spare another half-hour for you to tinker. I asked Hannah to bring us over some tea. We'll have a cup while you work.'

'Thank you ever so much, Mr Fitzallen!' His face alight with enthusiasm, the boy set off at a run towards the workbench, a smiling Lennox trailing behind him.

'I think you may have a budding inventor there,' Miss Standish said, smiling as well.

'He certainly has the interest. Lennox will keep an eye on him—and be able to determine, by how well he is able to intuitively discover how the parts come apart and go back together, whether he possesses any innate ability.'

'Ability like you had?'

Cam laughed. 'Mr Hughes used to say he gave me a workroom to keep me from disassembling his whole mill some night while he slept. Yes, I was enthralled with machines from the moment I first started working here. It turned out that I was pretty good at taking them apart and figuring out how to make them better.'

'I seem to recall at dinner that Mr Hughes mentioned you'd been granted a number of patents.'

He nodded modestly. 'I've filed my share.'

'If you've earned enough from them to buy a mill, you must be exceptionally talented.'

At that moment, the door opened and Hannah entered, bearing a tray. 'Set it down over here, please,' Cam instructed her, gesturing towards the cleared corner of his drafting table. 'Thank you, Hannah. Tell the foreman that I'll be back in the office in about thirty minutes to find out what he's discovered about that leaking machine in shop three.'

'Yes, sir,' the woman said, giving him a curtsy.

'Won't you have a seat?' he asked, waving Miss Standish to the chair in front of the drafting table. 'I prefer to stand—which is generally what I do when I'm drawing. The ideas make me too...restless to sit.'

'Shall I pour for you?'

'Please.' Looking over to the workbench over which Andrew was bent, his whole body tense with concentration, Cam added, 'I don't think you need to pour a cup for Andrew.'

She laughed. 'No, you shall probably need to drag him

away when it's time to leave. Though I don't blame him. It's fascinating even for me, little as I know about machinery. But it's an exciting age we live in, isn't it? I remember going to the kitchen for some of Cook's tarts as a child and being cautioned to avoid the open fire burning on the hearth. Now the whole hearth is taken up by a Rumford stove and Cook says she doesn't know how she ever did without one. At night, London used to be so dark, but now, many of the streets are lit by gas lanterns.'

Delighted that she seemed to share his appreciation for advances in technology, he nodded as he accepted a cup from her. 'And there's more, so much more!' he explained. 'The only part of being in London that I enjoyed was attending Mr Faraday's public lectures at the Royal Institution. The discoveries they discussed were not just about machinery, some involved the very fabric of life! Thomas Young proved that light—the very light that enables us to see in this workshop—moves in *waves*. And John Dalton conducted experiments to postulate that all matter—everything, from your skin to your gown to the tea in this cup—is formed from combinations of tiny, invisible particles called "atoms".'

She shook her head wonderingly. 'Fascinating! The Royal Institution gives public lectures? I must try to attend when next I am in London.'

'I regret to report that women aren't admitted—yet. A policy Mr Faraday does not agree with and one he is working to change.'

'I should hope so! Should Jenny become a teacher, why should she not be able to listen to such lectures and take new information back to share with her pupils? Should Andrew become an inventor, *he* would be able to attend!'

'I fully agree. One should be limited only by one's talents and interests, should one not? For me, that interest has always been machinery. Imagine, Henry Maudslay deciding to design a lathe that could turn out screws with accurate, standardised threads, every screw identical. Then Joseph Whitworth building a factory to manufacture them by the thousands. All of which made possible the construction of manufacturers like Hughes Cotton Works. Our large, heavy equipment must be assembled with a strong binding force, or the vibrations generated while it is operating would shake the pieces apart. But perhaps most exciting to me are the engines George Stephenson and his son Robert designed and are now manufacturing—the steam engines that drive railroad cars.'

'Yes, I've heard about Mr Stephenson. He resides near Leicester now, I believe. Lady Trent had invited him to join the committee for dinner the night when all the industrialists were present, but regretfully, he was unable to attend.'

'Have you ever travelled on a railway, Miss Standish?'

'No. I've never even seen one, except for the illustrations published in the newspapers when the Liverpool & Manchester Railway opened in 1830. Quite an event, I recall, with the Duke of Wellington and a number of cabinet members going on the inaugural journey.'

'You must ride one—it's the perfect symbol of our modern age! Although the investors initially supported the building of railways to more efficiently carry freight, the lines have become so popular with travellers, a number of new ventures have been approved by Parliament. I've invested in one myself, the line that runs from Derby to Birmingham.'

'From Derby? Why, that's just a short journey from Knively!'

'Yes, which is why I was willing to put my money

into that venture. I was able to visit several times while it was under construction, and have ridden on it numerous times since its completion to visit investors in Birmingham for Mr Hughes.'

The idea came to him suddenly, generating such enthusiasm he had to stop himself from seizing her hand. 'Would...would *you* like to ride on it? I'd be happy to arrange to take you—and Lady Trent, of course—on a journey.'

'That sounds marvellous!' she exclaimed, her eagerness delighting him. But then her excited expression faded.

'We would ride all the way from Derby to Birmingham? It wouldn't take us very long to get to Derby, but I doubt Lady Trent would want to travel for as many hours as it would take to reach Birmingham. And then return! Travelling...fatigues her.'

'It isn't really that long a trip—only a bit over two hours each way. The engines can sustain speeds upwards of sixteen to twenty miles per hour—almost as fast as a horse can gallop. But, unlike a horse, the engine can maintain that speed indefinitely.'

Looking thoughtful, she stared into the distance, apparently calculating. 'That would still make it a full day's journey—but she might agree. Oh, I hope so! I should dearly love to go!'

'Shall I follow you back when you return to Brayton Hullford and speak with her? I could answer any questions she might have about making the trip.'

'You could drive me back,' she murmured, giving him a look from under her lashes so provocative, it immediately fired his simmering desire.

For a moment, all he could picture was halting his curricle in some convenient glade on the road back to

Brayton Hullford—and kissing her, thoroughly and repeatedly. As he'd longed to do almost from the moment he moved away from her after the first, all-too-brief, caress.

His cravat suddenly felt too tight, as did his trousers. 'That…probably would not be wise.'

She made a little moue of displeasure and sighed. 'No, it would not—however delightful it might be. But if you can spare the time, I should love for you to come speak with Lady Trent.' She shook her head, laughing. 'I dare not think too much about it, for I shall become so enamoured of going, I will be terribly disappointed if she refuses.'

'I shall just have to make sure I convince her.'

And he would, using charm, recommendations, persuasion, wheedling—whatever it took. If he couldn't kiss Sara Standish, or make love to her the way his body urged him to, at least he could allow himself the pleasure of taking her on a journey she would almost surely find unforgettable.

In her company, he would certainly never forget it.

'Should I pour tea for Andrew and Mr Lennox now?' she asked, interrupting his scheming. 'I imagine you must all get back to work soon.'

He didn't need to consult his pocket watch to know she was correct. 'Yes, I'm afraid we must. I will have to talk with my foreman about a problem with one of the machines before I will be able to come out to Brayton Hullford. But I will come this afternoon, I promise.'

Engaged in pouring two more cups of tea, she nodded. 'A little delay will be fine. I intended to stop in to see how Jenny was doing on my way back anyway.'

'That will work nicely. So, after tea concludes, I'll escort you to the entry, where you may wait if your car-

riage has not yet returned, then set out for Brayton Hullford after my business is concluded.'

'Yes, I should like that.' Giving him a luminous smile,
she turned to carry the cups over to the boy and his supervisor.

Fired by a vision of her, bonnet strings blowing in the
breeze, her face alight with excitement as the railroad car
barrelled around a turn, Cam set his mind to considering
the most persuasive arguments to win over Lady Trent.

Chapter Seventeen

Several hours later, Cam arrived at Brayton Hullford and turned his curricle over to Rogers. 'Walk the team down the carriageway and back, if you would,' he told the groom. 'I won't be long.'

'Lady Trent and Miss Standish are expecting you,' Thurston said as he answered Cam's knock and took his hat and cane. 'If you would follow me?'

Cam trailed the butler up the stairs to a spacious front parlour. 'Mr Fitzallen,' Thurston intoned as he gestured Cam inside.

'Good afternoon, Mr Fitzallen,' the Marchioness said, nodding to acknowledge his bow as Miss Standish rose to give him a curtsy. 'Can you stay long enough for tea?'

'That's kind of you, but I must refuse. I'm afraid I need to return to the mill as soon as possible.'

Though he would much prefer to sit in this parlour and gaze at Sara Standish. Except for the dinner here at Brayton Hullford, he had always seen her dressed for walking, or in a carriage gown, her figure buttoned up under a heavy pelisse. He savoured viewing her in an afternoon gown that hugged her curves much more closely, while its low neckline showed off her lovely neck and shoulders.

Suddenly the absurdity of it all hit him and he had to restrain a chuckle. Ten years ago, he would never have imagined that he would be sitting as an invited guest in a marchioness's parlour, casting admiring glances towards a young lady of quality.

If the other orphans in the workhouse could see me now, he thought wryly.

'My companion tells me you have proposed a journey for us, one she finds very appealing,' Lady Trent was saying. 'Please, can you tell me more about it?'

Cam obliged, repeating to her details about the line, the transit time and the travelling distance involved. 'I think you would find it fascinating and much more comfortable than travelling by coach! There is a slight vibration as you travel over the rails, but nothing like the bumping and jolting one often experiences riding in a carriage.'

'It does sound more comfortable. Although I do worry about the amount of time required for the journey. I... don't travel as easily as I used to.'

'I wouldn't recommend something that would cause you discomfort, ma'am. We could bring extra blankets and cushions, as well, to pad the bench.'

The Marchioness looked from Cam to Miss Standish, her expression thoughtful. After several long minutes, during which Cam held his breath, she shook her head.

'I'm so sorry, Sara. Though I do believe I would find the journey fascinating, I... I just don't think I can tolerate it now.'

Miss Standish quickly schooled her initial expression of dismay into one of sympathy. 'I wouldn't want you to undertake a trip that would tax your strength.' With a visible effort, she put on a smile. 'Perhaps I shall have an opportunity at some other time to try riding on a railway.'

Cam longed to apply more persuasion, but seeing Lady Trent now, in the strong afternoon sunshine rather than under the dimmer glow of candlelight, he couldn't help observing how frail she looked. He also recalled hearing the apothecary gossip about what a boon she was to his business when she was in town, as he always needed to order additional quantities of herbs and medications in order to keep her supplied with the cordials she required.

So he made himself smile as well. 'Yes, perhaps we could make the journey on another occasion.'

Though when, he couldn't imagine. In just a handful of days, Lady Trent and her party would leave for London. She didn't often come to Derbyshire and Cam had no idea when she might return again.

Though it was like a knife to the heart to think of Miss Standish making such a journey not in his company, he still wanted her to experience it—even if he couldn't share it with her.

'The London to Birmingham line is under construction,' he said as he stood. 'Perhaps you could coax some of your London friends to travel on that with you once it is finished, Miss Standish. It's an adventure I wouldn't want you to miss.'

This was what he should make himself picture, he reminded himself. Not kissing her, but her returned to her proper place in London, sharing any adventures that came her way with her political friends and associates.

Not with an upstart inventor firmly entrenched in a far different world.

Still, that observation did nothing to lessen his stubborn desire to be the one who first shared with her the wonder of a journey by rail.

Mentally shaking off his irritation, he said, 'I'll take

my leave, then. I shall see you again when you visit the mill school, Miss Standish?'

In the wan smile she gave him he read her own disappointment. Foolish as it was, he was gratified that she looked as unhappy as he felt at the cancellation of their proposed excursion.

'I should be able to read to the students again in a day or so. I shall try to fit in several more visits in between preparing for our departure, which Lady Trent just informed me will take place ten days from tomorrow.'

Ten days! He stifled the protest rising in his throat. In his mind, he'd known she would be leaving, and leaving soon, but he'd always avoided dealing with that fact by leaving the actual departure date vague. Ten days was...far too soon.

And that reaction only reinforced how wise it was to have her leave, since her leaving was inevitable, before he became any more attached to spending time with her.

Suppressing his conflicting emotions, he said, 'Very well. Thank you for receiving me, Lady Trent, Miss Standish.'

'I'll walk you out. If I may, Lady Trent?' Miss Standish said.

She nodded. 'Good day, Mr Fitzallen.'

They had almost exited the room, both of them walking with dawdling steps to draw out their time together as long as possible, when Lady Trent said, 'Wait! Can you stay another few moments, Mr Fitzallen?'

Curious, Cam looked over. 'Yes, another few moments will not matter. What can I do for you, ma'am?'

'It's rather what I can do for you—and my dear Sara, who looked so woebegone after I denied her this treat, when she has been such a comfort to me, that I couldn't bear it. You shall have your rail journey, my dear, and in the next day or so. You must have a chaperon accompany you, of course, but it isn't essential that it be me. I shall survey the maids and see which one is adventurous enough to agree to travel on a train, and detail a footman to accompany you, to assist should something untoward take place. With a maid and footman to attend her, I can allow Sara to make the journey under your escort, Mr Fitzallen.'

Her body tensing, Sara studied Lady Trent. 'Are you sure you are comfortable, allowing that?'

Lady Trent sighed. 'Not completely, but I shall allow it anyway.'

With a little whoop of delight that made Cam laugh, Sara ran over to Lady Trent and gave her a hug. 'Thank you! Thank you so much! You can't imagine how excited I am about this journey. Imagine, travelling over twenty miles an hour—in a carriage! It will be so exciting!'

Lady Trent chuckled. 'Better you than me, my dear. Mr Fitzallen, you will let me know when the journey is arranged?'

Almost as exuberant as Sara, Cam would have liked to give Lady Trent a hug himself. 'Yes, ma'am. Is there a time that would be better for the household, so as not to interfere with your departure preparations?'

'Some time in the next few days would be best.'

'I shall try to arrange for day after tomorrow, then. Thank you, Lady Trent. I can't wait to see Miss Standish's reaction to travelling in a carriage that is moving at a gallop!'

Though Sara walked out with him at decorous pace, as soon as they proceeded on to the landing, out of sight of the parlour, she gave a little leap and seized Cam's arm.

'I'm going to ride on a railway! Behind one of those

marvellous steam engines I've read about. And watch the countryside fly by at twenty miles an hour!'

'So you will,' he confirmed, smiling at her enthusiasm and just as exuberant as she was at the prospect of sharing the experience, though he was trying his best to temper it. No point letting her know just how much being together for this journey meant to him, not with her about to exit his life for ever.

Turning his mind from that fact, he added teasingly, 'That is, you will experience it if you can find a maid brave enough to accompany you.'

'I'll bribe one if I must,' she tossed back. 'Oh, I can't thank you enough for offering me this opportunity!'

'It's as much a treat for me as it will be for you. To watch you as you see with your own eyes how marvellous machines are changing our world for ever, making it better for everyone, not just the rich and powerful.'

'To watch me see your vision for the future come to life.'

'Yes.' He was eager to share his visions with her— something he had never shared with anyone. Something he hadn't even *wanted* to share with anyone.

He pushed the alarming implications of that truth deep and determined to enjoy the moment. It would be fleeting enough.

It would all end in ten days.

By now, they had reached the front entry. 'Will there be many other people on the train with us?' she asked.

'Probably a fair number. Including your maid and footman.'

'So,' she said, her eyes dancing, 'no improprieties possible on *this* carriage ride.'

'Alas, no,' he said regretfully, surprised, but pleased— and aroused—to discover that her thoughts of what they might do if alone followed the same lusty direction as his. 'Not unless you want to entertain an audience of ten or twenty observers.'

She sighed. 'That would not be wise. So, you will let me know the minute you have everything arranged?'

'Of course. It should be possible to have everything set for the day after tomorrow, but I'll send you a note tomorrow to confirm that.'

Beaming, she looked up at him…and her gaze intensified. Her eyes locked on his face, she went up on tiptoe and leaned up, lifting her chin to him.

His heart stuttering to a stop, he froze, certain she meant to kiss him.

Dimly he heard the clomp of Thurston's approaching footsteps. She must have, too, for she stepped hastily away from him. An instant later the butler appeared, offering Cam his hat and cane.

It would have been madness for her to kiss him in Lady Trent's front hall, where they might be seen by any number of servants.

He was still furious with the butler for interrupting her.

'I shall see you soon, I expect,' she said, her cheeks rosy—with embarrassment that they had almost been discovered? Or chagrin that her clandestine kiss had been forestalled? 'By the way, what manner of clothing should I wear?' she continued. 'A riding habit? A carriage dress?'

Her question dispelling his irritation, Cam laughed. 'Just like a woman, to ask what she should wear.'

'Of course! One wishes to be properly dressed and I've never ridden on a railroad before.'

'I don't know much about female attire, but I expect whatever you would wear for a horse-drawn carriage ride would suffice. Make sure your outer garment is warm, though, and that your bonnet ties securely. The railroad cars have a roof over them, but travelling at such speeds, the wind can be strong.'

'I'll come prepared. Thank you again, Mr Fitzallen.'

'You are welcome. Good day, Miss Standish.'

'Thurston, I'm going to ride on a railway!' Cam heard her exclaim as the door shut behind him.

Grinning, Cam walked down the stairs and took the reins to his curricle back from the groom. Even the knowledge of how little time he had left with her couldn't put a damper on his delight.

England, his England, was becoming a modern world of ingenious machines. He couldn't wait to share it with Miss Standish.

Cam tooled the curricle along on the drive back to the mill, his euphoria fading as he remembered how soon he would be stripped of the pleasure of Miss Standish's company. Probably for good.

Everything within him rebelled at the idea, yet he couldn't see how he could prevent it. He ought not to *want* to prevent it. Coming to depend on the presence of another person for his sense of well-being was a recipe for being devastated by loss, as he ought to have learned at an early age. In any event, he didn't need a woman to distract him, as Miss Standish had so often recently, from the hard work of building his business.

He'd never really been spurred on by some need to prove himself to the gentry who, from his earliest memory, had dismissed him or thought him beneath them. The condescending young men at Cambridge who'd looked down on his commercial aspirations provoked only a mild annoyance, not any desire to best them. It had been his passion for machines, for mastering them, then improving them, and his vision of building better mills and safer workplaces that had driven all his efforts.

That passion, that vision, had been all the fulfilment he needed. It had indeed become his whole world, and concentrating on achieving that to the exclusion of all else had made him happy.

But now, as he thought of moving forward with expanding the mill, adding better safeguards and more programmes for the workers, sponsoring advancing schooling for promising students like Andrew...without Sara Standish to talk about them and share them with, the wonder and excitement of achieving them suddenly dimmed. The idea of doing all that without being able to tell her about it sent a deep pang of sadness echoing through in his chest, followed by a sense of...emptiness.

The horrifying realisation struck him that, much as he'd tried to prevent it, somehow Sara Standish had become far more important to his happiness and sense of fulfilment than he should ever have permitted.

Losing her, he suddenly recognised, would blow a huge hole in his life, as destructive as the stick of dynamite he'd once witnessed thrown down into a coal mine. Leaving the core of him empty.

What could he do to prevent it?

Get her to stay.

There was only one way possible to guarantee he could keep her with him. Much as his body exulted at the possibility of claiming her in all her sweetness, his mind immediately rebelled.

He had no illusions that asking her to share his world wouldn't, in effect, mean asking her to give up her own. Which was too much to ask of anyone.

He should forget this whole insane idea, lest he ruin

her chances to find a husband from her own world, someone to watch over and protect and cherish her beautiful, unique, shining spirit as much as he did.

Or at the least, allow her to continue in the independence she seemed to prize. Though it seemed unnatural for such a loving, giving person to live her whole life alone.

But when he pictured her face, heard in his mind the delight of her laugh, remembered her kindness to the children, her interest in his inventions, the fascination for books and scientific progress they both shared, he didn't want any other man to do the cherishing.

Just imagining someone else touching her, kissing her, made him feel like hitting something.

But what could a workhouse orphan offer that would make up for asking her to turn her back on everything she'd ever known?

He knew beyond doubt that if she gave herself to him, he would pledge her the same faithful love and passionate devotion he'd offered to his work. He would give her the chance to continuing working with mill children and the satisfaction of being able to help those of ability and ambition get the education that would allow them to realise their dreams.

She could devote her talents not just to writing letters, but to seeing her care and concern for children result in action that made lives better.

She'd already told him how energising and fulfilling she'd found it to work with Jenny and Andrew.

He couldn't offer her a social status equal to that conferred on her by birth, but she seemed to place as little importance on that as he did.

He felt himself hovering on the brink of a precipice. There was still a slender thread holding him back from fully committing himself. Difficult as he knew it would be, he could survive her loss…if he let her go now.

But he'd never got what he wanted by being timid or proceeding by half-measures, hanging back until the way forward was safe. He'd thrown himself into achieving his dreams with a single-minded devotion. If he were to declare himself to Sara Standish, he would do it in the same way—wholeheartedly, giving her all of him, his passion, his hopes, his dreams.

In short, he would risk everything.

But if she would agree to give the wonder that was Sara Standish into his care…the risk would be worth it.

Would she even consider it? With her time in Derbyshire about to end, he needed to find out.

Very well, he would ask. She could always turn him down. She probably *would* turn him down. It was the sensible thing to do, after all.

Would she be sensible?

He recalled her saying that she was interested in many things that were considered 'odd' for a lady, that her aunt had tried her best and failed to get her to confine her activities to those that society considered suitable.

Maybe she would find what he offered more 'sensible' than what her background—and society—dictated.

And if she did accept him…the soaring delight, the burst of euphoria that illumined his spirit at the thought was the final evidence he needed to convince him to take the risk.

Of course, not even a workhouse orphan would be gauche enough to blurt out a proposal in the middle of a train journey, with his intended surrounded by her maid, footman and a host of fellow travellers.

But somehow, he would find a chance to strongly hint of his intentions and see how she responded.

Thankfully, she wasn't one of those females who enjoyed flirting with every man she met, happy to lead on even ones in whom she really had no interest. Sara Standish wouldn't encourage him unless she were strongly inclined to accept him.

What had begun as a railroad adventure's glimpse of the future had suddenly taken on a much more far-reaching importance. Looking down at the reins, he found his hands were shaking.

He would do this. But his excitement and anticipation were now tempered with a healthy dose of terror.

Chapter Eighteen

In the early morning two days later, Sara sat with her maid in the Brayton Hullford carriage on the road to Derby, so excited she could scarcely keep still. Putting out of her mind that ticking clock warning of how little time she had left to enjoy with Cameron Fitzallen, she intended to revel in this marvellous day, in which she'd get to experience the greatest adventure of her life—with Fitzallen as her escort.

Could anything be more perfect?

Susan, the maid who'd agreed to accompany her, had been understandably nervous. Sara secretly thought the only reason the girl had agreed to go was that she was sweet on James, the big, strapping footman Lady Trent had assigned to assist them.

Her hostess had instructed the man to bring a basket of victuals and a purse with sufficient coin to meet any eventuality. 'For if your magical railroad breaks down and you find yourself stranded in the countryside or in some small village,' Lady Trent had told Sara as she bade her goodbye, 'you will need food to sustain you until the engine is repaired and funds to pay for lodging if you are forced to remain overnight.'

Though Sara would not mind a bit being stranded somewhere with Cameron Fitzallen, she doubted that was a possibility. The railway, he had assured her, was extremely reliable. But she was happy enough to have Lady Trent send the food and the footman along, so he might assist Mr Fitzallen if anything were to go amiss.

And to occupy Susan, so Sara might be able to steal some private conversation with Mr Fitzallen, if the opportunity arose.

She felt a tightness constrict her chest whenever she considered how very soon they would be leaving for London. And then last night, as she struggled to breathe against it, she suddenly thought of a way she might be able to continue their association after she left Derbyshire.

Mr Sellers had already agreed to correspond with her about any books or supplies he needed for the school. She'd also asked him to keep her informed about other students who showed as much promise as Jenny and Andrew.

If there were such children, surely she would need to make occasional trips back to Hughes Cotton Works to meet them and their schoolmaster and assess where it would be best to place them going forward? And if she returned to Hughes Works, she would certainly have to meet with its owner.

She hoped Mr Fitzallen would agree to such a partnership.

A little glow lit in her heart at the possibility that she would not lose him completely. She'd be able to tolerate the irritation of returning to society...and the loneliness of missing him...if she knew she would be able to see him at least occasionally. To ask about his latest interests and achievements, perhaps visit his workroom again and get a tour of his current projects.

Those few meetings were not nearly as much as her sore heart and needy senses were demanding. But the prospect of meeting him at all, however seldom, was far better than never seeing him again.

Such meetings would also be safe. Surrounded by others, the passion to which they both admitted would be constrained, so that they weren't tempted to rashness that would jeopardise her position and his.

Small planet Sara Standish, gazing at the blazing comet of purpose and achievement that was Cameron Fitzallen, would have to be content with that. And keep tight hold on what remained of a heart she was already far too close to giving over to him completely.

Which, as he had neither desire nor need for it, was a prescription for permanent misery.

A short time later, the carriage slowed as they reached the outskirts of Derby. Excitement fizzing in her veins, she straightened in her seat and craned her neck to look out the window.

'Are you sure you want to do this, miss?' Susan asked, her fingers nervously pleating her gown. 'Change your mind and we could be back home before Lady Trent finishes her breakfast.'

'Of course I want to do this! And you will love it, too. You'll see!' she assured the girl, whose face had paled as the carriage halted and James appeared to open the door and hand them out.

'We'll leave you ladies to rest and refresh yourself here at the Grouse and Hind,' Mr Fitzallen called down to them from his curricle. 'A private parlour has been reserved for you—the innkeeper's wife will escort you up. James and I will take the curricle to the stables, arrange our tickets, and return for you shortly. The train should be arriving in half an hour.'

An effervescent fizz of joy and elation filling her, Sara felt her lips curve into a smile. 'I can't wait to climb aboard!'

Fitzallen smiled down at her. 'It will be everything you are expecting and more. I promise!'

It was a good thing he was driving off in his curricle, Sara thought wryly as she walked into the posting inn. He looked so handsome today, his eyes so merry and full of anticipation at offering his treat that she'd been hard pressed not to throw herself into his arms and hug him fiercely.

Or kiss him, as she'd almost had the audacity to do, that afternoon at Brayton Hullford after he'd convinced Lady Trent to allow her to take the train journey with him.

Would he have let her? Or would he have drawn back in distaste, put off by her forward, unladylike behaviour?

She *thought* he would have responded with appreciation. The way he looked at her, the cryptic comments they sometimes exchanged and the strong physical attraction that simmered between them whenever they were together argued that he would have been delighted by her initiative.

She gave a little sigh. Now she would never know. And perhaps that was for the best.

But mourning the loss of his kiss or not, she intended to let nothing spoil her enjoyment of would be a glorious day.

Even the weather had co-operated, serving up a beautiful sun-dazzled, cloudless blue sky, June morning that was fragrant with the roses blooming in the cottage garden outside the inn's open windows. The views from the hills over the rolling countryside through which the train would pass would be magnificent.

She had just finished a glass of cider when Mr Fitzallen and James entered the private room. 'Time to go, ladies. Your conveyance awaits!'

Susan let out a little whimper, and Sara patted her hand. 'James will see that you come to no harm,' she assured the girl.

'That I will, Susan,' he said, giving the girl a wink that made her blush.

Taking the arm Mr Fitzallen offered, Sara walked down the stairs.

The waiting train reminded Sara of a powerful thoroughbred being readied for a race. The engine with its tall smokestack, like a chimney mounted on a long iron barrel with wheels, puffed smoke as the operators prepared it for the journey.

The passenger cars resembled long wagons with canopy tops and were accessed by short doors leading to padded benches. With their wheels rolling on parallel iron rails, they sat high enough off the ground that passengers had to use a wooden platform in order to reach their seats.

Within a few minutes, Mr Fitzallen and James had helped them both to clamber aboard, Sara having to hold herself tightly in check to resist leaving her hand on Fitzallen's arm. But she did allow herself to give his arm a squeeze before releasing him, smiling at him as she took her seat. 'Thank you again. This will be the most exciting adventure of my life!'

'Only hope it's not the last one,' Susan muttered.

Other passengers entered, filling up almost all of the available seats, although their party of four had one corner of the car to themselves. 'Will the engine be quiet enough that we will be able to talk?' she asked him.

'Yes. It's not nearly as loud as the machinery in the mill,' Fitzallen replied. 'You will be able to tell me about your impressions as we travel, which I very much look forward to hearing.'

At that moment, a whistle blew and the train began to move, slowly at first, but then gradually accelerating. 'The operator won't bring the engine up to full speed until we are out of the town,' Fitzallen told her.

'It's already moving faster than a horse at the trot,' Sara observed, a little apprehension mixing into her jubilation. But she would have none of being timid Sara Standish today—today she was brave, bold Sara, keen to embrace all the possibilities of the future.

She cast a sideways glance at Mr Fitzallen. Almost as keen as she would be to embrace this man of the future.

They had gone only a short way outside the town when the train crossed a long stone bridge. 'We'll cross many bridges,' he told her. 'Stephenson soon figured out that engines lost power and burned more fuel if they had to go up and down hills. So when the railway lines are built, every attempt is made to maintain the track at a constant level, with bridges constructed as necessary to cross steams and low places, and the rail bed built up in others, so that the angle of rise or descent is kept as small as possible.'

'Mathematics at work already.'

He smiled. 'A great deal of mathematics, along with the artistry of stonemasons and road-builders.'

She caught her breath as the train began to accelerate, until it seemed to her that the countryside was flying by. A beautiful collage of fields, houses, distant hills crowned with trees, flashed by her, the wind rushing at her face and snatching at her bonnet. 'This must be what a bird feels like when it's flying!'

'Perhaps,' he said with a smile. 'And did you notice? The ride is as smooth as a bird on the wing, with none of the jolting of a horse-drawn carriage.'

'It is smooth,' she marvelled. 'No wonder people are so enamoured of travelling in this manner.'

'I believe that soon, people will not want to travel any other way, especially long distances between cities,' Fitzallen said. 'When you think of going all the way from Derby to Birmingham in just over two hours, in a much more comfortable fashion than by horse-drawn coach, why wouldn't one choose to? As a matter of fact, since the Liverpool and Manchester railway opened five years ago, all the stagecoach lines connecting the cities have shut down.'

'Good for the passengers. Not so good for the stagecoach drivers and the innkeepers at the posting inns along the way.'

'They can become railroad drivers and local travellers will still patronise the inns. But seeing this—the speed, the efficiency, the beauty—just imagine how many more improvements to life wait ahead, as men create more and more machines to help them travel and do their work. The whole world will be changed, for the better, I am certain, and the possibilities are limitless as man's imagination!'

She nodded, looking at him with pride and admiration. 'Limitless for men like you, who have the vision to foresee more uses for machines and the brilliance to invent them.'

He waved a deprecating hand. 'Fascination and perseverance.'

'Intelligence and skill.'

He grinned. 'If you insist on paying me compliments, I'll not object. But the countryside just ahead is breathtaking. You should settle back and enjoy the view.'

And so she did, marvelling at the swiftness of the ever-changing scenery. But more than anything else, revelling in the presence of the man seated beside her. His strength, intelligence, vibrancy, and purpose.

How dull and colourless her life was going to be, bereft of him for months at a time.

Once again, she beat back any negative thoughts. He was with her today and she was immensely grateful for that.

Chapter Nineteen

It seemed but a short time later when the train began to slow. 'We're approaching Birmingham,' Fitzallen said. 'You should see the city appear over that rise.'

'Already?' she asked. 'It seems hardly any time at all since we left Derby.'

'I told you the transit was quick.'

'Unbelievably so! Only about twice the time it takes to go from our London house out to Richmond Park! To think we've gone many times as far today... Mr Fitzallen, you must tell me how I can invest some money in railways!'

He laughed. 'Give me the name of your solicitor and I'll send him a list of the most promising railway bills now before Parliament.'

They were nearing the city now, the track beginning to pass by buildings and roads and crossing several bridges until the train finally slowed to a halt by another elevated platform.

'We'll disembark here,' Fitzallen told her. 'The next train returning to Derby doesn't depart for another hour. I thought you ladies might enjoy driving up to the heights above the city. With the day so fine, there will be a wonderful view over the city.'

'That sounds delightful. James brought us that basket of provisions, so we can have some refreshment. See, Susan,' Sara said as Fitzallen helped her down, 'wasn't it wonderful? You did enjoy it, didn't you?'

'Well, miss, it weren't quite as terrifying as I feared it would be,' the maid allowed.

Especially not since the maid, after initially uttering a little shriek each time the train picked up speed, let James hold her hand and put a protective arm around her shoulder.

Sara thought the girl would ride any number of trains to repeat that experience.

She only wished she'd been able to let Mr Fitzallen hold *her* hand and put his arm around *her* shoulders. That edgy, heated swirl of attraction had pulsed between them the whole length of the journey, simmering under her excitement over the ride and the views.

A little sizzle of heat went through her at the thought of embracing him. Though it wouldn't be fear or nervousness that prompted her to hold him close.

Not for the first time, she regretted her position as a Lady of Quality, whose behaviour was held to certain standards. Ah, to have the freedom from scrutiny of a maid or a footman!

'I'll see to hiring a carriage and be back to fetch you in a few minutes,' Fitzallen was saying. 'James, you'll look after the ladies?'

'Yes, sir. We'll watch for your carriage.'

Half an hour later, the foursome had descended from the carriage on the heights, admired the view, and were finishing up the victuals Lady Trent had provided. 'Shall we walk a bit before we must return to the train?' Mr Fitzallen asked Sara as the maid packed up the basket.

'Yes, I'd like a chance to stretch my legs before we are seated again for the journey home,' she replied.

And to her delight, as she'd hoped, James beckoned to Susan, who came over to take his arm. As they strolled off to admire the view at the edge of the summit, Mr Fitzallen offered her his arm—and led her in the opposite direction.

They would get that private conversation she'd longed for after all.

'I hope you won't be annoyed by my repeating it, but I simply must thank you again for today. Riding on the train—it's a harbinger of a different world.'

'It *is* the harbinger of a different world, and the changes have only begun. A different and wonderful world, where machines will take over the burden of performing many of life's most difficult tasks.'

'I so admire your vision. It's as inspiring as your talent.'

'More compliments! You will make me quite vain.'

'I doubt I'm the first female to pay you compliments. You must be universally admired wherever you go.'

'Ah, but yours are the compliments that matter. Because you never say anything you don't mean. And you apply an inquisitive mind and a discerning intelligence to everything you do and say.'

She chuckled. 'I have also been described as "intrusive and prying", enquiring into matters that are none of a lady's concern. But while I'm being intrusive and prying, may I ask you something I've wondered about?'

He lifted an eyebrow. 'Something "intrusive and prying"? I can't imagine what, but ask away.'

Since she might never have another chance, she might

as well forge ahead. 'Have you always been...alone? It seems you know everyone, but I don't ever see you with, or hear you speak about, any...particular friends.'

He shrugged. 'I suppose, from the time I was small, my passion for machines and my desire to tinker with them, perfect them and invent them, occupied me so completely I never felt the need, or took the time, for friends.'

'I envy you that self-sufficiency.'

He shook his head. 'I'm not sure you need to envy it. If I am perfectly honest, remaining alone became... something of a protective choice.'

The odd note in his voice prompted her to ask, 'You... lost someone close to you?'

He gave her a half-smile. 'You are discerning.'

She waited, but he added nothing else. She wished she might probe further, but she'd already been rudely inquisitive enough.

She'd concluded that he didn't intend to comment further on the subject when he said abruptly, 'There was an older girl at the workhouse when I was first sent there from the foundling home. You...remind me of her, with your warmth and concern for the unfortunate. Molly took me under her wing, protected me from the bigger children who would have preyed upon me. It was not until much later that I realised that she'd...died for me.'

'Died for you?' she echoed, shocked. 'What do you mean?' And then immediately added, 'I'm sorry, I don't mean to pry.'

'You might as well know the whole.' He shook his head. 'It was a terrible winter, with snow and storms, the workhouse always cold and swept by draughts. I was about six at the time. Children were sickening and dying all around us. Molly had developed a terrible, rasping cough. I suppose she knew, as I did not, that her end was near. She started giving me her morsels of bread and soup, saying she'd already eaten at the factory. I was young, trusting—or perhaps, to my shame, I was just so hungry and sick myself, I didn't question her. She slipped away in the night, in early March that year.'

Heart aching for him, Sara chanced reaching out to squeeze his hand. He left his fingers in her grip, not pulling away, as she'd half-expected him to. 'I'm so sorry. It must have been…devastating. I know what it is to lose… people who care for you, although my experience was by no means as tragic as yours.'

'You lost people who cared for you—when your good friends married?'

'Yes. I'm struggling to be independent, without their support. Although Lady Trent has been a kind mentor, it's not the same as having a…true friend of your own age, who understands you and shares your interests. Someone you…long to be with.'

Which was as close as she could come to admitting *he* was now that person for her.

Both were silent for a moment. Then, gazing into the distance, he said softly, 'I was so…bereft and miserable after Molly's death, I walled myself off, never wanting to experience such loss again. But now… I'm no longer so sure I want to live my life alone. I know you are to leave for London in just a few days. Is there any chance you might…stay on in Derbyshire?'

Shock sizzled through her and her heart leapt. Was he asking what she thought he was asking?

'If someone were to ask me to stay on…as his assistant and…intimate helpmate… I might remain.'

He looked back at her then, his face alight and a brilliant smile on his lips. 'Perhaps someone had better ask, then. But not here and now—surrounded by strolling visitors and hovering servants. Even an orphan from the workhouse knows certain questions must be asked in proper form. And in private.'

She knew her answering smile beamed even more brightly than his. Certain now that he meant to ask what she'd not dared to hope for, everything within her exulted. Though in her giddy delight, she'd not mind at all if he went down on one knee before her in front of a trainload of observers, he was probably correct.

A certain amount of decorum and discretion should be preserved.

'I suppose so,' she answered at last. 'We depart for London in barely a week. But today you've shown me the vision of a brave new world to come. We need to be brave enough to meet it, to discard the rules and conventions holding us back and choose what is right for *us*, without fear or hesitation.'

He studied her face. 'You truly believe that?'

'With all my heart.'

He seized her hand and drew her further along, to where a stand of trees bordered the path, then stepped her into the shadows behind them.

And as she had dreamed about and craved for weeks, he bent down and kissed her.

As before, he began gently, but the kiss quickly became more passionate as he stroked and sampled her lips, then delved his tongue into her mouth. She gasped as the shock of it set off an explosion of warmth deep within her, a tingling that rippled through her body in waves.

She leaned closer, matching the exploration of his tongue with the tentative touch of her own. He groaned, tightening his grip on her.

She felt his strength and heat against the whole length

of her. Felt the hardness of him pressed against her belly—the realisation of what that meant sparking another wave of tingling arousal. She put her hands around his neck, holding him closer still, wanting everything he offered and more. Wanting this moment to last and last. Wanting to stay in his arms for ever.

His hands roved down her body, moulding her breasts through the heavy material of her gown and pelisse, intensifying the building tension within her. She murmured her impatience, wanting the encumbering clothing discarded, wanting the feel of his hands on her bare skin.

All too soon, he broke away, panting. 'Darling tormentor! You drive me to madness, trapped within that mechanical cage of garments.'

'Thank heaven you are good at taking apart mechanical things.'

He laughed. 'I burn to show you just how skilled I am! But…not here and now. We really must start back, lest we miss the return train.'

With him having made a delicious start on her sensual education, the last thing she wanted was to stop now. Unfortunately, as sense wrestled control back from passion, she knew he was right.

'I hate it, but you are correct.' She gave a giddy laugh. 'My, oh, my! That second kiss was even better than the first. I can't imagine how wonderful the third—and everything else—will be.'

The gaze he fixed on her was so tender, this time it was her heart that tingled. 'It will be wonderful. More than you can imagine.'

'When?' she demanded.

He chuckled, running his gloved fingertip over the lips he'd just kissed. 'Soon, my impatient one.'

'You promise?'

His gaze turned sober. 'I promise. With all *my* heart.'

And then he laughed, the merry sound of it echoing the joy that flooded her. This was better than all her dreams and imaginings—Cameron Fitzallen would really be hers.

Who would have imagined shy, quiet Sara Standish would ever have won such a prize?

Gently he tucked an errant curl back under her bonnet and straightened her pelisse. 'We must collect Susan and James and get back.'

She sighed. 'If we must.'

His tender gaze roved over her face. 'How did I ever survive without you in my life, my darling Sara?'

'How could I survive without you for the rest of mine, my beloved Cam?'

'Neither of us will have to, ever again,' he promised.

Almost dizzy with delight, she let him lead her back to the summit, where the team was tethered. Susan and James scurried towards them from the opposite direction—the footman red-faced and the maid rosy cheeked, her ruby lips looking thoroughly kissed.

'I believe they may have been occupied in the same manner we were,' Cam murmured.

Sara put a hand to her mouth. 'Oh, dear! I hope I don't look that obvious!'

'They are too wrapped up in each other to notice and, by the time we reach the station, you will look your usual calm, ladylike self again.'

She gave him a wry grin. 'I doubt I shall ever be calm or ladylike again.'

He grinned back. 'I certainly hope not.'

As they waited on the platform to board the train after Cam returned their hired carriage, Sara heard a voice call out his name.

'Cam, my boy! What are you doing here?'

Cameron turned towards the caller. 'Good day to you, Mr Hughes! I took leave from the mill for the day so I might introduce Miss Standish to the wonders of travelling by rail.'

'Good day to you, Miss Standish,' Hughes said, making his way through the throng to give her a bow. 'Marvellous advancement, isn't it? So fast, so comfortable! Never want to travel any other way, once you've gone a distance by rail coach.'

'I've been very favourably impressed, and I am grateful to Mr Fitzallen for suggesting the journey.'

'Good tactic, Cam, my boy, to impress a lady who has the ear of a Parliamentary Committee,' Hughes said, giving Cam's arm a pat. 'Now, if I might interrupt your afternoon to have a word of business? With your permission, Miss Standish.'

'Of course,' she replied, curious what the former owner would want to discuss with the man to whom he'd turned over his operation.

'I've just spent some time in Birmingham with Mr Carlisle, who, as I believe you know, owns the largest group of iron foundries in England. We met at a gentleman's club and I told him all about you—your vision to improve and expand the mills, the inventions you've come up with to make machines and operations more efficient. He is very interested in talking with you about factory management and operation. And he hinted he might be willing to invest a sizeable sum in your plans to expand Hughes Works and acquire other mills.'

Cam smiled at Hughes. 'You have always had the touch, recruiting investors.'

'Well, that talent must now pass from me to you, my boy! It's forward of me, I know, but I promised him I'd send you back to Birmingham forthwith! Carlisle wants to show you around his various operations—have you take a close look at his machinery and perhaps suggest improvements. Should take four or five days, I'd imagine. Don't worry, I'll fill in for you at the mill while you're gone.'

'What an opportunity for you, Fitzallen!' Hughes continued. 'And much sooner than I expected you to land something like this. You must go to Birmingham at once, though. Carlisle said he's leaving within the week for London and expects to be gone a month or more. If I've learned anything in the years I've spent finding backers for the mill, it's that one must net investors while they are first hooked, before they can wriggle away. Carlisle is one good, fat fish indeed.'

After giving her a dismayed glance, Cam turned back to Hughes. 'Must I return to Birmingham at once?'

'Always best to strike while the iron is hot—especially in the case of an ironmonger,' Hughes said with a chuckle. 'Don't expect it should take you long to pack a few things and ready yourself to return. Why do you hesitate? Are there problems at the mill needing your attention?'

'No, no problems at the mill. I suppose there is no reason I couldn't go back tomorrow.'

'That's the spirit! If you find you need anything, the shops in the city are almost as fine as those in London. Now, I expect the impression you make on Carlisle to live up to the glowing report I gave of you, so have your most persuasive arguments prepared. This is your chance, son! Don't let me down.'

'Of course I won't,' Cam replied—the only thing he could reply, she knew, in the face of the prompting from the man who had been his earliest and most loyal supporter. 'I'll arrange to return to Birmingham tomorrow.'

'That's the spirit! Ah, time to board, I see. Well, glad I chanced to see you—saves me trying to track you down tonight! Good to see you again, too, Miss Standish. I hope you enjoy your return journey. Kind, as well as shrewd, of Fitzallen to have arranged it for you, eh? Capital fellow!'

'He is, indeed, and thank you, Mr Hughes. I'm sure I shall enjoy it.'

'I'll expect a full report when you return, Cam,' Hughes said.

'Of course. I hope I'll live up to the expectations you've created,' he said wryly.

'Ah, you'll do me proud, I have no doubt. Good day to you both!' Giving Cam a slap on the back, Hughes made her a bow and walked back into the milling throng on the platform.

Cam looked subdued as he assisted Sara to climb back into the rail car. 'I'm afraid I shall have to go tomorrow,' he said with a sigh. 'I'll return as soon as I can. Hopefully, Carlisle will not need me for four or five days.'

'I hope not. That would put your return dangerously close to the time Lady Trent intends to leave for London. And I will be waiting impatiently to be asked a question—in the proper manner.'

He smiled then. 'I'll be waiting very impatiently for your answer.'

They settled on the bench side by side, both pensive.

Sara knew Cam was disappointed to have to postpone the interview that would turn vaguely worded promises into a formal offer—an offer she was even more impatient and anxious to answer with a formal acceptance.

How was she to contain her excitement and delight for the handful of days until he returned and called at Brayton Hullford, and they made their commitment to each other official?

Joy fizzled in her veins. Until, for the first time since they'd exchanged those promises, Sara considered how others would view their declaration.

Lady Trent was not likely to be joyful.

All right and fine to talk of bravely venturing into a brave new world, but she was too honest not to recognise that none of her family or acquaintances would view a liaison with Cameron Fitzallen with anything but shock and disapproval.

Not that she meant to let that sway her decision. But it would hurt to lose Lady Trent's good opinion, if, in fact, after hearing the news, that lady chose to cut their connection. Although she was certain that Emma and Olivia would support her, her aunt would be devastated, her mother only less so.

But it was *her* life she must live, not the one society or her family would choose for her.

No longer would she let the caution of her failed relationship restrain emotions that now had her yearning for Cam. Unbelievably, he not only looked with approval on her intellect and activities—he actually loved *her*.

Which outweighed even the pain of disappointing her family.

The life she chose for herself, the prospect of which filled her with jubilant anticipation, must be shared with Cameron Fitzallen.

Chapter Twenty

In the late afternoon five days later, Cam sat at his desk, looking over reports and orders processed in his absence. He'd arrived back the previous evening, too late to call upon Sara at Brayton Hullford.

By his calculations, he still had two days before the Marchioness's party departed for the capital. He'd rather call there after having previously arranged the visit with Sara, so that he arrived when she would be free and expecting him. Having confirmed with Sellers when he stopped by the bookkeeper's office this morning that she intended to read to the children today, he'd decided to catch up on as much work as possible before she arrived.

Then he'd meet her at the schoolroom, enjoy her performance for the pupils—and arrange for that call at Brayton Hullford.

A thrill ran through him to think that soon, lovely, marvellous, caring Sara would be his. Assistant, helpmate, critic, partner—ah, what they would accomplish together!

He would make sure she never regretted taking that bold step into his brave new world and leaving hers behind.

In truth, as the afternoon advanced, he was having a harder and harder time concentrating on his work, too often falling into glorious daydreams of what the future held for them.

As a knock at the door startled him out of his latest fond imaginings, his spirits leapt. This must finally be the summons to the schoolroom he'd been awaiting.

Just a few more moments and he would see her again. And in just another day or so, he'd finally have the right to kiss her, take her hand and boldly announce to the whole world that she belonged to him.

Feeling lit from within with joy, he nodded to the lad who'd knocked and stood, straightening his coat. But before he could walk out to follow the boy, the lad instead entered his office.

'There be a lady to see ya, Mr Fitzallen.'

Not Sara? He couldn't imagine Lady Trent paying a call on him—unless something had happened to her?

Before alarm could seize him, he looked up to see an employee conducting a woman towards his office. An older lady, just a bit younger than the Marchioness, whose voluminous skirts, huge bonnet and intricate, elevated braided coiffure must be the latest London fashion.

He hadn't the faintest idea who she was.

The man opened the door and motioned her in. 'Lady Patterson to see you, sir,' he said before closing the door behind her.

Wary, Cam stood and gave her a bow. 'What can I do for you, Lady Peterson? That is—nothing has happened at Brayton Hullford, has it? Miss Standish is well?'

'So you know who I am. I wasn't sure you would. I should like to sit, if I may.'

Puzzled, but with a sense of dread building in his gut, Cam motioned her to a chair.

'If you know who I am, then it probably won't require much reflection for you to figure out why I am here.'

'Sara—' he halted as Lady Patterson winced at his use of her niece's first name '—Miss Standish told you about me?'

'She most certainly did not, or I would have come to Derbyshire much sooner! No, I learned of your... association from a friend who happened to be travelling on the Derby to Birmingham railway about a week ago. She spotted my niece on the train, in your company. That is, she thought at first it was Sara, but when her companion identified *you,* realised she must be mistaken, as Miss Sara Standish would never have been travelling alone in the company of a *mill owner*! My friend felt fortunate to have discovered her error before she embarrassed herself by coming over to speak to a person whom she would not, after all, wish to acknowledge. She thought the episode so amusing, she wrote me about it. I found it...much less amusing.'

Cam had expected they would meet with opposition from Sara's family. He hadn't expected it quite so soon—and he resented it far more than he'd anticipated. 'So why did you want to see me, if I'm so *undesirable*?'

'I want to remove my niece from Derbyshire and away from your influence, immediately. But I shall need your help to accomplish it.'

'My help?' he echoed. 'And if your express purpose is to put an end to our association, why should I help you?'

'The fact that Sara did not mention you leads me to believe your feelings for each other must be...more than casual. Am I correct?'

'And if you are?'

'If you truly care about her, I wanted to appeal to you to do the right thing—and let her go. Oh, you mustn't think I have no sympathy for young people who imagine themselves in love! I was enraptured when I married my late husband. But rapture is too intense an emotion to last. If one is fortunate and well matched, that excess of feeling mellows into a deep, sustaining affection. If one is not so fortunate, or ill matched, once passion is slaked and the novelty of the union wears off, those initial feelings dwindle until all that is left is uninterest, boredom—or even dislike.'

'I can assure you, that will not happen in my case. And knowing your niece, how could you imagine a man fortunate enough to have secured her affection would not love her dearly until the end of time?'

Her expression softened. 'I could not imagine that. But a man's attachments are often more…fleeting.'

'This man's are not,' he said tightly.

She nodded. 'I believe you—or rather, I believe that *you* believe that. But what of Sara? Yes, perhaps she wants to be with you here and now, continuing that regrettable political work that brought us to this impasse in the first place! But what about five or ten years from now? When she has tired of being surrounded by those who don't understand and can't appreciate her love of books, art, learning? You share those interests, I suppose; though I grant you are handsome enough, Sara would never have become enamoured just of a handsome face. But how many others in this vicinity share her interests? You will always have your mill, which will likely occupy most of your time. She…would not be nearly so occupied. Increasingly, she would be isolated and alone.'

He wanted to argue that the country contained people of sense and discernment. But it was quite possible that middle-class shopkeepers and solicitors and craftsmen would not feel comfortable befriending someone born a lady. And the local gentry would likely refuse to associate with her, once they learned she made so great a mésalliance.

'And what if you are not here in five or ten years?' Lady Patterson pressed her point. 'Illness or accident can happen to anyone; you have no guarantee of long life. Even worse than having you buried in your work, if she had to bury you in truth, as a tradesman's widow, she would be left alone. Isolated for the rest of her life, with no possibility of returning to polite society. For make no mistake, if she takes the drastic step of throwing her lot in with you, she will be exiled permanently from the society of her birth. Her status isn't sufficiently grand to make you acceptable and your wealth isn't sufficiently large to safeguard her status.'

'She has good friends who will still see her—and I would hope her family would not abandon her.'

'No, we would not. But we are not *here*. Here, she would be alone. Can you guarantee that she would not one day come to regret having given up everything for you? Or come to resent you, for leaving her with without alternatives? Being Sara, she would likely bury her misery and resentment deep, living out her life in quiet desperation. Would you condemn her to that?'

Lady Patterson hadn't told him anything he hadn't already told himself about the dangers of luring Sara out of her world. But hadn't that all been nullified, when she affirmed she was willing to take those risks?

'Shouldn't Sara be able to choose the life she wants for herself?'

Lady Patterson shook her head and sighed. 'Young lovers always believe their love will last for ever—who would risk their heart so foolishly, if they had doubts?

Asking her to choose is really no choice at all. Here and now, of course she would choose you.'

'So what do you intend?'

'I shall go to Brayton Hullford and tell Sara that her mother is ill and requires her presence in London at once.'

'You think she will believe you?'

'Her mother's health has been poor for years. She might not be sure her mother is in real danger, but she will be uncertain enough that she *will* go. In any event, I shall only be advancing her departure by a day or so. Once I have her back in London, I intend to do my utmost to reattach her to the society to which she belongs. Oh, I have no doubt she will miss you keenly. But if you give her no encouragement...'

'You think she will settle back into the life she left, content to abandon her work in Derbyshire.'

'I certainly hope so. I believe she can do anything, if she sets her mind to it. The question is—do you love her enough to let her go?'

In the euphoria of their adventure together, Sara might have declared her intention to dispense with the rules that had restricted her and do what *she* wanted.

But would it be what she wanted...for ever?

'I would never do anything to hurt her,' he said at last.

Lady Patterson exiled a profound sigh. 'I have been hoping to hear you say that, ever since I received that horrifying letter from my friend. Now, I don't make light of what you are giving up. She's my niece and I know just what a treasure she is! Which is why I want her to be happy, and not just for a short while, but for all of her life. That's why I had to see you, to fight the battle she wouldn't wage to ensure that long-term happiness. So, you will let her go?'

He couldn't, wouldn't give her up—not on the advice of this woman who, Sara had told him herself, had done nothing but press her towards a future she didn't want.

But this was also the aunt who loved her and wanted the best for her. A woman who'd had a husband and family and had experience with the emotional dynamics of those relationships.

Something he knew absolutely nothing about.

He'd like to meet her demand with defiance…but he knew her plea came from the heart. That she genuinely wanted Sara's ultimate happiness.

He wanted the same thing.

Which one of them was right?

Once again, he felt Sara should have a choice in this. Yet he suspected Lady Patterson was right—if she were with him right now, she wouldn't be able to make a dispassionate, rational decision. Her heart—and the powerful physical attraction between them—would overrule every other consideration.

So, although everything within him wanted to lash out and tell Lady Patterson to go away and mind her own business, that he and Sara together would decide their own destiny, he couldn't help but take her warning seriously. 'I will consider it,' he said at last.

'You will not try to see her before she leaves.'

He held on to his temper with an effort. 'I said, I will consider it.'

Lady Patterson nodded. 'Time, and caution, is always best in these matters.'

'Only if you want to lose.'

'Easy enough for you to say!' she snapped back. '*You* wouldn't lose, no matter how things turned out in the end. You remain in *your* world, with your business and your interests intact. But Sara *could* lose—more than you could imagine.'

'I said I would consider it,' he repeated again, not sure he could say any more without giving in to frustration and fury.

'Thank you.' Looking him up and down, she shook her head. 'You are a very impressive young man. I can see why Sara was so tempted by you.'

'What a shame that I wasn't born with the correct pedigree.'

Seeming oblivious to the bitter irony in his voice, she nodded. 'A shame indeed. But, alas, past mending. I shall take up no more of your time. And, Mr Fitzallen, I do appreciate your display of honour.'

'Rare as that quality is among those of humble birth?' he spat out.

'Quite. Good day to you, Mr Fitzallen.' Giving him a regal nod, she rose and glided in fashionable splendour from the room.

Stunned and frozen, Cam watched her walk out.

Then he wandered over and sank back into the chair she'd just vacated, only to spring back up.

He would have to go out—leave the mill. He couldn't be here when Sara arrived to read to the students. He wouldn't be able to resist seeing her and, before he saw her—if he saw he—he needed to think.

With her whole life and happiness in the balance, for once, should he heed Lady Patterson's warning to be cautious?

Anger at her aunt's interference faded, replaced by a jumbled mix of uncertainty and anguish that made him feel as though he'd been dealt a body blow.

Out of that mix, an odd memory surfaced. He recalled the first time he'd tasted pineapple, while he'd been at Cambridge. The sweet fruit, which could only be raised in hothouses in England or imported at such high cost, his host told him, that it had become the symbol of hospitality in the American colonies, a treat offered only to the most favoured guests.

He'd loved the savoury sweet feel of it on his tongue, like no other taste he'd experienced. He'd never forgotten it.

Sara was like that, he thought. Sweet, precious, unique, no one he'd ever met able to compare to her. Having tasted her, knowing she was willing to give herself to him, how could he give her up?

How could he live without her sweetness?

How could he live with himself if, in claiming her, he destroyed her?

He was absolutely certain he would love her for ever. But her aunt had sowed the seeds of doubt that she would always love him.

True, she'd vowed on their train journey that she was brave enough, and ready, to abandon the restrictions society placed on her and embrace his world. But would she feel the same in five, ten, twenty years?

As Lady Patterson had asserted, he would often be occupied with business—as he had been just now, when he'd been away for four days to confer with an investor. With her friends far away and the local people polite but distant, would she feel increasingly isolated and alone?

He knew how wearying it could be to work with the disadvantaged, poverty and apathy grinding them down, leaving too many like Thomas, who had no desire to better his situation, too few like Andrew and Jenny, who aspired to more. Would Sara eventually become worn out and disillusioned by her work with them?

True, she could always return to London, if she were fatigued by her work and discouraged by the poverty around her. There would be theatres to attend, museums to visit. But would being there, perhaps passing in the street people she'd once known, who would look past her without acknowledging her, only deepen her distress and discouragement? Make her feel even more alone, weary, and useless? If she stayed in Knively, would years of mill noise and mill dust dull her life, strip it of beauty, meaning, happiness?

Because she'd chosen him?

He remembered her asserting that she'd not dared become a 'conformable wife', because she hated angry words and dissension too much to protest, even if she were unhappy. She would just quietly endure. Having chosen him, she would live with that choice, no matter how miserable she might become.

It was like a lance through his heart to imagine her living in quiet desperation, because of him.

He had, and would again, gamble with his own life and prospects.

He couldn't gamble with hers.

If he did not declare himself… Sara would remain free, with all her possibilities still open. She could continue her work with the mill children, but reclaim her place in London society whenever she chose to.

The only way he could forestall declaring himself would be if he avoided her. He didn't dare meet her, look into her glorious blue eyes, or his resolve would break. That ferocious sense of self-preservation that had propelled him from the workhouse, despite slights and competition and adversity, to attain what he had, would make him seize what he knew would bring him joy, regardless of the consequences.

So he dared not see her.

As he sat, staring unseeing into the distance, the full implications of that decision gradually settled in his mind.

From the depths of childhood pain, the wolf of desolation howled.

He thought he'd held something of himself back. But he was wrong. Some time over the last week, certain she would accept his proposal, he'd demolished the last barriers he'd erected long ago to protect his heart and fully embraced loving her.

When he'd lost Molly, he'd lost a protector, the only mother he'd ever known. In Sara, he'd found a true partner, his equal, a sharp observer, a keen intellect—and a woman he desired more than any other.

This was not just loss. What he felt now was utter devastation.

A searing wave of pain gashed through him, its pressure so intense he literally couldn't draw a breath.

The wave finally subsided, leaving an icy wasteland in its wake.

Numbly, he rose from his desk and paced out of his office into the din of the factory. Dimly he noted the foreman waving to him as he passed his office, but he didn't stop. As he walked through the carding room, someone grabbed at his sleeve. He brushed them off.

Mechanically, he went down the stairs and out the front entry. But instead of heading to the stables to get his curricle and return to his rooms, as he'd initially intended, he turned and headed to his workshop. Once inside, he slid the bolt, locking out the outside world.

He walked over to his drafting table, the site of so

many of his discoveries, revelations that went on to become lucrative patents.

Sinking into the chair before it, he put his head in his hands and wept.

Chapter Twenty-One

An hour later, Sara arrived at Hughes Cotton Works, hoping today would be the day Cam returned. Over the time he'd been gone, her emotions had climbed to a towering peak of exhilaration every time she thought at the idea of pledging her life to him. Beneath that euphoria surged a simmering arousal at knowing she would soon claim the sensual education he'd promised.

Her friend Emma, who before her marriage to him had shocked them by daring to have an affair with Lord Theo, had tried to explain to her the all-consuming power of passion. Though she had appreciated what her friend said, she hadn't really understood it. Now that imagining Cam's touch made her tremble with need, she sympathised completely.

Not that she hadn't had her moments of doubt. The idea of severing irrevocably her ties to society didn't worry her as much as knowing what a disappointment, quite possibly even an embarrassment, her choice would be to her mother and aunt. Though they had both constantly harangued her to do what would never make her happy, she knew they only wanted what they thought was best for her.

But she'd vowed to be shy, timid Sara no more. Better to risk the possibility of paining them than to miss out on the magnificence of sharing her life with him.

By now she was more than ready to cast aside every last doubt, invite him to call at Brayton Hullford and throw herself into her new life.

As soon as she entered the schoolroom, Sellers informed her that Mr Fitzallen had indeed returned and sent Thomas up to let him know of her arrival. Joy effervescent within her, she waited impatiently for him to join them in the schoolroom, yearning once more to see his beloved face.

Instead, a few minutes later, Thomas returned alone, looking puzzled. 'He weren't in his office, Mr Sellers,' the boy announced. 'The foreman said he seen him walking out 'bout an hour ago, but nobody seems to know where he went.'

A chill went through Sara. 'Is there something wrong?'

Mr Sellers frowned. 'It's…unusual for him to go out unexpectedly, especially without telling the foreman where he is going. Perhaps there was a problem with one of the suppliers in the village. He probably won't be gone long. He seldom leaves the mill for any length of time during working hours.'

'Perhaps he's going to stop by and see Jenny while he's in the village. She's improving daily and I know she'd love to see him. But the minutes are passing swiftly and I don't wish to delay your lesson too long. Shall I begin reading without him?'

'Yes, please, miss!' Alice exclaimed.

'Very well. What story shall we have today?'

And so she began reading, trying to lose herself in portraying the voices of the different characters. Still, a part of her remained distracted, anticipating that at any moment, he might walk in.

By the time she finished the story and the students took out their slates to begin their lessons, he still had not returned.

At last, just as she was about to leave, the schoolroom door opened.

Relieved, excited, she looked up. But instead of Cam's lithe form and handsome face, it was Martin who strode in.

'I just got a message from Lady Trent, telling me to come fetch you at once. She needs you back at Brayton Hullford.'

Alarm coursed through her. 'What's happened? Is she ill?'

'I don't know, miss. Rodgers, the groom who rode over, just said it was important and I should bring you back at once. Thompkins has the carriage waiting outside.'

'I suppose I must go, then. Mr Sellers, will you tell Mr Fitzallen that I'm sorry to have missed him and hope to see him soon? If possible, I should like him to call at Brayton Hullford tomorrow. I'm promised to help Lady Trent with her packing, so I won't have time to come to the mill. There are still some details I need to discuss with him about getting Jenny settled.'

'Very well, I'll tell him. We will all certainly miss you once you return to London.'

She nodded absently, acknowledging the chorus of agreement from the students as she followed Martin out.

Anxiety sat like a boulder in her gut. She was promised to attend Lady Trent for the entire day, and they were scheduled to leave the day after. But Cam knew those plans as well as she did. Surely, now that he was back in Knively, he would arrange to call on her before she had to depart.

And what was so important that Lady Trent needed her to return immediately to Brayton Hullford?

A short time later, the carriage deposited her at the front entry and Sara hurried up the stairs. 'What has happened, Thurston?' she asked as he ushered her in.

'Nothing to alarm you, Miss Standish. In fact, it should be a happy surprise.'

She exhaled a breath of relief—immediately followed by curiosity. 'A surprise?'

Thurston gave her a genial smile. 'Follow me up to the front parlour and you'll see.'

A soaring hope filled her. Had Cam come directly here, rather than waiting to meet her in the schoolroom?

Smoothing down her skirts and giving her coiffure a pat, she hurried after the butler. But as she swept into the room, beaming, she saw…her Aunt Patterson awaiting her.

'Sara, how good to see you again! It's been so long!' her aunt said, coming over to give her a hug.

Still puzzled, Sara hugged her back. 'It's good to see you, too, Aunt Patterson. But…why have you come? I wrote you that we intended to leave for London the day after tomorrow.'

'Come, sit with me, child. I'll explain—and then you shall have to get busy.'

'What is going on?' Sara asked impatiently as she took a seat beside her aunt.

'It's your mama, I'm afraid. She had another one of her spells. Only this time, it was much worse that the ones she's had before. The doctor was quite concerned about her—so concerned, he recommended that I fetch you back as soon as possible.'

Worry flickered through her—but also scepticism. Her mother liked her daughter close by and had not been at all pleased when she'd discovered that her sister had given Sara permission to sojourn in the country, playing hostess to a group of politicians. 'Are you sure she is genuinely ill? You know how she can…exaggerate her symptoms.'

Her aunt sighed. 'It's impossible to know for sure, but the physician was genuinely worried.'

Her mother might well need her. But how could she possibly leave Derbyshire before she'd spoken with Cam?

Using that reason to plead for more time would lead to explanations that would have her aunt scooping her up and returning her to London this very minute.

'Are you sure we need to rush? We are not ready to depart just yet. I promised Lady Trent that I would help her finish closing up the house tomorrow and we can then depart the day after, as planned.'

'Lady Trent has maids aplenty to see to that. And though I cannot vow for certain exactly how dangerous your mother's condition might be, could you live with yourself if we delayed and she were to expire before we arrived?'

Sara blew out a frustrated breath. There was only one answer to that question, of course. Distressed as she was about the turn of events, it appeared she was going to have to depart for London—tomorrow.

Did she dare try to get a message to Cam to come at once?

But then he would encounter Lady Patterson. And though she fully intended to inform her aunt, as well as Lady Trent and all the rest of her family, of her decision to marry Cameron Fitzallen, trying to do so in the midst of the worry over one of her mother's periodic crises of health wasn't an ideal time.

'In any event, Lady Trent has already agreed to let Thurston take charge of closing the house and will travel with us. Tomorrow! And since it will be time for the dinner bell before we know it, you must scurry up to your room and supervise the packing.'

Lady Patterson leaned over to give her a kiss. 'I'll see you at dinner, my dear.'

Confused—and profoundly disappointed—Sara walked with heavy steps up to her room. If only she had seen Cam at the mill today!

How were they to proceed, if she were forced to go back to London before she'd talked with him?

She supposed all she could do was write a note to let him know that she'd been called away by her mother's ill health, but was still eager to answer that question he promised to ask her at his earliest opportunity.

Should she add a request for him to leave the mill and call on her in London?

She knew he didn't like leaving the mill for long and he'd just been away for five days. And she really would prefer to remove the last bit of lingering uncertainty about his intentions—after all, he'd strongly *hinted* he intended to declare himself, but he'd never said in plain language that he meant to ask for her hand—and discuss with him the best strategy to employ in breaking the news to her family, before she presented him at Standish House in London.

But where else would she be able to meet him?

Would he follow her—and ask the question she so yearned to hear?

How long might she have to wait to find out?

As irritated as she could ever remember being with her mother, Sara stalked into her chamber, where her maid had already pulled out her trunks and begun to pack. As she gathered her belongings, her angry frustration gave way to resignation—and an ache of loneliness she suspected was going to haunt her until she saw Cameron Fitzallen again.

In the early evening a month later, Sara sat at her desk in the small back parlour at Standish House, looking over the letter she'd just completed for the Ladies' Committee. With the second reading of the Chimney Sweeps Act due to take place shortly, Lord Lyndlington had asked his wife to have her committee put out a barrage of letters to resistant members of Parliament, pointing out the advantages of the bill.

As she set the letter on top of a stack of several similar missives, she thought again about the climbing boy of the chimney sweep's, who had touched her heart so long ago—and set her on the path that had led to her involvement in political work and animated a fierce desire to better the lives of poor children. She hoped that child had survived and perhaps moved on to a safer occupation. At least, after this bill passed, any lads who followed him in the trade would be better protected.

She ought to feel satisfaction at having played a small part, finally, to assist in bettering the lot of boys like that. And she was satisfied—at least in her head.

But that sense of satisfaction did not reach her heart. It seemed, in the weeks since she'd left Derbyshire, as she heard little from and saw nothing of Cameron Fitzallen, that her capacity for both joy and satisfaction had been extinguished.

After dispatching a brief note explaining her abrupt

departure before leaving Brayton Hullford, she'd sent him another letter as soon as they settled back in London. Letting him know that her mother had improved rapidly once her daughter was restored to her, she repeated again how eager she was to see him and finish the discussion they'd begun on their train journey together. Impatient, filled with longing, missing him desperately, she'd waited…and waited for an answer.

It was ten days before she received his reply, expressing his satisfaction that she'd arrived in London safely, his pleasure that her mother's condition was no longer considered dangerous, and hoping she was pleased at being able to resume her work with the Ladies' Committee.

She'd read it over and over, but could discern nothing that hinted he had any immediate intention of coming to see her in London.

She'd written back again, telling him she hoped before too long to visit Knively and bring along any supplies Mr Sellers needed for the schoolroom. Once again, she waited ten days for an answer, this time a polite thank you for her kindness to the students at Hughes Cotton Works. A reply that did not include an offer to assist her with planning a visit or indicate that he had any wish to see her if she should travel to Knively.

As the days slipped by and his dispiriting letters arrived, she went from hope and joyous anticipation, to confusion and distress, to quiet anguish, to a hollow resignation.

Perhaps, despite her repeated written avowals of how much she wanted to see him, he believed that her abrupt departure represented a betrayal, her choosing a return to London and her family over a life with him.

Or perhaps, as he considered all the obstacles society would put in the way of their creating a happy union, he'd concluded that making a life together would be too difficult. Or that having a woman around, to whom he was required to pay at least a modicum of attention, would take too much time away from the concentration he needed to devote to his inventions and the expansion of his business, the two endeavours that had motivated, energised and rewarded him for most of his life.

She just wished, she thought as a painful throb of desolation rippled through her, that she could actually see and talk with him, to know for sure what was responsible for his puzzling, heartbreaking change of mind.

For as the days apart grew into weeks, it seemed indisputable that he *had* changed his mind about wedding her.

It seemed she had been right all along. Like Lucius Draycott, he could admire her intelligence and dedication, and enjoy discussing with her his visions for the future. But in the end, shy, quiet Sara Standish didn't possess enough charm or allure to hold the heart of a handsome, dynamic, driven man like Cameron Fitzallen.

How foolish she'd been, thinking his belonging to another world would protect her from letting herself be drawn in close enough to get burned.

After initially finding excuses to avoid accompanying her aunt to social events, as hope faded and numbness set in, she'd become docile and indifferent. She wore the gowns her aunt chose for her, came along to whatever function her aunt wished to attend, smiled and nodded at the appropriate places when forced into conversation while her mind drifted and her thoughts were worlds away.

After three weeks had passed, and resignation set in, she decided to resume working with the students at Ellie

Lattimar's school, hoping that endeavour would revive her energy and enthusiasm.

But she made, and then cancelled, two appointments to visit it. Each time, on the point of setting out in the carriage, she was overwhelmed by the memory of Jenny's voice asking her to read to them, or Andrew's excited face as he looked at the machines in Fitzallen's workshop. She didn't think she could look into the eyes of Ellie's students without thinking of Jenny, and Andrew, and even Thomas, the one she hadn't quite caught yet in the net of her stories.

The truth was, she missed working with the mill children almost as much as she missed Cameron Fitzallen. For a moment, she allowed herself to remember how energising and satisfying it had been, surrounded by their rapt faces as she read to them, feeling that, for the first time in her life, she was really making a difference.

She had been *good* with the children, she realised with a quiet satisfaction.

A knock on the door distracted her, followed by the entrance of her maid, the girl's face alight with excitement. 'Miss Sara, there's a gentleman to see you! A Lord Cleve.'

Chapter Twenty-Two

Sara suppressed a groan. She'd seen the Earl's son at several of the social functions to which she'd been dragged and he'd been attentive enough to attract her aunt's attention. Delighted, Aunt Patterson had urged her to make more of an effort to attach this well-born Member of Parliament, 'Who is everything you have always said you wanted in a husband, if you were to be enticed to wed.'

Everything, except they shared almost none of the same views.

Everything, except he wasn't Cameron Fitzallen.

But if there were to be no Cameron in her life, perhaps she ought to re-examine the prospect of Lord Cleve.

She wouldn't ever love him, but he hadn't given her any indication that he required a wife who loved him. As his wife, she would have a permanent household of her own, not dependent upon the favour or continued existence of some family member or friend. She could remain in the political world, not just as a writer of letters and participant in the Ladies' Committee and volunteer at Ellie's school, but as a hostess sitting at table as the men of power who shaped the direction of the nation were deliberating.

A faint interest stirred. Enough that she would see what he wanted.

So instead of instructing the maid to inform him she was not at home, as she'd first intended, she said, 'Very well. Tell Lord Cleve I'll join him in a moment.'

After waiting a suitable interval, staring into her mirror, feeling only emptiness, she walked down to the parlour.

'Ah, Miss Standish, how wonderful to see you again!' Cleve enthused, bowing to her curtsy as she entered. 'That will be all, Mary,' he told the maid.

Resentment stirred at his ordering this Standish servant about, too faint for her to bother protesting. Though he might well mean to declare himself, if he were dismissing the maid. Otherwise, a circumspect *ton* gentleman wouldn't risk being left alone with a gently born maiden, lest her relations decide he'd compromised her.

'Would you like tea?' she asked, the rituals of courtesy coming automatically to her tongue.

'No, I shan't stay long. But after the marked attentions I have paid you, both in Derbyshire and since your return to London, you can't be unaware of my…intent.'

So he did plan to declare himself. The only emotion that thought evoked was distaste.

Not sure she could force herself to accept him, despite all the advantages a political marriage of convenience might offer, she would make the interview as short as possible by forcing him to get to the point.

'And your intent is…?'

He cleared his throat. She suppressed a slight smile at the thought that he was finding this as difficult as she was. He must want a competent hostess with excellent political connections a great deal more than she'd previously suspected.

'First, let me say how…relieved I am to have you back in London. Away from the…harmful influences of mill towns. Although a concern for the unfortunate is commendable in a lady who will be mistress over an estate, supervising the parish relief committee and so forth, it's best to leave the actual intervention in such places to those hired to oversee them. One never knows what sorts of disease and…unfortunate associations one might be exposed to there. That is, I trust you have given up those…unfortunate associations?'

A vision of Cam's face came to her, laughing as she clutched her bonnet against a buffet of wind as the train wound around a curve. After swallowing hard against the pain, she said, 'And if I have?'

'I would be prepared to offer a…partnership I believe would be of mutual benefit to us both. You have strong and enduring relationships with people of political influence. And I could give you a position that would allow you to exercise that influence to the fullest.'

So he did want her contacts and her competence as a political hostess. Were intelligent and diplomatic maidens of good birth so thin on the ground? But the position he might offer wouldn't be enough. Once she…recovered sufficiently, she had every intention of continuing her work in Derbyshire.

'And if I have not…given up these associations?'

He frowned. 'In what manner would you continue them?'

'I have contacts with the schoolmasters of the mill schools. I intend to continue visiting them, delivering supplies and consulting about the students, perhaps sponsoring further education for those who show aptitude and enthusiasm.'

'And might you also be associating with...certain mill owners?'

'As I cannot visit mills without the co-operation of the owners, I would be.' She hadn't yet figured out how she would steel herself to see the children at Hughes Cotton Works, which would mean the anguish of encountering Cam, but eventually she would sort it out.

Lord Cleve stood silent for a moment. 'I suppose I could allow my wife to write to the schools, rally her committee to obtain supplies they need and send them on. But any further contact with actual...individuals, I would not be prepared to tolerate.'

'Then it appears we are at an impasse. I'm sorry to have taken up so much of your time, Lord Cleve.'

She curtsied, intending to leave the room. He stayed her with a touch to her sleeve.

'I would strongly urge you not to pursue that path. Up to now, I have refrained from making generally known certain...questionable activities in which you were engaged in Derbyshire. Particularly your unsavoury association with a certain factory owner. But should you persist in this association, I would feel it my duty to warn others, especially those responsible for safeguarding the character of unmarried maidens, that it might be best for them not to include you in their entertainments. So that their innocent charges are not infected with dangerous ideas.'

For a moment, she stood, staring at him. 'You are threatening to spread vicious rumours about my character, to isolate me socially and embarrass my family, unless I marry you and behave as you want?'

He straightened his shoulders. 'I wouldn't describe

it as "threatening". After all, I would be merely telling the truth.'

'You must be in greater need of my political connections than I thought.'

He grimaced. 'If you must know, there's a by-election coming up and I've been informed the party…might not support me. My father, who controls the purse strings, would be extremely displeased if I were not returned to Parliament. The head of the election board is Lord Lyndlington, husband of your dear friend. Who, I'm sure, would give great credence to anything you say.'

Distaste turning to disgust, she nodded. 'She would indeed. Spread your stories as you will, Lord Cleve. I will live in expectation of shortly being able to congratulate the electors of your district on returning a worthier candidate to the House.'

For a moment, his eyes blazed and she thought he might strike her. Then, his expression murderous, he snarled, 'You'll be sorry', and stalked out.

As Sara wandered back up to her room, she thought that after his anger faded, Cleve would probably be happy she'd refused his not quite proposal. As the Earl's heir, he would inherit the title one day, regardless of how disappointed his father might be in him. And as the heir, he was well born enough to find a wealthy lady to wed, solving his financial difficulties. He would probably enjoy idling about society, spreading malicious gossip, much more than he enjoyed performing his duties in Parliament.

And he'd be right about society. She could already envisage the gossip over teacups as the salacious stories sped about town… *Have you heard about Lady Patterson's niece? The girl has been keeping company with a factory owner!*

Her aunt, and likely Lady Trent, would be embarrassed and chagrined. At the moment, she was too dispirited to think of a way to prevent that.

She'd just reached her chamber when the maid reappeared, an expectant look on her face.

'No, Mary, I have no interesting news to announce,' she said flatly.

The girl's excited look fading, she said, 'Then I expect you shall have to prepare to dress. You're to attend the Cheddingtons' dinner tonight.'

Sara sighed. She vaguely remembered she'd nodded assent when Aunt Patterson informed her where they'd be dining, noting dully that it likely represented another of her aunt's attempts to find her a suitable husband.

For the Cheddingtons had an unmarried son—with a passion for ferns. Sara liked ferns as well as the next person, but if she had to sit at dinner and listen to Thomas Cheddington prose on about rhizomes, fronds and spores, she feared she might try to drown him in his soup bowl.

Suddenly, from out of the hitherto bottomless pit of her misery and paralysis, a reviving anger roared up.

Why was she wasting her life, marking time here in London, attending boring events to which she contributed nothing while she dodged her aunt's matchmaking attempts? Having to deal with men like Cleve, so arrogantly sure of their worth and so dismissive of those who didn't share their views that they felt no compunction about slandering those who didn't agree with them?

How ironic, she thought bitterly, that the gossip mills would heap scorn upon her, should Miss Sara Standish dare to throw her hand away on the mill owner she loved—but would applaud her for securing a marriage of convenience with an earl's son she could barely tolerate.

If she were going to be ruined socially anyway, she

might as well do what she really wanted. Abandon a society into which she didn't fit and return to Derbyshire, where she could make a difference in the lives of children who really needed her.

From deep within her, a sense of purpose bubbled up. Cameron Fitzallen might not want her any longer, but those children still did.

How could she manage to get back to them?

The answer occurred to her almost at once.

'Mary, fetch my bonnet and pelisse, please, and have Jameson summon me a hackney. I must visit Lady Trent at once.'

A short time later, Lady Trent's butler led her to the Marchioness's salon and announced her.

'Sara, my dear, what a lovely surprise!' the Marchioness cried, patting the sofa beside her. 'Please, come sit with me. I know you were supposed to assist me on Thursday—but we didn't have a meeting scheduled tonight, did we?'

'No, ma'am.'

'Then to what do I owe the pleasure of this visit?'

'I wanted to ask for your help.'

'Certainly, if it is within my power to give.'

'I intend to return to Derbyshire. I appreciate all Aunt Patterson's attempts to get me settled and your efforts to introduce me to young men who might make suitable partners, but after a month back in London, I'm now certain that I am simply not suited to be a conventional society matron. I miss visiting the mills and working with children. I want to return to Derbyshire and take up my work there again.'

'I see,' Lady Trent said, looking thoughtful. 'Are you sure you want to do this? You do realise, if you absent yourself from London now for any length of time, your chances of wedding will dwindle to almost nothing.'

'As I informed you from the first, I don't believe marriage is my future. Besides,' Sara added with a wry smile, 'after I describe my interview with Lord Cleve, I think you'll agree that possibility will soon be zero.'

After she'd finished detailing that encounter, Lady Trent exclaimed, 'I may be a widow, but I am still *somebody*. If Cleve tries to destroy your reputation, he shall have to go through me to do it!'

'By all means, do what you can to counter anything that would reflect badly on you or my family. But the longer I've been back in London, the more convinced I've become that my calling is to work with the mill schools and the mill children. Why should I be concerned if society decides to shun me—since I've already decided to abandon it?'

'Oh, dear! You are that determined?'

'I am. However, there's the practical matter of where I can reside once I resume my work. As I remember, there was a lovely cottage on the grounds at Brayton Hullford. Would you allow me to rent it?'

'This...wouldn't have anything to do with a certain mill owner?'

Sara took a breath as a needle of anguish jabbed her. 'Regrettably, no. I'm going back for the children. Not to run after Cameron Fitzallen.'

'Though you will doubtless run *into* him, if you visit the mill schools. Are you...prepared for that?'

She shrugged, trying to convey a nonchalance she didn't feel. 'I shall have to be.'

Lady Trent nodded. 'So, what have Lady Patterson and your mother said about this plan?'

'I haven't informed them yet, as there is no point until

all the arrangements are made, most particularly deciding on a place to reside. They won't be happy, of course. But I am determined to do this, with their blessing or without it. I'd rather rent your cottage than put up at the Thistle and Bobbin, or try to find rooms in some private home, but—'

'Of course you may stay at the cottage. If you truly are set upon doing this.'

'I am. My income is modest, but I think I can cover the rent—'

'No need to discuss that, dear. Your family's solicitor can settle that matter with mine later. So, I am to lose you?'

'I shall miss you, ma'am. But you can always come visit me at Brayton Hullford.'

'When do you mean to leave London?'

'As soon as I can pack, arrange transport and inform my family.'

'Won't you be lonely, all alone in the countryside?'

Without Cam, she would be lonely the rest of her life, no matter where she lived.

'I will have the children to energise and entertain me. My work and reading, and, I hope, visits from friends. I shall be content.'

Contentment being the most she could now hope for, she thought.

'I must say, I'm not completely shocked. Saddened that we will lose you in London, naturally. But also, proud of you, my dear. Few women have the courage to strike out on their own, as you plan to do.'

'I'm lucky enough to possess financial resources to do so. And it doesn't take courage to go where you feel you are meant to be.'

'Embrace me, then, and promise to visit me before you leave!'

'Thank you, Lady Trent. I would have taken this step regardless, but it will be much easier with your support.'

'You shall always have that.'

After giving the Marchioness a hug, Sara walked back out, already planning which supplies and clothing she would take with her. No need for fancy ball or dinner dresses, but she should take all her plainer day dresses, even the ones Aunt Patterson said were outdated and should be handed down to her maid.

After weeks of listlessness and misery, she felt a quiet sense of satisfaction that she was finally moving forward—towards a future that suited *her*.

If only Cameron Fitzallen could have been a part of it.

As Sara rode in the hackney back to Standish House, the sense of excitement and anticipation that had been suppressed since the crushing of her hopes of wedding Cameron finally stirred again.

The decision to resume her work in Derbyshire settled in with a solid sense of rightness that convinced her she'd made the proper choice. Her family wouldn't like it, but she was now certain she was a cog that no longer fit in the wheel of London society—if she ever had. She was a different piece of machinery altogether.

Already she was thinking in the vernacular of the mill.

Three spinsters living together in London, as she, Emma and Olivia had intended, would have been thought eccentric. Lady Trent was correct; a Lady of Quality leaving society to work with the poor would be thought worse than eccentric—she'd be considered radical.

Was she a radical?

With her modest looks, moderate dowry and genteel, but not important, family, she'd always thought of herself as ordinary. Her lack of enjoyment of society and its activities meant she was ordinary and *odd*.

But maybe she *was* more than just odd. Maybe she was, as Cameron once told her, extraordinary.

The very whisper of his name in her mind sent a stab of pain to her chest. Putting a hand over the ache, she considered again the contrast between how she drifted indifferently on the edges of London society, her chief delight writing letters, and the pleasure and energising sense of accomplishment she felt working with mill children in the schools.

Perhaps she was a radical after all.

A radical with the courage to seize control of her life and make of it what she wanted.

Perhaps even a radical brave enough to approach the man she loved. And find out, once and for all, whether he truly wanted her.

Chapter Twenty-Three

A few days later, Sara drove herself in her new curricle from the cottage on Brayton Hullford estate to Hughes Cotton Works. Excitement, trepidation and a strong sense of purpose filled her, along with a bubble of joy at the thought of seeing the children—her children—again.

Yes, returning to Derbyshire had been the right thing to do.

What would Cameron Fitzallen think about it? She'd tried to prepare herself for whatever his reaction might be—displeasure, uninterest, mild approval.

And if his response were warmer than that... Having been so cruelly disappointed once, she wouldn't allow herself to even think about that possibility.

One way or another, soon she would know for sure.

After turning her vehicle over to a boy at the stables, she entered the mill—and almost ran into Alice. To her delight, the girl beamed at her.

'Are you going up to the schoolroom now?'

At her nod, she said, 'Everyone at Hughes will be glad to see you again.'

'I hope so,' she murmured before continuing on. She expected a warm welcome from Mr Sellers and the children.

She wasn't nearly so certain how Mr Fitzallen would greet her return.

Quickly she mounted the stairs, Mr Sellers looking up as she walked into the schoolroom.

'Miss Standish, what a surprise! I know you'd written that you hoped to return for a visit, but I had no idea it would be this soon! Welcome, welcome! The children will be so excited!'

'I'm just as excited to be seeing them! How is Andrew getting along? Has he been back to the workroom? And Thomas—is he finally mastering his letters?'

'You can ask them both—they should all be here shortly. As will Jenny. She's not yet strong enough to work, but as you know, the family will soon be moving to your brother's estate in Kent. Mr Fitzallen encouraged her to return to school and keep up her studies until they are ready to leave. After the children arrive, shall I send one of them up to let Mr Fitzallen know you are here?'

Apprehension fluttered in her belly like fallen leaves stirred by a strong wind. Calming herself, she said evenly, 'By all means, let him know.'

Would he come—or avoid her? she wondered.

Then the children began trooping in, greeting her with exclamations of surprise, delight and a few hugs.

'You will read to us straight away, won't you, miss?' Alice asked.

'Of course. Which story is your favourite?'

'Read "Rapunzel",' several of them chorused together.

Memories of Cameron's comments about that heroine had anxiety stirring in her gut again. But a radical young woman in charge of her own life had no place for missish nerves.

'"Rapunzel" it shall be.'

* * *

She had almost finished the story when the noise of the factory intruding into the schoolroom announced someone's arrival. Sara looked up from her book—and for a moment, her heart stopped.

Cameron Fitzallen stood just inside the doorway, seeming frozen in place, his gaze locked on her—with such a look of uncertainty and longing on his face that a resurgent hope flooded through her.

'Miss Standish!' he exclaimed. 'I... I wasn't expecting you.'

'I imagine you were not,' she said drily. 'None the less, here I am. Let me finish reading this story and you may walk me to my curricle. I should like to speak with you.'

'Of course.'

Telling herself once again she was a bold woman in charge of her own destiny, Sara swallowed her nervousness and returned to her book—though even she would admit that her rendition of the rest of the story was not her best.

Then, her heart thumping so hard in her chest she was surprised he couldn't hear it, she bid the students goodbye and walked out with Mr Fitzallen.

Though it was too noisy inside the mill for conversation, the wordless connection that fizzed between them was as strong as ever, further bolstering her hopes.

Once they exited the building, Cam said, 'Why did you come back?'

'I once told you that I thought working with the mill children was what I was meant to do. My return to London just confirmed that for me.'

'Was that...the only reason?'

'I can't answer that yet.'

'Do you intend to...stay for long in Knively?'

'I intend to stay on permanently. Walk down the lane with me and I'll explain.'

'You didn't come in the Trent carriage?'

'No. I recently purchased a curricle and drive myself now. I shall retrieve it after our talk.'

He shook his head. 'You truly are an independent lady now.'

'You helped me discover that I could be.'

'Does Lady Trent approve?'

'Lady Trent is still in London. I'm not staying at her manor, I'm renting a cottage on the grounds. I hadn't previously thought I had sufficient funds to maintain a place on my own, but country rentals are much less expensive than those in the city. I plan to stay there indefinitely and work with the mill schools at Knively, Wirksworth and Bakewell, allowing the Ladies Committee to assist, not just the students at Hughes Cotton Works, but those at all the mill schools in the area. Lady Lyndlington approved my acting as a liaison for the Committee, to inform them about conditions, recommend projects and supplies that would benefit the schools, and arrange for promising students to have additional training elsewhere. As well as having me report about other needs that might develop—such as retraining stagecoach drivers to be able to work on the railway.'

'That's an ambitious undertaking!'

Gathering her courage, she waited until they'd left the mill yard and proceeded a little distance down the lane, where a copse of trees hid them from view. Halting there, she turned to look up at him. 'Why did you let me go, Cam?' she asked softly. 'Did you change your mind?'

'No, never that.'

'My aunt talked with you, didn't she? Pointing out all the reasons why you should give me up?'

'Did she tell you that?'

She smiled. 'No, but your answer just confirmed it. I thought it suspicious when she descended so suddenly with that claim about Mama's deteriorating health. When we reached London, Mama seemed no markedly worse than she'd been when I left the city. But...why didn't you tell Aunt Patterson it was none of her business and send her on her way? Why did you just...give up on us?'

'I had to,' he burst out. 'She pointed out that if I called on you and asked you to choose between me and your life in London, the power of the connection between us would guarantee your answer. It wouldn't truly be a dispassionate, reasoned choice made after carefully considering all the implications. Standing beside you now, feeling what I feel when you are near me, I know *I* couldn't have been dispassionate.'

He looked away. 'Don't you see, I *had* to let you return to your own world. Let you discover for yourself, away from the spell we cast over each other, whether or not you were truly ready to give up everything you'd ever known. I couldn't bear thinking that if I forced an immediate decision, you might later regret it. That you'd grow to resent, maybe even hate me, for ruining your life.'

With her certainty growing that, this time, he *would* ask the question she longed to hear, the bubble of hope within her ballooned, carrying her spirits soaring.

'And if I had not come back to Knively? You would have just...forgotten me?'

'I doubt I would have been that selfless. But I promised myself I *would* give you time alone to think and reconsider. I told myself I could stand waiting for a week. And after I managed that, for just one more week and then another.'

'And gradually, the waiting got easier.'

'No,' he said flatly. 'It never got easier.'

She put her hand on his arm, the sizzle of connection sending a shock through her. 'Then I have just one more question. Do you love me, Cameron Fitzallen?'

With a muffled cry, he seized her and pulled her into his arms, crushing her against his chest, his face buried in her hair. 'I never want to be parted from you again, my heart, my life. Will you take me, Sara Standish, to love and cherish, for the rest of your life?'

'Yes, a thousand times yes, my darling Cam!'

And then he was kissing her, hard and deep, his passion and fervour leaving no doubt about how desperately he wanted her. Not until they were both breathless and panting did he stop kissing her and pull her back against his chest.

'When I thought I might have lost you for ever, I wasn't sure I could bear it,' he murmured. 'Letting you go was the most desperate gamble of my life. But now, knowing one day you will be mine, I can wait as long as it takes. You may not have to give up everything of your former life, either. When I spoke with Carlisle, that wealthy iron manufacturer in Birmingham, he told me he'd be happy to back me as a candidate for Parliament.'

'I can't think of another man who would be a more eloquent advocate for manufacturers and mill workers alike.'

'I'm not ready for Parliament yet—I have much more to do here first. But if I were elected, you could return to London and become the political hostess you've always wanted to be. I'll never be accepted in society, but if you can be patient for a few more years, I can offer you almost everything else you deserve. In the meantime, I can cash in some investments and buy you a proper house— unless you'd rather build one.'

'I don't want to wait several years!' she protested. 'It would be wonderful if you decided to enter Parliament, but I'm equally happy to be a mill-owner's wife. And we don't have to delay until you find a house. I already have one. Lady Trent's cottage is charming, with several bedchambers, a large kitchen and dining room, and a fine front parlour for a library. I've already engaged Susan and James and borrowed the undercook. I think it would do nicely for us.'

'But you are used to living in much grander accommodations.'

'True, I grew up on a large estate and lived in an elegant London town house. And for most of my life, until I met my friends at school, I was lonely and neglected. It's love, not empty grandeur, that creates a home. So I see no reason we can't wed immediately. Besides, I'm very impatient to discover what happens after kissing. In fact, let's return for my curricle. You can drive me to the cottage and begin to teach me right now.'

Laughing, Cam bent down to kiss the tip of her nose. 'Stop tempting me, vixen! You'll soon be the wife of a factory owner. Excessively moral, the merchant class. They don't tolerate the sort of amorous antics that occur among the upper reaches of society. You just told me you have a cottage staffed by three servants whose loose tongues would start wagging the minute I escorted you in. I'll not have my wife's reputation ruined before the ring is even on her finger.'

She frowned, not at all pleased by that turn of events. 'I must wait until we are wed, then?'

'I'm afraid so, my impatient one.'

'Can't there at least be kisses?'

'Only out of sight. Like now.' And with that, he treated her to another series of deep, bone-melting, toe-curling, logic-destroying kisses that left her almost too dizzy to stand.

'More!' she protested weakly when, his heartbeat thundering against hers, he broke off the last kiss.

'That's all I dare for now. I'd better walk you back to collect your curricle before desire overpowers sense completely.'

'You mustn't leave me yet!'

He groaned. 'Oh, yes, I must. I'm just flesh and blood. There's only so much temptation I can resist.'

'No, we must drive together right now and call on the vicar, so that the first of the banns can be called this Sunday. I'll wait the three weeks to discover what happens after kissing, but not a moment longer.'

Laughing again, he picked her up and swung her round and round. 'What a life we will build together!'

'I don't care what happens, as long as I can share it with you.'

Setting her back on her feet and giving her one last kiss, Cam tucked her hand on his arm and walked her towards the stables.

A little more than three weeks later, on a glorious, sunny, warm July day, Sara stood with her two dearest friends in the vestibule of Knively's small stone church.

'And here we always thought you were the quiet one,' Olivia Overton, now Mrs Hugh Glendenning, said as she pinned the bonnet on Sara's blonde braids. 'Soft spoken, always avoiding confrontation. Then you go on to live *completely* on your own, thumb your nose at society and its rules, and find yourself a handsome, brilliant entrepreneur to marry. You're the most radical of us all!'

'As long as she will be as happy as we are, that's all I ask,' Emma Henley, now Lady Theo Collington, said.

'But my, how differently our lives turned out from what we imagined when we were schoolgirls at Mrs Axminster's Academy!'

'I have to admit, I wasn't happy about waiting to wed Cam, until he reminded me that calling the banns would give us enough time to summon all of you—and my family—to attend.'

'Bravo to your Aunt Patterson for deciding to come. And Lady Trent!'

'My aunt had palpitations when I first told her I meant to marry him, of course. But after I made her confess the lengths to which she went to try to keep Cam from proposing, she felt so guilty, she had to try to make it up to me by attending.' Giddy with happiness, Sara giggled. 'Now that she's met him, he's charmed her completely, just as I knew he would. She's even invited us to stay at the Standish town house in London, so he can meet my mother!'

Sobering, she continued, 'I'm so glad the two of you have chosen to stand by your "radical" friend.'

'Of course we would,' Olivia said. 'Besides, any man who could win your heart had to be seen and inspected. He'd better be worthy of you!'

'Oh, he is,' Sara assured her. 'He's *perfect*.'

'Besotted,' Emma and Olivia said together, shaking their heads.

'You are the only one of us to actually work at the new schools our political efforts have brought into existence,' Emma said. 'You must let us know everything we can do to assist you.'

'I will. We may not have ended up where we thought we would, but we've all fulfilled our goal of finding places in the world where we can be useful, rather than just idly drifting along in society.'

'We have done that. At the wedding breakfast, we shall raise a toast to us—and our wonderful husbands.'

'And to the next generation?' Olivia added, smiling as she patted Emma's belly.

'To us and the next generation,' Sara agreed, her happiness bubbling over. 'After some instruction from my husband, I hope to contribute to that very soon.'

'First, the wedding,' Emma reminded. 'Your impatient bridegroom awaits.'

'He can't be more impatient than I am,' Sara muttered.

The three friends dispersed to take their places, Emma and Olivia joining their husbands in the congregation, Sara walking over to the church's entry, where Cam awaited her. 'Ready, my heart?' he asked quietly.

'Ready to pledge you my heart and my life.'

'As I will pledge mine to you. Let's go walk boldly into our brave new world!'

With a quick kiss, he tucked her hand on his arm and walked her down the aisle to the waiting vicar.

A few hours later, after a joyful wedding breakfast on the green shared with her friends, the villagers and most of the employees from Hughes Cotton Works, who had all been given the day free, Cam took her hand.

'Is it finally time for that lesson?' she whispered.

The heated look he gave her promised she was going to enjoy every minute of his instruction. 'Almost.'

He pointed to where Martin was driving over his curricle, now covered with flowers and ribbons. 'We need only say our goodbyes and drive back to the cottage.'

'Can you spring 'em?'

Chuckling, Cam walked her over and handed her up, then took the reins from Martin. Just before he set the horses in motion, he turned to the crowd, flinging into their midst a bagful of gold coins that had the cheering throng scrambling.

Then he drove Sara quickly to their cottage. And proceeded to show her just how expertly he could dismantle a mechanical cage of garments.

* * * * *

*If you enjoyed this story, be sure to read the first
two books in The Cinderella Spinsters miniseries*

The Awakening of Miss Henley
The Tempting of the Governess

*And why not check out Julia Justiss's
Sisters of Scandal miniseries*

A Most Unsuitable Match
The Earl's Inconvenient Wife